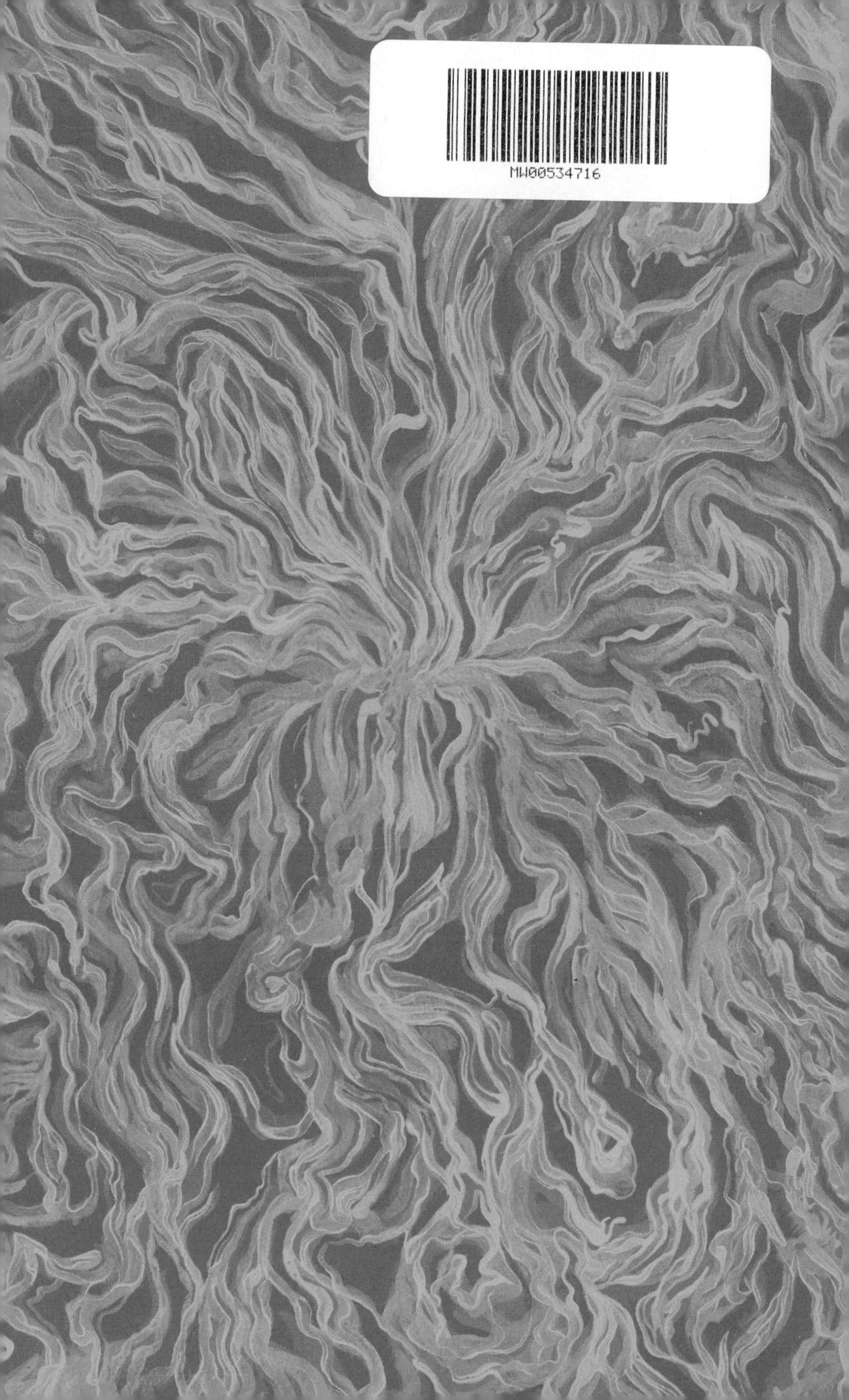

PRAISE FOR *NIGHT OF THE WITCH*

"Set against the backdrop of the medieval German witch trials, Raasch and Revis weave a fantasy and heart-pounding tale full of history, love, witchcraft, and war that will have you gripping your book, waiting for the next shocking twist."

—#1 *New York Times* bestselling author Jennifer L. Armentrout

"*Night of the Witch* is an irresistibly compelling page-turner, distinguished by vivid descriptions, a fascinating magic system, and crackling chemistry between the two leads. Best of all? When I finished reading, I wanted more. Bring on the next book!"

—Claire Legrand, *New York Times* bestselling author of *Furyborn*

"A breathtaking adventure from beginning to end. Full of wild magic, stunning twists, and a romance that burns on the page, *Night of the Witch* is an addictive read that will leave readers desperate for more."

—Rachel Griffin, *New York Times* bestselling author of *The Nature of Witches* and *Bring Me Your Midnight*

★"The authors sustain tension via Fritzi and Otto's alternating perspectives, and harrowing descriptions of body horror and trauma alongside quiet, tender moments of connection round out this beguiling series opener."

—*Publishers Weekly*, STARRED review

"Raasch and Revis have brewed a brilliant novel that combines history and fantasy in the best of ways. Be prepared to stay up late reading this one. If it isn't the action keeping you on the edge of your seat, then it'll be the sizzling romance."

—Tricia Levenseller, *New York Times* bestselling author of *Blade of Secrets*

"*Night of the Witch* is the most original fantasy I've read in a long while, full of stunning world-building, fierce heroes, and bewitching romance. I am not exaggerating when I say it's a knockout, unputdownable story by two of the best YA authors today."

—Evelyn Skye, *New York Times* bestselling author of *Crown's Game* and *Damsel*

"Sizzling with magic and searing with forbidden romance, *Night of the Witch* is a spellbinding enemies-to-lovers historical fantasy as incisive in its exploration of grief and prejudice as it is tender in its portrayal of love and hope. Raasch and Revis have me enchanted from start to finish."

—Amélie Wen Zhao, *New York Times* bestselling author of *Song of Silver, Flame Like Night*

ALSO BY
SARA RAASCH AND BETH REVIS

Witch & Hunter duology

Night of the Witch

THE FATE OF MAGIC

THE FATE OF MAGIC

SARA RAASCH
AND
BETH REVIS

sourcebooks fire

To everyone seeking magic:
May you realize it isn't a search.
It's a self-discovery.

Jacket art © David Curtis
Jacket design by Erin Fitzsimmons/Sourcebooks
Internal design by Laura Boren/Sourcebooks

Published by Sourcebooks Fire, an imprint of Sourcebooks
P.O. Box 4410, Naperville, Illinois 60567–4410
(630) 961-3900
sourcebooks.com

Cataloging-in-Publication Data is on file with the Library of Congress.

Printed and bound in the United States of America.
LSC 10 9 8 7 6 5 4 3 2

CONTENT WARNINGS:

Domestic abuse (memories), body horror, murder, physical torture, psychological torture, emotional manipulation, loss of body control through magical means, self-harm through possession, grief and loss of life, scenes of battle, blood, and gore

1

OTTO

"So, let me get this straight," I say. Brigitta looks smugly down at me. "I am supposed to participate in a mock battle, after which the guard will toss me into an ice-cold pond, then I have to climb to the top of the waterfall before running through literal fire?"

"Yes, that's about the sum of it," Brigitta says, chuckling. We're at the outskirts of the Well, in the shadows of the trees that hold most of the witches' homes. A safe distance away so that none of the others will be caught in the crossfire of today's activities.

"But...*why*?"

"Tradition." Brigitta shrugs. "You may be a goddess-chosen warrior, Otto Ernst, but you've not yet been chosen by *us*." Joining the elite guards of the Well will cement my place in the coven, despite my lack of magic.

"And the way to get chosen is to first fight and then be tortured by you?"

Brigitta smiles. "That'd do it."

I stare at her flatly, but I can appreciate the activity. Call it bonding, call it hazing—after I survive tonight, I'll be an accepted and respected member of the society in the Well, inducted into the Grenzwache itself.

But first I have to survive.

Alois snickers, his shoulders shaking. Of them all, the redhead is closest to me in age, but even then a few years my senior. Behind them, I can see the other members of the guard openly laughing at me, elbowing each other and whispering.

They're witches. They have spent their whole life in the Well coven, and most of them have spent decades in the guard, every day honing their skills in both combat and magic to ensure the protection of the Origin Tree. They've been so secretive about the damn tree that I've yet to even *see* it, despite being here for months and being a goddess-chosen warrior. But I suppose that's the point. When the Origin Tree is the literal source of all magic on the entire planet, it gets protected.

Regardless, though, they have not only years of training, but intimate knowledge of the land and magic on their side. I eye Brigitta's tattoos swirling over her biceps and up her shoulders, the sharp lines of the black ink competing with the sharp lines of her clavicle. The ancient Celtic markings aren't just tradition, as Brigitta implied. Each one enhances the warrior's skills, protects the body, strengthens the muscles. The sigils and runes are further magic. And, once all this bonding with the guards is done, Fritzi is going to mark *me* with tattoos of her choosing, gifting me magic through my skin.

Witches who fight, Brigitta told me, do not always have time to craft a spell, carefully gathering ingredients to brew a potion or whatever the witch's specialty may be. The heat of the battle requires *action*. That's where the tattoos come in. The traditional Celtic designs serve a purpose, a way to draw from magic without the sometimes slower and more tedious spell work.

This would not be the case if the Guards used wild magic like Fritzi, I think, but I press my lips closed. This is one of the secrets she wants me to keep. The Well coven is deeply traditional, and wild magic is decidedly not.

For now, my skin is still blank. I'm just a human without magic, who's spent most of his time as a soldier...but a soldier who never intended to truly fight. My time as a captain of the hexenjägers was a front; I never wanted to be a witch hunter. I just had to pretend to be one to bring them down from the inside.

"Don't worry so much, Ernst," Brigitta says, laughing at my serious face. "Today is just for us, the border guard. The real induction comes later."

"And on the day of the actual trial, I'll be scaling waterfalls and leaping through fire while Fritzi..." I say, waving my hand, "Fritzi will be taking a bath?"

"That's a bit of an oversimplification," Brigitta says. "But essentially. Yes."

"A bath." Alois laughs. "Is that what you want, warrior?"

"It would be nice," I grumble. I quite like the baths here. I shift in my seat, hoping the others don't notice how much my mind has wandered at the idea of Fritzi in a bath.

"I think he's grown a bit soft," Alois says. My mind panics for a moment, but then Alois steps closer and pokes me in my belly. I'm pleased that he winces, his finger finding no fat to cushion the jab. "Lazing about in the trees."

Fritzi, Liesel, and I have been in the Well for months. It's become our home.

Brigitta tosses me a pouch. Inside are a dozen red sacks sewn shut. I weigh one in my hand, and a red powder coats my palm. "You must 'kill' twelve of us before you win," the captain says.

Twelve to one. I glance behind her. There are easily thirty people participating in the battle. I only have to hit twelve with the red markers, but I'll have to go through more than three times that many to make a hit.

"There are only twelve markers in the bag," I say, counting again.

"So don't miss." Alois grins with all his teeth.

"Meanwhile, we'll have these." Brigitta makes a movement with her hand, and Alois picks up a basket and starts distributing five spell pouches to each member of the guard.

"What do they do?" I ask warily.

"Each hit will freeze you just a little more," Brigitta says cheerily. "One will tingle, like pins and needles at the spot where you're hit. It'll get progressively worse with each strike until you're numb."

"Numb's not so bad."

"Yeah," Alois calls back, shooting me a wicked look I don't trust. "It's not so bad at *all*."

My stomach twists. *Got it. Don't get hit.*

"Game's over when you mark twelve of us, or when you can no longer move." Brigitta smirks. "Well, 'warrior?'" She somehow makes the word sound like a mockery. "Are you ready to be truly worthy of Holda?"

Holda? No. I could care less what a goddess thinks of me.

But I'll be damned to any hell that exists before I let Fritzi down.

Brigitta raises a horn to her lips. "The hunt starts when I sound the horn."

"I thought this was a battle, not a hunt," I say, already staggering back.

Brigitta towers over me, her lips curled into a sardonic snarl. "Every battle is a hunt until you figure out how to fight back."

Skokse, I think as I dash through the underbrush, using the scant grace Brigitta allowed for me to make the first move. I skulk through the trees, already hearing the horn signaling that the hunt is on.

I need my horse. Skokse is the closest thing I have to an ally in this battle, and if I'm mounted, I can be faster. I can have a chance.

I circle back. In my time here at the Well, I've gotten a feel for the place, both in the trees with Fritzi and on the ground with my sister, Hilde, who has been embraced by the coven despite not having magic herself.

Hilde. There's an idea. She might help me to hide.

I shake away the thought as soon as it forms in my head. First, she is my sister, not a soldier. Second, I don't want to hide. I want to win.

Another blow of a hunting horn. Louder this time.

"Skokse," I remind myself, cutting through a copse of saplings toward the stables.

I break out into a run, not caring about stealth.

An arrow whizzes by, close enough that the fletching stings my skin.

"Hey!" I shout, spinning around to see Alois on the wooden fence near the animal pen, giving me a mocking salute.

"If it hits you, I promise to heal you!" he calls, already knocking another arrow.

"If!" I shout back, zigging over the worn grass where the horses graze. "I thought you were supposed to use the spell satchels?"

"Oh, I'm just having a bit of fun!" Alois laughs.

Another arrow flies, missing me by a whisper.

I pause long enough to point behind him. "Hi, Cornelia!"

Alois spins around, already squaring his shoulders and tilting his head to show off. I laugh so loud that I blow the ruse; he aims another arrow at me with lightning speed, letting it fly just as I reach the barn and throw myself into the stable, eyes frantic. I have seconds at most. There. Last stall. Skokse's head, black as night, dark eyes watching as I race to her.

"Help me out?" I gasp, throwing open her stall door.

Skokse's steps are heavy thuds as she strides forward. She has no saddle, but I kick a bucket over to use as a step and grab her withers, swinging my leg over her side. Before I have a chance to give her a command, Alois and three others of the guard burst into the far side of the stable, and Skokse pivots, kicking dirt and hay as she darts toward the other side. I lean low over my horse's back, clinging to her as more arrows land with thunks into the wooden wall, and Skokse leaps over the low, wide door.

A burst of green and blue as we enter the meadow. I straighten on Skokse, then nudge her with my right foot, circling her back around the stables to the other door. As I'd hoped, Alois and his three fellow guards are racing down the long, wide stretch of barn in the direction of Skokse's stall. Behind them now, I get one of the witches in the back with a red marker. She shouts and cranes her head, cursing as she steps to the side. Out of the game.

I throw another—missing the witch I'd aimed for, but thankfully hitting Alois right in the face, a giant stain of red powder sliding over his cheek.

"Just a bit of fun," I say, and Alois snorts in appreciation.

The witch I'd aimed for hurls a spell satchel at me, and my arm burns from the hit. *Much* worse than just pins and needles, as Brigitta said, but at least it wasn't a direct blow. I hit him with a marker, and he steps back. One more down. I whirl Skoskse around in the limited space of the barn's corridor.

The last guard—a young woman with slick black hair named Mella—must be hiding in a stall. I twist my head around, my scalp tingling, wincing at an attack that hasn't come.

Skokse blows out a breath. My hands tense in her mane.

Suddenly, the horse kicks, slamming both back hooves into the stall behind me. I hear a groan and turn to see Mella crumpling under the remains of the wooden door. I curse. It's a game to us, but Skokse doesn't know that.

"We've got her, don't worry," Alois says, rushing over. The two others have potions and spells at the ready to heal their comrade.

I toss a red marker on Mella's limp body. Alois shoots me an annoyed look, but I just shrug, turning my horse around. Four down. Eight to go.

Skokse and I charge out of the barn. The commotion in the stable was loud enough to summon more of the Grenzwache, but they're too far away to risk my throwing a precious red marker. I kick Skokse, and we head down the hill. My horse is pure muscle and strength, barely showing any signs of exertion as she races toward the relative cover of the trees.

Every battle is a hunt, I think. *Time to fight back.*

Behind me, I can hear horse hooves.

I squeeze Skokse with my legs but let go of her withers. The bag with the markers is securely tied to my waist. My heart thuds as I look around.

There. A relatively low branch that's thick enough...

Carefully, I pull my legs up. Sensing my movements, Skokse slows, but not by much. Her pace is even. I nudge her toward the tree, and before I can tell myself what a stupid thing it is to do, I kick up with my legs and grab for the branch with my arms.

Oof. The wind is knocked out of me as I cling to the branch. I scramble, pushing my feet against the trunk to launch myself higher. Skokse wheels around, nodding her big head at me.

"Go," I gasp, pointing.

The horse thunders into the thicker trees as I climb higher. This fir has enough cover that I won't be easily spotted. I stand on the branch, leaning my back against the trunk, watching. Waiting.

Six guards on horseback race toward Skokse. I see one wave to the others, pointing toward the trees. Skokse is visible, but only just. The riders slow, fanning out along the edge of the grove.

Skokse, bless her, moves closer to a path near my tree, drawing them in. The riders start heading into the denser woods.

Six. I take a breath, holding my markers in my left palm, gripping one with my right. I have to be quick. I throw one, aiming for the second rider, and my next marker is already leaving my hand before the first hits. In quick succession, I get three hits. The remaining three riders circle around, looking erratically, everywhere but up. I get one more hit before the other two pinpoint my location. I toss a fifth marker, striking the penultimate rider, then I leap from the tree—right at the last guard. She screams in surprise as I land on top of her, mashing the red marker on her back.

Her horse bucks, and we both fall off, a tangle of arms and legs. The others rush, making sure no one is gravely hurt. Now that each of the six bears a red mark from my attack, they're friendly. Out of the game.

"Better hurry," one says as I whistle for Skokse, who weaves between the trees back to me. "Brigitta's coming."

I use a stump to help launch myself onto Skokse's back.

Sweat and dirt streak down my face as I lean over Skokse, letting the horse skirt the edges of the dense trees. I'm reaching the end of my ideas, and exhaustion and fading adrenaline are making it hard to think. I've gotten ten of the guards with my markers. I need two more.

I could head deeper into the forest, into the areas that have been forbidden. I know the Origin Tree is...somewhere there. But that area will likely be guarded even more heavily.

I narrow down the locations. As captain of the Grenzwache, Brigitta is the most elite warrior, and she knows the game better than any. *Where would she be?*

On my tail.

She would follow the blood trail—even if the trail is red powder and not literal blood. I close my eyes, envisioning her seeing Alois in the stable, finding the riders at the trees. None of them moved, I realize. They stayed where they were after I marked them—dropped like bodies. Dots for Brigitta to connect, making a line straight to me.

I pull Skokse up to the tree line and hop down, patting my horse on the neck. "Thank you," I tell her. She stomps, her sharp hoof cutting the soft earth.

I slip into the trees. I'm not that far from the riders I struck down. I move silently through the forest, careful of every step, creeping closer, closer. Back to the very guards I've already marked.

Hunting.

None of them hear me as I position myself behind the trunk of a huge oak.

I wait.

The riders are all chatting, laughing. Horse hooves approach. They hail someone.

"He got all six of you?" Brigitta's voice. She sighs. "Honestly, pathetic. He doesn't even have spells."

"Well, he has muscles," one of the witches grumbles. I smirk, tensing my biceps. Nice to be appreciated.

"He was in the trees," the rider I knocked out of the saddle says.

"Hardly an excuse." Brigitta sounds caught between amusement and exasperation. "He used to be a jäger."

"Not a *real* jäger," one of the riders protests. "He's on our side."

I grin silently.

"*Still*," Brigitta says, laughing at the others. "You're all on extra night patrols for failing so spectacularly."

Some more chatter.

"He rode off," one of the other riders says. I don't even peer around the trunk.

I wait.

Footsteps crunch through leaves and forest detritus. Brigitta steps closer to my tree.

She stops. "You three go east. You three go west."

Horses gallop off, the group splitting up to cover more ground and find me.

"Where are you going?" A male voice. I think that may be Theodar.

Brigitta moves slowly, carefully.

She's guessed my play.

I hear the sound of heavy pouches thudding. She's testing the weight of at least one in each hand.

I wait.

"Come," Brigitta commands Theodar, and they stride into the forest.

Closer.

Closer.

I see the tip of her boot. In another moment, she'll be beside me.

I scream, the sound raw and jagged, and it works—Theodar shouts, whirling around as I leap in front of them both. I toss one red marker, smacking his panicked face.

Brigitta, however, is not so easily distracted. She raises her hands, both heavy with spell bags, and I dodge, rolling through the leaves and sticks and mud, tossing the red marker up. She ducks, easily avoiding the hit.

I've lost my red marker, and she has spell pouches in each hand, still very much my enemy.

"You can just give up," Brigitta offers. "You don't have to win."

"You're wrong there," I say.

Brigitta kicks at me; I scramble over the forest floor. One spell bag slams into the back of my thigh, and my whole leg goes numb so abruptly that I stumble again and nearly fall over. Brigitta advances as I struggle.

"Give up," Brigitta says good-naturedly, tossing the other spell pouch in her gloved hand.

"Never going to happen," I say. I roll, grabbing the red marker that I'd hit Theodar with.

I stagger, limping—but my injured leg and the red marker in my right hand distracts Brigitta enough that she doesn't notice that I have a rock in my left hand.

I slam the stone into Brigitta's knuckles.

Stunned, she drops the spell pouch to the ground. I raise my hand to throw the red marker at the same time that Brigitta grabs up two more spell pouches from her belt.

I could duck.

But then I'd miss the shot.

I lunge for her, the red marker in my palm slapping against her chest at the same time Brigitta slams both spell pouches on either side of my head.

The hunt is over, I think as I drop like a stone to the forest floor.

2

FRITZI

Morning light cuts through the council room's high wide windows, searing the headache behind my left eye; tension or sleeplessness, I'm not sure. And though I could easily grab a remedy from the shelves that rim this meeting room, vials of herbs and potions, I stay planted on the chair at the table, hands demurely on the beaten wood, focus pinned on Liesel, across from me.

She busies herself going over a worn piece of parchment, dragging her finger down, back up, down again, lips moving in soundless recitation of notes and lines and details.

I silently try to get my ten-year-old cousin to look at me. I want her to remember that I'm here, that I won't let the council be cruel to her; I want her to remember that Cornelia, at my right, is also here for her and is just as unwilling to let Rochus and Philomena get away with any of their usual combative comments.

Rochus clears his throat from his seat at the head of the table. "Liesel, dear, if you are unprepared to give us this information, we can seek it elsewhere."

"She's fine—" I start.

At the same moment, Cornelia cuts in with, "Give her a chance to—"

Liesel flies to her feet, slams her palms against the table, and hooks Rochus with a glare so sharp that he drops back down into his seat, brows to his receding gray hairline.

"It began," Liesel says, her voice pitched purposefully low, like a growl, "in Birresborn."

I bite my bottom lip. Hard.

All my fears of her being nervous for this recitation were unfounded, it seems. She wasn't quiet to hide her anxiety.

She was...*preparing.*

Philomena sighs, a quill poised in one hand over a blank sheet. "Yes, we know quite well where you are from—what we need are the details of your journey to the Well, so we might have a record of the things that transpired. We need the details *only*, so you do not have to—"

Liesel sweeps her arms wide, face going gaunt and tragic. "The day was cool. Cold. *Frigid.* The air not yet fully winter, not yet autumn. Oh! The *chill*—"

Cornelia puts a hand over her mouth. Fighting a smile.

I'm not even fighting mine. I grin, wider still, headache forgotten, as Liesel puts a hand to her chest and sways.

"A morning like any other! Until my deranged cousin attacked our village and kidnapped me."

Her voice falters, and she consults her notes, but my chest squeezes, smile dropping off my face.

It is good, though, that she is able to make light of what we went through. This is her way of dealing with what happened to her, and I'm more grateful than I can say that Brigitta has been encouraging Liesel to create this story. And while I had thought it would be more...direct... than what the council needs to put in their records, I can't deny the part of me that's softening and melting at the sight of Liesel so obviously enjoying the act of storytelling.

"Ah," she restarts. "I mean—*oh*! The horror of his vile hexenjäger brigade as it did descend upon our unsuspecting coven! The barriers had fallen, brought low by—" she stutters. Glances at me, once; I almost miss it, but she flurries her hands around in an approximation of something intangible. "By *forces*! Mysterious forces—"

"Your other cousin, you mean," Philomena corrects. "We know Friederike lowered your coven's barrier, allowing Dieter and his hexenjägers to attack. Do not try to soften her role in—"

Liesel makes a crooning mewl, the back of her hand on her forehead. "The vile Kommandant abducted me! I was taken far, far away, across the untamed lands, through desolate forests and churning rivers—"

"Liesel," Rochus tries, "we only need—"

"—to Trier! The capital of the vile hexenjägers. There, I was imprisoned, unjustly I may add, at the hands of my vile cousin—" She stops. Squints. Realizes, perhaps, that she said the word *vile* quite a lot already, and frowns at herself before looking down at her paper again. "Only to be rescued from certain death by my cousin! My...other cousin. Not the vile one. His sister. And her brooding warrior!"

My chest squeezes again, but with a snort I can't stop. I wish Otto had been allowed into this council meeting rather than being whisked away to some apparently very important Grenzwache trial; I can only imagine the look on his face at being described as *brooding*.

Liesel bats her hand in a dismissive wave. "He's not important to the story. I didn't like him at first." She thinks for a moment, shakes her head tightly. "No, the story is better without him—"

"He is a part of your journey," Rochus cuts in. "We need to hear of his contributions as well."

Liesel pouts. "But he didn't do anything. Except carve me a dog." She thinks again. "Well. That part *was* nice, I guess."

Was it a dog? I remember him saying it was meant to be a horse.

"You cannot discount him as it suits you," Rochus says. "We must hear everything that occurred. *Truthfully*."

I turn a distrustful scowl at Rochus. Why is he so interested in Otto's part of this story? Is it merely to know every detail, as he says—or do they hope something happened that they can use to discredit Otto, even with him being chosen as my warrior?

"*Truthfully—*" Liesel drags out the word "—back across the untamed lands we went!" She flares away from the table, pacing before the high windows that show the treetops of the Well sanctuary rippling off into the distance. "Back through desolate forests and churning rivers—we were on a *tiny* boat; it was so small. The water, frigid! Now it was winter, fully and wickedly—Fritzi washed my hair and it *froze—*"

"I did not—" I stop. Think back.

Well. Perhaps I did do that. We were filthy though, having narrowly escaped the explosion of the basilica imprisoning a hundred innocent people that my brother had intended to burn in Trier. Cleaning the ash and grime out of our hair, even with winter-cold river water, had been a necessity.

I cannot believe that *that* is the detail she fixates on. Not the run for our lives. Not the nights huddled around smoldering campfires, worried that every snap of a branch in the dark was Dieter, come to get us.

No. The worst thing we experienced was frozen hair.

"*Child*." Philomena pinches the skin over her nose. "We agreed to let you be the one to give the official account, but we truly need only the details of where you were, what you encountered, and how you passed. This *performance* is highly—"

"A CRONE!" Liesel shrieks. "Not *the* Crone, of course, not Abnoba. But an old woman. In a little cottage outside Baden-Baden. Into her home we went, and she captured us three in a pit of thorns and bones."

I frown. "Liesel, the old woman didn't capture us."

"And FRITZI!" She whirls towards me. "Fritzi harnessed the powers of her connection to the Well and freed us from the thorns! Plants bow to her command; greenery is hers to control!"

"I didn't—"

"And that was not even the worst we faced!" She leaps onto her chair, blond braids snapping around her shoulders, blue eyes wild, and face reddening. "Into Baden-Baden we went, me, Fritzi, and her sulking warrior—"

"Sulking," Cornelia echoes, and buries her face in her hands with a giggle.

"To face terrors previously unknown by witches: the most heinous of Christian holidays, a perverted festival of merriment—"

I scoff. "Liesel, do you mean *Christmas*? The Baden-Baden Christkindlmarkt?"

"None other!" She teeters in the chair, corrects herself, and gets a far-off look of horror. "They stole our Yule traditions and made them so—so—*Catholic*."

"The *hexenjägers*, Liesel," Philomena drones. "How did you evade the *hexenjägers*?"

"A CASTLE!" Liesel points at nothing. "A castle, high on a cliff, dark and brooding—or, no, that was Otto—" She scowls, looks down at her notes. "No. He's not important. FRITZI. Dieter came up the hill on horseback, and Fritzi *saved* us—"

Cornelia has both hands over her face, making a high-pitched, desperate whine that I think is a poorly restrained laugh.

I stand from my chair. "Liesel, I think that's—"

"The trees of the Black Forest awoke at her call! They rushed to our aid! Branches snapped in the morning mist—splinters flew—"

"*Liesel.*" I try hard not to laugh her name. "I think that's quite enough for now."

Her shoulders sag. "I haven't finished."

"We have enough information," Philomena says to her blank sheet of parchment.

She has been trying to get the exact details of our journey for weeks, for the council's posterity. Cornelia has kept her delayed with insistence that we needed to rest and heal, which were far too true. I had merely intended to just never recite any sort of tale to her, but Liesel had been the one to insist.

I lower back down into the chair, the scars pulling at my chest, my thigh, my stomach.

Philomena only asked once for details of what happened after Dieter magically ripped me out of the Well, what he did to me when he had me chained up in a room in Baden-Baden, what spells he might have used.

The look I gave her was enough to shut her up.

I was barely able to tell Otto. The thought of repeating what Dieter did to me, and having that account written down, made a record—

Absently, I scratch at the brand Dieter left on my sternum. My headache pierces, pain a lightning bolt behind my eyes, and when I snap them shut, briefly, I see—a tree. The Tree, the Origin Tree, the guardian of our magic—

I shake my head, and the image fades. Or maybe it was never there—the light from the windows flares against the veins in my eyelids like branching arms.

Cornelia shoves to her feet. "If we are quite finished?" She doesn't wait for their response; she locks her fingers around my arm and hauls me up, but my gut stays in the chair, a sudden, intense jerk of nerves.

Philomena sets her quill down with a huff.

Rochus manages to look up with a rather sincere smile. "Yes, of course."

Cornelia bows her head. "We will have proper council meetings after she's bonded."

Philomena shoves away from the table wordlessly, lips pursed. Rochus's face goes tight.

For being the leaders of the Well, the sanctuary ordained by the triple goddesses as a haven for witches, they are remarkably bad at hiding their true feelings. Each flash of disdain for me is carved across their faces.

"Yes," Rochus says stiffly. "We look forward to our council bearing Holda's champion."

As though summoned, Holda makes a low hum in my head. *He will show my champion proper respect*, she tells me, as though I will snap at him to swear fealty to me.

I shrug away her concern, an annoying itch at the back of my mind, and I think that might be the cause of my headache. Her presence comes and goes, and even after months of it, I haven't gotten used to having a goddess not only in my head, but also invested in my life.

"And her warrior," I add.

They will not downplay or warp Otto's contributions to this. Liesel may have, but that's their relationship; she barely tolerates him, he dotes on her, and she goes away with armfuls of sweets and toys and whatever else he's able to scrounge up for her. It's a brilliant system she has, honestly. I don't think he's yet figured out that she truly does worship him.

But as for the council...

Cornelia has accepted Otto, of course. She was the one I did not have to sway, the one who eagerly accepted my role as a goddess-blessed champion and Otto's role as my protector, both of us harbingers of change.

Rochus and Philomena, however, still act as though it will all go away, and they will return to a normal secluded life of being secreted away in the deep dark of the Black Forest, without the troubles of violent hexenjägers and meddlesome girls from beyond their borders.

Dieter's defeat has made them complacent. Instead of seeing his threat as a need to act to prevent more dangers from others like him from forming, they believe we are safe from any dangers now.

Rochus's jaw tenses. "And her warrior."

Cornelia tugs my arm, and I reluctantly peel away from the table. Liesel has gathered her notes and meets us at the door, her bright eyes snagging on mine.

"Was I good?" she asks, breathless. It is only now that her nerves show, the anxiety I'd thought she had blossoming to the front.

Cornelia leads us out into the pale morning, the sun gleaming down on the little deck that juts off the council meeting room. All around and down below, the Well spreads out, a tangle of bridges and ladders and stairs, cottages nestled in branches and buildings formed to flow with the bends of trunks. The trees are just beginning to think of budding, small bundles of coming greenery clinging to the tips of branches, giving the faintest promise of spring against the gray and brown of winter's palette.

I stop Liesel and cup her face in my palms. "You were brilliant."

She beams. "Really?"

"I was riveted, and I lived through everything you said. Although"—I smile—"I don't remember some of those details."

She shrugs happily. "The stories they tell in Baden-Baden always have things like that—daring rescues. Big heavy words. I may have added a few things."

She's been listening to storytellers down in the village. She goes with Brigitta and her contingent of guards, along with a dozen or so other Well children, the barest beginnings of friendship between the hidden witches of the Black Forest and the mortals who have lived unknowingly as their neighbors all these years.

It's been an adjustment, to say the least. Yet another reason why Rochus and Philomena distrust me and what I represent.

And they have no idea about the truth of wild magic.

"Now," I say to Liesel. "I believe you've missed almost a morning's worth of lessons?"

Her face puckers. "I don't *need* lessons. Abnoba teaches me."

And as comforting as it is to rely on whatever the Crone might be teaching her chosen champion, my very young cousin...

"Humor me, will you?" I tap her nose. "You are making friends with the other students, at least, aren't you?"

That earns me a reluctant sigh. "Some of them are all right."

"I'm glad; that's—"

"None of them are as good at fire as I am."

"Well. For all our sakes, I should hope not."

She glares at me. Then smiles.

Her arms clamp around my waist in a throttling hug before she tears off across the treetop bridges, blond braids swinging behind her.

"In truth," Cornelia whispers as Liesel scampers off, "I think the instructors of our little school here are all too relieved when Liesel is called away. Did you hear she threatened to burn one of them *inside out*? What does that even mean?"

"I could almost understand such a threat—he *did* try to get her to do arithmetic."

Cornelia's flat look in response has me backtracking.

I sigh. "We worked through it. She did *not* actually burn him, which I have learned to take as a win."

Cornelia laughs and loops her arm with mine. "Come on, then. The ceremony will begin two mornings from now, but the purification will start tomorrow at dawn, and we have much to still plan for it."

I roll my eyes, but let her drag me down a staircase. "How have we not planned everything already? Though I do appreciate you giving us an excuse to leave the meeting early—"

"That was not an excuse," she tuts, flipping her red hair over one shoulder. "We still have hours of work ahead of us. *And* I hear your potion should be almost completed, yes?"

The bonding potion. I've been brewing it for the past three days—with, surprisingly, Hilde's help. Otto's sister lives in a little cottage at the base of the haven's trees, the perfect sequestered space in which to *think*, to brew and measure and create. And Hilde has added some helpful suggestions about beer brewing I've incorporated, ways to heat and add ingredients that complement the bonding potion's particularities. Because this potion, if brewed wrong, will strip me of magic and kill Otto.

But do I even need a potion like this anymore? Couldn't I just focus wild magic on Otto, on connecting him to me, and forgo any of this dangerous game?

Yes, Holda says. Immediate and sure.

I do not think now is the time to bring up wild magic's potency to the council, I say back, even though I'd been toying with that very idea.

It will never be a good time, says Holda.

I grimace. What would Rochus and Philomena say if I refused the potion and performed the bonding with Otto on my own, with just wild magic? I'm still so new with it. So untested. Is *now* the time and way to both try my abilities and make the announcement to the whole of the Well that they have been lied to about magic's true power?

Playing by Rochus and Philomena's rules is still necessary. They don't trust me. I can't think about broaching the subject of wild magic now; Otto and I have to bond; we have to continue fostering relations with people outside the Well; we have to do a dozen other things first. Maybe then, the council will trust me, and it will be easier to begin taking wild magic seriously.

My head aches, and I rub absently at my forehead—

—before coming to a stop in the middle of the staircase.

"Hold a moment," I say and turn to Cornelia. "You said we have *hours* of work ahead of us? What could possibly take that long?"

We've been over what the bonding ceremony entails. Otto's preparation will be physical exertion, the skills he will need to hone as my warrior, which he is already off on. My preparation, from what Cornelia told me, involves tinctures and herbs, simple spells of purification and cleansing.

But from the look of sly glee on Cornelia's face, I completely misjudged what she intends to do with me.

That slyness softens into true happiness, and she brushes a blond curl back from my face. "This is the first bonding ceremony the Well has seen in ages," she tells me. "We must get it right. Not just for you, but for us"—she waves around, at the whole of the village, the treetop community bustling—"and all we have accomplished. This is the mark of our future, Fritzi."

"So it's hardly an important thing Otto and I are doing, then."

She gives me a look. "Don't pretend you wouldn't *bond* with him anyway."

A smile creeps up over me, unbidden and traitorous, verdammt.

I bat at Cornelia. "We hardly need a ceremony for *that*."

"Oh, I know. My home is not nearly far enough away from yours. The neighborhood gathers together to complain about your...*bonding noises.*"

My face heats as my eyes go wide. "No. Truly? No. We're careful not to—"

She laughs, and it's evil, and I have half a mind to push her off the tree.

"I hate you," I tell her, but she hooks my arm again.

"Ah, this is excellent energy to have going into preparations. Annoyance and hatred."

"Well"—payback occurs to me, and my smile is devilish—"maybe you'll also be a cause for complaints once you tell Alois how you feel."

Cornelia chirps her offense and bumps me with her shoulder, but she purposefully shifts the conversation as we continue on, talking idly of the preparations she'll need, the herbs for potions we'll brew. Burdock root and rosemary, mint and sage, all things to burn away impurities and ensure the bonding ceremony is true. And final details of outfits she's arranged for us both, stylings and preparations for every event over the next few days.

Another twinge behind my eye signifies my headache hasn't left, and I fight not to rub at my temple, not to wince.

If Rochus and Philomena only knew how justified they are in distrusting me.

If they only knew how very much change I'm destined to bring to the Well.

Not only opening our hidden society to magicless mortals. But maybe, eventually, opening up *all* magic to *all* witches.

The world that the council oversees, that the goddesses ordained, is one of strict adherence to defined rules to access magic. Witches like me, green witches, access the magic by plants, by potions and herbs and green growing things. Witches like Liesel, through fire; witches like Cornelia, through spells that let her bridge the line between life and death. We do not reach beyond our set rules. We do not cross our defined areas.

To do so is to access wild magic. Wild, wicked, corrupting magic.

Or so we were told.

Wild magic, though, is nothing more than what it sounds—magic that is boundless. Magic that, once accessed, allows a witch to do *anything*.

The day my brother was defeated, I broke my tether to the Origin Tree and gave in to wild magic—just as Holda was always trying to get me to do—so I could realize what she knew, what her sisters deny: that wild magic is a stronger source of power than the stifled, narrow sieve of the Origin Tree. And with the rise of threats like the hexenjägers, who burn us without cause or trial, we need all the tools we can get.

It is time for witches to reclaim their true power.

It is time for us to stand against the burnings and death and slaughter.

But doing so…is all on me. I'm Holda's champion. After this ceremony, Otto will be my warrior, my bonded guardian, someone I will be able to call on through a connection established by the bonding potion. He'll be in this with me, whatever my fate may be, and my stomach cramps, my headache rages. All I wanted was to free my cousin from Dieter and to make sure Otto was safe.

I don't…I don't want to be a champion.

I'm not sure I can be.

The sooner you are bonded to Otto, the stronger you will be, says

Holda in a suddenly clipped voice. *Do not let anything get in the way of it, Friederike. This is what you need.*

No, it's what our society needs. All the tasks laid before me, the parts I must play, are what our coven needs; what the Well needs; what the council needs.

Cornelia leads me to her cottage, and I go, half-present, half wishing I could glare at Holda.

Is something wrong? I ask.

No, she says too quickly. It's nothing.

It's *something*. It's always something with these goddesses.

But I do want this ceremony, just not in the way Holda means, not even in the way Cornelia foresees.

I just want him. Otto.

All this, all the uncertainty, and as long as I have him, I think, maybe, I can endure whatever is to come.

3

OTTO

Despite staying up late and celebrating in the aftermath of the mock battle with the guards, I'm wide awake. I had a pretty good nap in the middle of the day thanks to the spell pouches, and once I was revived, the feasting and drinking had turned raucous. Alois told me that none of them had ever gone down quite so hard as I had, but Brigitta told me privately that few of them had never gotten a speck of the red powder on her. Pretty sure the pride in her face at my taking her down will carry me through the next few days leading up to the actual trial.

I stare at the moon, almost hidden by the new leaves unfurling outside. I can't sleep, but I dare not move. Fritzi is curled against my body. Her hair splays out on the downy pillow, a halo of gold. I want to tangle my fingers in it, pull her to me. I want to claim her lips, her body. I want to wake her with my love.

But I also want to let her sleep.

Since the end of Advent, things have been peaceful for the most part.

Dieter fell for my ploy, drinking a poison that stripped him of his magic and nearly killed him. He is one threat that has been dealt with.

But I know there are a million more.

Fritzi wants to open up the world to wild magic. Which will put her at odds with nearly every person, witch or not, in the world. She has to convince the magical council here at the Well that wild magic isn't an evil, sacrificial, corrupting influence *and* that they should trust her despite the fact that she's violated their laws and *already* cast off their restrictive version of magic.

And even if Dieter and the hexenjägers of Trier are gone, it's not exactly as if the world will embrace witches, no matter what type of magic they use.

I don't know what the future will hold for her.

I only know that I *have* to keep her safe.

A low crescent moon hangs on the horizon. We're high enough up in the trees, in our safe and cozy home nestled among the branches, that I will see the sun rise before my sister, whose cottage is on the ground below. A gentle snow drifts down; the last stray flakes as spring awakens.

It's been months. I know Fritzi still mourns her brother, but she mourns a version of him that no longer existed, perhaps never did. Her memories of her brother are shadowed; how long did he wear a mask, pretending to be someone he wasn't, someone she could love?

What an utter fool Dieter was. He was malicious and calculating; he rose in the ranks of the hexenjägers to Kommandant. He had the archbishop of Trier in his pocket. His cruelty was so extreme because of his genius. And yet—what a fool. To see Fritzi, to know her, and to toss away her love.

Hers is not a heart to toy with.

Soon, I shall prove that to her. The bonding ceremony has been used to threaten Fritzi multiple times. Once a witch drinks the bonding potion with someone, they are irrevocably linked, their powers intermingling. It requires absolute trust, something Fritzi did not share with the council when they tried to force her to commit a binding and sever the Well's magic with the world, and something she especially did not feel for Dieter, her brother, when he tried to use the spell to steal her magic.

But she trusts me. She loves me. And soon, we will magically bind our souls together.

Fritzi moans in her sleep, her hand clenching, releasing. Her eyelids flutter.

"Fritzi?" I'm not surprised she's waking; it's hard to sleep with such an important event happening so soon.

She shakes her head, still waking up. "Nightmare," she mumbles.

I reach for her, but she swings her legs over the side of the bed, the covers draped over her body. She's wearing her shift, and she grabs the robe from the hook by the door, shrugging it over her shoulders, her long blond hair still obscuring her face.

"Where are you going?" I ask, standing up.

"I have to do something." Her voice is raspy from disuse. She blinks at me. "I... It can't wait. I have to do it now." She bites her lip, nervous. "Library," she adds in a low voice.

"Is this about the council?" She and Liesel both have reason to be wary. Not only did the council try to coerce both girls into a binding; they have not been fully honest. Neither have the goddesses. Even with Fritzi being chosen by the goddess Holda as a champion, and that same goddess selecting me as Fritzi's warrior, we both know there are still secrets. Too many.

"It's important..." Her voice trails off.

She probably wants to keep the council out of this, I think, remembering that ass, Rochus.

"I understand," I say. They all have their secrets. We can have ours. "Can you tell me more about what you're looking for?"

Fritzi hesitates. Lets out a breath. Finally: "Do you trust me?"

"Always." The word bursts from me. Trusting her is one of the few things I'm certain of.

Fritzi shoots me a thankful smile and opens the door. I grab my cloak, squeeze my feet into boots, and follow her outside.

It's still early enough that no one else is around. Fritzi's been given a room close to the heart of the community, and while there are guards on the walkways and bridges connecting the trees, there are few here. I follow her, my muscles tensing.

Fritzi pads silently over a short bridge suspended high in the air, connecting to the council's inner sanctum. I cast a look behind me. The maze of bridges and landings built into the very trees of the Black Forest was once confusing to me. Now I can easily spot the school Liesel attends with other children, the homes of my friends, the quickest route that will take me to my sister's house.

Fritzi kept going without me. The door to the council room almost closes before I can slip in behind her. My stomach is tight, my senses alert. It's odd for her to act this way. It's clear she doesn't want to be seen by the others, but does she not want me to follow her either?

Everything is dark. Even the fires are cold, and I can see my breath in a cloud before me. The council room isn't used daily. There's a musty scent in the air, like damp earth and petrichor, a cold smell that I know the big hearth at the end of the hall would burn away if it were lit.

My footsteps echo, and I realize that Fritzi's feet are bare, despite the cold. I reach for her, intending to grab her arm and pull her to me, wrap my cloak around her shoulders, but she pivots suddenly, shifting in a way I didn't expect.

She opens a door I'd never noticed before. There's no light in this room—it's on the western side of the tree, beyond the sun's early rays, and there is neither fire nor torches. I stop by the door where a candle sits on an iron holder and use the tinderbox to spark a small flame.

Fritzi's already gone.

"Fritzi?" I say, my voice barely louder than a whisper.

I thrust the flickering candle out, sweeping back and forth, illuminating long rows of shelves. A library, the likes of which I'd never seen before. Even the archbishop back in Trier didn't have this many texts, scrolls and bound manuscripts and books and folios. A treasure trove of books, a wealth more precious than gold, all stored neatly on shelves.

I hear a noise to my left, and I whirl around, the flame on the wick smoking and sputtering. Smoke obscures my vision, and for a moment, all I see is a pair of eyes, pale and empty, unblinking. My heart lurches, but then I realize—

Fritzi stares up at me.

"Where did you go?" I whisper.

She tilts her head, and I notice another door on the far side of the library, closed.

"You must be freezing. Did you get what you need?"

She's silent for a long time. "Not yet," she finally whispers.

"Let's go back then?" It comes out as a question.

She nods, her hair sliding over her face. I reach out, tucking a lock of gold behind her ear.

"Is everything okay?" I ask softly. For a moment, her eyes seem darker than normal.

"Let's keep this our little secret," she says. She leans up and blows the candle out, the smoke swirling around us as she presses her lips to mine.

4

FRITZI

The next morning, I find that the bathing grove has been transformed.

Moss-covered stones surround a narrow offshoot of the river that runs through the Well. Folding wood panels cordon this space off from others, dozens of candles now filling this little cove, their light adding pecks of flickering orange to the late afternoon sun that shines down through gaps in the trees. Strands of herbs have been hung between sapling branches, and the whole area smells of them, but tart as well, where some have been burned: spicy mint and bitter rosemary and floral lavender.

I inhale as deeply as I can, willing the scents to elicit the intended calm, but a knot holds in the bottom of my belly. One that tugs, and winds, and tightens as I stand just outside the entrance, holding a robe tight around my body.

Hilde gives up on a purple flower she'd been trying to weave into the plaits across my hair. "Scheisse, I never could figure out how to do things like this. Why did Cornelia give me this task?"

"Maybe it's your test." I force a smile for her. "Otto is busy abusing all of his muscles. You get to solve a complex hair problem. And I get to take a bath."

She sighs heavily and starts in on the flower again. "Did I miss where I have to be involved in the bonding ceremony too? Because as much as I've come to like you, I don't think I want to be a part of that."

"That's not what—why does everyone keep making jokes about it like that? As though I would be so crass as to talk about such things with my lover's sister."

Hilde gags. "*Lover*."

My smile becomes truer. "My darling? My truest one? My tender—"

Hilde pats my cheek. Hard. "There. You're finished and ready to be baptized."

I cringe. "That's not what this is."

"You're purifying in water. Cleansing from sin. Dedicating yourself to a deity." Her tone is honestly curious. "How is it not?"

"This isn't meant to dedicate me to anything. This is to get rid of negative energy and reset my internal balance." It's easy to recite the words Cornelia has been drilling into my head for days, why this is so important, as important as Otto jumping around a...waterfall? I had to have heard that incorrectly. "And *sin* has nothing to do with it. I have done nothing for which I should feel guilty."

My gut thuds at that.

If the council knew where I got my true magic from, they would certainly disagree. Which is why it's so important I adhere to these traditions, to their rules, so as not to arouse suspicion.

But that's where my reticence comes from. Not in actually thinking I've done something wrong in connecting with wild magic, but in knowing that it will be a source of contention with the council.

Hilde cocks her head, a bewildered look falling over her. "I'm still not used to that," she says softly.

I straighten my robe. "Used to what?"

"Not being ashamed."

My eyes fly up to her.

I have gotten to know her well these past months. She's only similar to Otto in moments like these, when she is serious. Most of the time, she is uncouth and loud in a way that blends all too well with my own natural state, to the point Otto frequently regrets having us both in his life. Especially when we team up against him.

But now, when she stares up at me, her eyes are all Otto's, dark and sincere, and I can easily imagine her turning those same eyes heavenward in a cathedral, searching for answers in votive candle smoke.

I squeeze her shoulder. "Have I told you today that I'm glad my magic sent you here?" The errant spell that transported her to the Well so long ago is the reason for all of this, her presence here, mine, Otto's.

She beams. Wide and pretty. "No. But I do like to hear how much you adore me, so go on, go on."

My squeeze on her shoulder turns into a pinch, and she chirps. "I'll let Brigitta be the one to properly fawn over you."

Hilde blushes, and with a satisfied sigh, her eyes drift out. "And, oh, she is so very *good* at fawning."

My turn to gag. "All right, truce on talk of our...exploits?"

Her smile turns devilish. "I don't know. You did promise you'd give me all the details of that time you tried to woo the traveling merchant's daughter in Birresborn."

From one angle, I want to smirk—it was a rather silly moment that involved trying to steal a dried flower hanging in the rafters of my aunt's house, only for me to topple headfirst into the fireplace and come out covered in soot. Instead of swooning over my attempt at romance, as I'd hoped, the girl had laughed at me.

But even as I remember it, grief punctures holes in the story. I remember my aunt's house. Liesel's mother.

I remember it standing empty, bodies littered at my feet in the wake of Dieter's attack.

With a hard shake of my head, I drop my eyes from Hilde and straighten my already straight robe. "Can you see if Cornelia is ready for me yet?"

Hilde pats my arm, misreading my shift for nerves. "Of course. You'll do great."

She ducks into the cove, and for a moment, I'm alone.

Birds chirp somewhere overhead. The sounds of the Well are more distant, the bulk of the hidden city farther back, but I can imagine the bustle of day-to-day life, makers selling wares and people working looms and lessons underway. Liesel and all the other school-age children are missing more lessons for the upcoming ceremony; she was all too thrilled about that.

These normal thoughts serve as enough of a distraction that when Cornelia dips out in front of me, I'm able to square my shoulders without hesitation.

"Ready?" she asks.

I nod.

She slides away, and after a beat, I follow her in.

A path is laid out for me through the bathing area where two rows of women create a funnel to guide me toward the pool. At the edge, ankle-deep on a stone that lets them stand just within the water, are Liesel and Hilde, with Cornelia joining them.

If any of the women lining this path raises an eyebrow at a non-witch being part of this purification ceremony, they don't show it. With Hilde's help creating the bonding potion, watching over it as it brewed, and her relationship with Brigitta, she's become an honorary member of the Well.

The headache I can't seem to get rid of thuds behind my eyes, and I fight a wince as I step down alongside them, the cool, clear water lapping at my bare feet.

Will any amount of cleansing spells ready me?

I can pretend all I like for the council. Play the part, obey their rules and traditions, make it look as though, when I use magic, I am doing so through casting spells and harnessing ingredients. But it's a lie, all of it, and I have done far worse than that.

Holda chose me to do this; Otto eagerly fell into his role as my warrior. But I know, after this ceremony and the bonding one tomorrow morning, that I will be forced to the front of Holda's crusade. It will fall on me to convince the council—well, to convince Rochus and Philomena—that wild magic is no different than the magic they painstakingly protect in the Origin Tree. That the limitations we put on witches on how to use our power are unnecessary and harmful. That our entire way of life is a lie, and we should undo the very systems they've upheld for decades, and—

I drop the robe before I sink down into the bathing pool, and the shock of the chilly water silences my inner turmoil. The thin white shift I'm wearing billows up around me, dispersing herbs that bob across the surface of the pool, and with the nearby glow of candlelight and the soft, steadying presence of all the women behind me, it is, for a moment, peaceful.

I did not choose you idly, Friederike, Holda tells me.

My muscles go slack, and I lean against the edge of the pool, head and shoulders out of the water, my back to all the people in this cove.

So you chose my brother with the same careful intent? I can't help but snap. He had been her champion before me.

She goes silent.

The grotto fills with the velvety murmurs of chanting. The voices of the women rise around me, swelling high in a gentle litany. A spell. A prayer.

Water sloshes as Cornelia, Liesel, and Hilde kneel behind me.

After him, Holda says, *I made sure I did not choose incorrectly again.*

I don't respond.

Fingers tug at my head, tipping my face up to the high blue sky above. The murmured words catch, gain in volume:

"Water to wash. Plants to grow. Smoke to carry. Fire to ignite."

You may not believe it, Friederike, says Holda. *But you are the most suited to this task. I will not downplay the size of it, nor what I ask of you. I know I demand too much. But I will be at your side through every moment. I will not abandon you.*

I almost reply with an observation of how much good her allegiance did me when Dieter ripped me out of the Well and had me chained at his mercy in Baden-Baden. I almost respond with how much good the favor of a goddess does against potent cruelty.

But I agreed to this. I agreed to be her champion, however misguided I was, however desperate. I'm here, and I'll face the confrontations and struggles I know are coming, so pouting about it will get me nowhere.

The voices chanting, the smells of herbs and candle smoke, the velvety warmth of the water and air—it all combines, egged on by my sleeplessness, and for a moment, I think it worked. This cleansing ceremony. I feel made anew suddenly, shoved into a dazed aura—

You ask too much of this one, sister, snaps a voice. Recognition shatters the brief aura of fogged drifting. Perchta, the Mother goddess. *She will fail you and hurt what we have built.*

You do not wish to change our ways, Holda says. *You have made your stance clear. But you and Abnoba agreed, even so, to allow me to try.*

Still in the water, still wrapped up in the chanting of the people around me, I go immobile.

Holda could have this conversation without me hearing. So she is letting me hear it.

The other goddesses are aware of what it is she wants me to do: remove the restrictions on magic so all witches can access it without the requirements of tapping into the Well. But last I knew, Holda was shielding my connection to wild magic not only from the council but from her sisters too. It is not surprising that the goddesses saw through her scheming.

I do not move, skin gone cold in the water, pinned in place by the sensation of being near something forbidden, something sacred.

"Water to wash. Plants to grow. Smoke to carry. Fire to ignite."

The chanting continues, Cornelia, Liesel, and Hilde closest to me, but even their words are monotone, as though those who chant are no longer aware that they speak, like the whole of this cove has fallen into a lull under the conversation happening in my head.

Our priest and priestesses will never allow wild magic to be accepted, Perchta says, undeniable haughtiness in her tone. *Especially when it is this one presenting such an ill change. She cannot be trusted. She will only disappoint you the way her brother did.*

My chest bucks, heart wrenching hard, but I keep my lips pressed together, teeth digging into my cheeks until iron sours my tongue.

Holda doesn't respond right away. Does she think I will argue with Perchta? That I will fight for my abilities and swear I am not my brother?

Where is Abnoba? What side of this argument does she fall on?

I say nothing. I do nothing. I just sit in the water, trapped beneath Perchta's condescension, and stay silent.

You will not interfere, Holda tells Perchta. *Friederike will have the best chance I can give her.*

I will not interfere, Perchta says. *But if she endangers us, you will not be able to keep her safe from me.*

The air sucks out of the cove in a jarring pop that vibrates in my ears.

The chanting around me continues, but there is a livelier note to it now, not the droning, dizzying quality it had before. And behind me, Cornelia dips a cup into the pool, scoops water and a few pieces of rosemary, and dumps it down my hair.

"Water to wash," she says again, in time with the other women. "Plants to grow. Smoke to carry. Fire to ignite."

Her fingers on my scalp ground me. They still my shaking, shaking I hadn't even realized I was doing.

Perchta's words linger in my head. Holda's defense and certainty.

My palm presses flat on the brand on my stomach. A spot on my thigh aches. A third on my chest.

Dieter's brands. The scars he left behind.

I smell the stench of burnt flesh suddenly, hear distant screams—my screams—and I just want to *rest*, I just want to *run*—

Cornelia shifts aside, making room for Liesel, who repeats the action, scoop, dump, recite.

This spell is unnecessary. This whole cleansing ceremony is unnecessary. All the spells we memorized because they were *the only way* to access the Well's magic—lies. All the herbs we use, the potions we brew—lies. Catalysts, at most, ways to focus our intent. But they were just rules inflicted on us by the goddesses, who sealed away as much magic as they could in the Origin Tree so they could divvy it out in a controlled, methodical way, as opposed to the unpredictable, unrestrained might of wild magic.

Hilde is next. She repeats what Cornelia and Liesel did.

Their voices lock together, the women all behind me, a faceless, chanting sound rising, rising in volume.

"Water to wash. Plants to grow. Smoke to carry. Fire to ignite."

My eyes flutter shut, and I see the outline of the Origin Tree again. Its branches twisting, reaching for the sky.

Water. Plants. Smoke. Fire.

Four elements twist up around it, streams of each that lock together in a braided rope of protection—or, no, they contract, and the Tree shudders—

I gasp, but the image is there and gone so fast, a twinge of nothing more than ghost pain.

I've been sleepless. The headaches are getting worse. My nerves are rubbed raw.

That's all.

It has to be.

Cornelia squeezes my shoulder, and I rise up out of the water, shivering. Even though it is a wet spring in Baden-Baden, in the Well, it is perpetually warm, but that does nothing to stop the bone-deep shudder.

I see the Tree quaking under the tightening of that elemental rope.

A blanket is wrapped around my shoulders. I huddle into it, and when I turn, the women have gone silent, a dozen shining eyes watching me.

They have not had a witch-warrior bonding ceremony in decades, much less a *champion*-warrior bonding ceremony. And I feel the weight of their hope tenfold, an invisible power even more intense than wild magic.

My knees wobble.

I take a breath, spicy mint, bitter rosemary, floral lavender.

My eyes meet Cornelia's, and she beams, a wide, excited grin.

"Now," she tells me, "we get to have some fun."

Fun turns out to be a rather lengthy dressing process, where Cornelia, Hilde, and Liesel twist my hair with flowers and cocoon me in a gown that had to have come right out of one of the fantastical stories Liesel loves listening to. It's more or less a kirtle—a fitted dress—but the sleeves have been removed so my arms are free, and slits up the side leave my legs bare to midthigh. The deep green color is offset by stitched plants, herbs for protection, and flowers, bright, beautiful, violent bursts of orange and blue and gold, and a thinner cover is placed on top, sheer gray fabric that almost makes up for how much skin I'm showing.

If we were staying in the Well for the final piece of the purification ceremony—the bonfire—then I wouldn't mention it. But as I trail Cornelia through the forest, our procession of women making for Baden-Baden, I can't help but clear my throat awkwardly.

"I think this outfit may cause the Catholics to collectively turn on us again," I say.

Hilde laughs. Boisterously. "Rest assured, *this* Catholic is *manically* in favor of this sort of fashion."

Liesel's big eyes blink up at her. "Why?"

Hilde blanches. "Oh. Um. You see—"

I nudge her with my elbow, and she tumbles a few steps like I tripped her. "Nothing, Liesel. Hilde thinks she's funny."

Liesel scowls, clearly knowing she's missed the joke, but she relents.

All around us, the woods are darkening with dusk, but lanterns dot the gray-black trees like fireflies determined to emerge before summer.

Hilde clears her throat. "Is my role done? I'm off to—"

"Yes," I say instantly. Then grin when, for a second, she looks offended before realizing the game.

She rolls her eyes. "Such gratitude. I don't know *what* Otto sees in you."

"With this dress, he'll see quite a lot."

Liesel giggles. "*Ohhhhhh*. I get it now."

Scheisse.

Hilde chortles and playfully punches me in the shoulder. "*As I was saying*, I'm off to find Brigitta." And she's gone with little more than a backward wave.

Cornelia chuckles at Hilde's departure, but she edges closer to me and sobers. "Do not worry about the dress," she tells me. "We aren't hiding from them anymore, remember?"

Her smile doesn't counter the intensity in her eyes.

No. We aren't hiding. We declared the existence of magic and witches quite spectacularly when my brother overtook Baden-Baden, and while the distant reaches of the Holy Roman Empire may be able to deny us still, the people of this little hamlet no longer can. Most have embraced us, no doubt for saving them from Dieter, but how long will those good graces hold? We're having this bonfire ceremony in their town square as another good-faith outreach. What if seeing our practices is too much, too soon? What if—

I cut myself off, balling my hands, eyes rolling shut on a groan.

The Three save me. Is this how I sound to Liesel, to Otto? How are they still tolerating me?

Yes, there are terrifying things to be done. But we *survived*. We survived my brother. We survived his crusade. We're here, and people without magic *know about witches* and are willing to at least attempt to embrace us.

This is good.

Whatever happens after the bonding ceremony.

This is *good.*

I repeat that to myself as we wind through the forest, emerging into the town of Baden-Baden.

There is no city wall, not like the fortress that is Trier, and I'm glad there's no comparison between those two cities. Trier was dark and smoke grimed, a war of Roman architecture and Catholic oppression. Baden-Baden is sprawling and open in a way that matches the untamed mystery of the Black Forest, as though it remembers its roots, even under the Empire's hand.

We weave through the streets, most buildings shut up against the late hour, past nightfall now. The sky is clear and star speckled, the air cool but not frigid, and I'm grateful for that, dressed as I am.

A hand tugs at my wrist. I accept Liesel's fingers between mine, and she squeezes.

"Don't be nervous," she whispers up at me.

I cock a smile down at her. "Me, nervous? Never."

"You don't have to—*whaaaaat?*"

Her words end on a long, drawn-out gasp, eyes plastered ahead of us, to where the road spills open into the town square.

I turn, and my smile grows.

The bonfire in the middle of Baden-Baden is truly impressive, a pile of logs that sends fingers of orange and yellow dancing up into the black sky. Music plays from somewhere, tinny instruments and tapping drums that shoot urgency into everyone as they hurl their bodies around the fire. Most are from the Well, witches all too glad to no longer be forced into hiding. Some, more than I'd expected, are from Baden-Baden, and their tentative smiles grow as they watch members of Brigitta's Grenzwache toss themselves in daring leaps over the flames.

There are pockets of discontent too. Some people have come merely to fold their arms and glare at the celebration, muttering to each other and shaking their heads disapprovingly. But they are far, far fewer than I expected—errant groups, hardly the majority. And most of their discomfort seems to lose its force against one man in particular: the town priest, who is clapping alongside witches, smiling at the music, dark robes lit by the flames.

He is accepting of us. Of this.

And so the dissenters hardly have support to turn their muttering into action.

Liesel bounces next to me and points at the people leaping over the flames. "Oh, I want to try that! Fritzi, *Fritzi*, oh my—"

Before I can say anything at all, she takes off, darting through the crowd in a blur of blond curls and blue dress.

Cornelia laughs. "She gets it." Her elbow pierces my side. "Why are you so sour, then? This is *your* party, after all."

"I'm not sour." I frown at her. "And I'm not nervous either. I don't know why you and Liesel are so set on me being upset when I am clearly *fine*."

Cornelia gives me a flat look. "Yes. You're terribly convincing. All I'll say is—ah." Her eyes dart over my shoulder and a coy smile takes her. "All I'll say is that you had better do something tonight to purge yourself of all this being *fine* before you undergo the bonding ceremony tomorrow. That is the *point* of all this purification, after all, and, oh look, there is *something* coming up to you right now."

I whirl, feeling his eyes on me even before I see him.

5

OTTO

Fortunately, after the mock battle with the Grenzwache, being dunked in an ice-cold pond and then climbing up the rocky side of a waterfall was *nothing*, and the freezing water actually helped revitalize me despite my exhaustion at the trial. By the end, beer and laughter and a lot of back-clapping hugs assured me I passed. I am now both a member of the guard and a citizen of the Well.

All around me, the celebrations roar just as loudly as the flames.

A heavy arm falls over my shoulder as Alois pulls me closer. "We should absolutely be doing this more often!"

"The trial, or the party after?" I ask, grinning at him.

"Both, as long as it's not me scaling rocks." He laughs loudly, even though his joke wasn't that funny, and I smell the beer on his breath. Before I can say anything, Alois seems to sober. "It's a little intimidating, isn't it? To bond with someone else? To irrevocably declare yourself as the warrior of a witch?"

I blink, surprised. I hadn't considered that. I had only ever thought of Fritzi, and how I could best help her.

"You're going to be her shield," Alois continues, his eyes growing distant. "If there's a battle, you'll be in front of her."

I push his arm off my shoulder. "No," I say. "If there's a fight to be had, I'll be *beside* her. That's the point."

Alois opens his mouth to say something, but then his face goes slack. I follow his eyes. Cornelia is in front of a procession of women, and I have no doubt whatsoever that she's the cause of Alois's sudden awkwardness as he scurries away, too shy to actually approach the priestess.

But then I see Fritzi.

She walks through the darkness toward me. A different sort of heat washes over me at her scorching gaze, stronger than the bonfire at my back.

"What are you wearing?" I ask, the words barely clawing through my tight throat. There's cloth—some sort of gauzy material draped in panels over her kirtle—but there's also skin, so much of Fritzi's skin visible it's decadent, and—

"You like it?" she asks, twirling, knowing *exactly* what she's doing to me.

"Love it." The words come out strangled, barely audible.

She slows, the cloth drifting over her legs and arms, a cloud of beauty, then stops, raking her eyes over me. "And look at you."

I glance down at the green tunic and brown leather leggings I got after my pond-dunking. At the time, I'd just been grateful I didn't have to climb the waterfall nude, but after that and fire-jumping, I realized this wasn't just the standard fare of what the Grenzwache wear on patrols, but magically enhanced garments. The tunic is thin as cotton but sturdy as leather; the leggings are supple, easy to move in but impervious—so far, at least—to fire or sharp rocks. The boots Alois laced for me make my movements in the forest silent.

I don't know if there is anything magic about Fritzi's dress, other than the way it makes my body flush at the sight of her in it.

"So, you survived your trials," she says, oblivious to the way I cannot rip my eyes from her.

Although I felt that the Grenzwache had come to accept me already, the tasks had not been easy, and I dread to think of what failure might have meant. The witches bandaged me up after, giving me a potion for healing, tinctures for the cuts and burns on my body. But hard as the trial was, I'm grateful. If I could not have passed this test among friends, how could I even be close to worthy as Fritzi's protector?

"You survived your bath," I say, giving her a smile I hope doesn't reflect how grueling my day was.

Fritzi pauses, and my stomach tightens at the dark look that flickers over her face. But then she glances at me, her smile cutting across my worries.

"Well, it was pretty questionable there at the end," she says, a mischievous glint in her eye. "I'm fairly certain Hilde tried to drown me."

I cast my glance over Fritzi's shoulder and spot my sister, her arms draped around Brigitta.

"Oh yes," I say dryly. "She's a burgeoning murderess. I'll have a talk with her. If I can muster up the courage to face someone so vicious."

"Please do. It was a very trying day for me. My fingers got pruney, Otto. *Pruney*. While you were making merry in the forest, I'm sure."

She holds her fingers up for me to see, and it's all I can do not to grab them, to pull her to me, to claim not just the tips of her fingers but her whole body.

But there's something she's not telling me. Even though she speaks lightly, I think there must have been something more to her bath than scented soaps and warm water. I recall last night, the strange way that she crept to the council's library.

"Fritzi—you know you can trust me, right?" I ask.

She looks at me curiously.

"It's just..." I pause. She has a right to her secrets, especially when it comes to magic, something I cannot advise her on. But I want her to know that I will do anything to help her, and that she is not alone in whatever worries her. That I will be beside her, no matter what the fight entails. "Last night..."

Fritzi frowns, her gaze sliding away. "Last night, I had a nightmare." I can see the muscles in her jaw clenching, and I stroke the side of her cheek until she turns to me. "I really don't want to talk about it. Not now."

I nod. I can only imagine the sorts of terrors she dreams about. She hadn't seemed distressed, but if she woke up with dark memories, going to the library, where there are spell books... She may have been seeking a way to drive those thoughts from her head.

I curse myself. Maybe she actually did want to be alone, and I forced my presence on her. She's had nightmares before, and she'd wanted me to hold her after, but now... Her fears could have a different tenor; perhaps the only way to drive them out is through magic.

"Whatever you need from me, I will give to you," I promise her, my hands sliding down her arms to grip her hands. *Even if that means you want me to leave you alone.*

"Always so noble and serious." Her lips quirk up in a smile, and she lifts on her tiptoes, a swift kiss fluttering against my lips.

"As for tonight," I say, "there is one other task, no?"

Brigitta had informed me that the last part of the night would need to be the marking of my body. All the guards of the Well have black tattoos etched in their skin, each a sigil, a spell, that aids them in their defense.

Brigitta explained it to me before we left for Baden-Baden. *"Typically, I would use this night to determine your weaknesses and needs as a soldier, and then I would mark you with counter sigils that would strengthen you where you need it most, infusing the tattoo with magic."*

But I am a goddess-chosen warrior with a powerful witch who will bond with me tomorrow.

This ceremony is ours and ours alone. And only Fritzi will ever mark me.

Cornelia, the one member of the high council that Fritzi likes and trusts, approaches. I look over her shoulder and spot Alois watching her some distance away, as if he is entranced. "We need ash," she says, oblivious to Alois's adoration.

The raucous celebration doesn't abate as Cornelia leads us around the fire. It's good, I think, to see so many people out tonight, sharing in joy. There is a fervor surrounding us—witches from the Well mingling with the people of Baden-Baden. There's a unity here that I appreciate; the priest of the local parish may be willing to dance with Liesel at the bonfire, but I know he'll continue to hold Mass. That's fine. No one is trying to convert or change anyone; we're all simply allowing the others to exist, sharing in the joy of life, not any god or goddess.

How different life in Trier would have been, had this been the attitude from the start.

The thought makes me stop in my tracks. I have spent my whole life focused on one goal at a time. Stop my father from hurting my stepmother. Protect my sister. Infiltrate the hexenjägers and tear apart their reign of murder from within.

But it's not until this moment, seeing the joy of shared respect and acceptance of humanity among all, that I realize my goals were always leading me to this point.

Peace.

Not a peace achieved through uniformity and control or even tolerance. One achieved through acceptance.

It's obvious not everyone approves of tonight. There are people in the houses unwilling to join us in the town square, glaring down from behind cracked shutters. And it makes me wonder how long this peace can last.

Fritzi walks with her head held high, even the blooms in her curling hair standing at attention as she looks out at the crowd. Does she fear the same things I fear? It is not yet fully spring, and the witches of the Well brought not just fire but food and beer to the townspeople. The dark night is lit; the long hunger between harvests is sated. Can this unity survive in the bright light of day when there is no night to hide behind, no need to be grateful for an extra feast?

This celebration has brought two peoples together, but such unity is fragile.

Despite all my doubts, I find that hope burns vivid. This one sparkling moment has proven a peace like this is possible. And now that I've seen it, I know I can fight to make it last.

Trier had joy too. Once. But the yule nights gave way to other fires, and in the end, terror divided the people in a way no shared love of life could withstand.

Now, though, I can't help but believe the joy of a bonfire is a greater bond than the fear of a witch burning.

No one stops to stare at us as we near the flames, so close that I feel a sheen of sweat on my skin. Even though we are in a crowd of people, there is some privacy here. The people around us are all celebrating their own joys, taking their own tentative steps toward linking with others of their choosing. Brigitta has swirled Hilde into a boisterous dance; Liesel is now regaling a group of children from Baden-Baden with her tales, hands splayed and arms thrown wide as she exaggerates; even stuffy Philomena accepts a sip of beer from a brown-robed monk who offers her a taste.

Cornelia starts to pull Fritzi away, but I grab her, spinning her to me, searing a kiss on her lips that would make the fire beside us wither to ice in comparison. There's a nervous tension between us. We are crossing several thresholds, each ceremony a reminder of a tie that binds, a net woven around us, drawing us closer together. I cannot ease the worry lines between Fritzi's eyes, but I want to assure her that this is what I choose.

Her. Us.

Every time.

"If you're quite done," Cornelia mutters as she kneels with Fritzi to scoop up a palm of ember-filled ash from the base of the fire, adding oil from a vial, turning the mixture into black paste in Fritzi's open hand.

"I don't know how to mark him," Fritzi says, a rare moment of vulnerability.

"Let the goddess guide you," Cornelia says. "Remember: magic is about intent. The two of you are bound in ways beyond the potion you'll drink tomorrow."

Fritzi dips her finger into the puddle of black in her palm and lifts it. A slow smirk that spells trouble smears across her face. "Lean down," she instructs me, and I almost do it, but I'm well aware of my Fritzi and instead take a step back. "I'm just going to draw a big smile on your face so that Liesel doesn't think you're so *broody*."

"My *face*?" I say, gaping. A tattoo is indelible. I do not need a black smile across my face permanently. Or ever, really.

"Well, where do you want the sigil?" Fritzi says, rolling her eyes but smiling regardless.

I grab the hem of my tunic and pull it off, exposing my torso. "I was thinking my arm or my chest..." I know very little about what this process would include, only that the end result will be a black mark staining my skin, imbuing me with magic.

Brigitta is marked all over her body, from her neck to her toes, various swirling designs. She has shown me some—the fox at the base of her skull to give her cleverness, the runic symbol over her heart to bolster her courage, the black line on her lip to make her inspiring in her speeches to her soldiers. "*There are two limitations,*" Brigitta told me earlier this night. "*The marks enhance, but do not create—they will not make an evil heart good or a severed limb regrow.*"

"*And the second?*" I asked.

"The magic must come from somewhere. Usually, it is a witch who earns the marks, and their magic focuses through the sigil."

But I have no magic of my own. I am not a witch. Whatever mark Fritzi gives me will mean that, when I need to draw power from the sigil, I will be drawing power from *her.* Brigitta has dozens of tattoos, not only because she needs them and earned them, but because she has the magic to focus them. They enhance her natural skill, and the power for that enhancement comes from her own resources.

Resources I do not have.

Once I understood that, I resolved to only take one mark tonight. I do not want to steal from Fritzi. She is the champion. She needs her magic more than me. But Brigitta assured me that it would not drain Fritzi's magic to divert power toward one tattoo, and such a thing may help me be strong enough to aid her. Being bonded will mean that I can work with Fritzi's magic and that we can work together.

"I don't know what to draw," Fritzi says, turning to Cornelia. "I'm not sure… What if I get the sigil wrong?"

She is so worried, but I'm not.

Cornelia shakes her head. "It's not like that. All you have to do is hold the ash to his skin and *will* the magic into the marking that will best enhance his own strengths."

Brigitta had explained this to me, too, showing how the more intricately woven designs created a tighter spell casting, reflecting not the skill of a tattoo artist but the magic behind it.

"It's okay," Cornelia starts to tell Fritzi, but I ignore her. I take Fritzi's trembling wrist, rubbing my thumb over the rapid firing of her pulse. I look right in her wide eyes, noting the flickering flames reflected over the cool blue.

And I press the flat of her palm against my chest, right over my own heart.

For one moment, I feel the warm black paste made of ash and oil.

The bonfire disappears.

The *world* disappears.

My mind floods with memories so vivid that I cannot see anything else. Kneeling in the parish church at Bernkastel, Hilde to one side of me, my father to the other. The priest stooping to smear ash on my forehead, the ritual reminder of Ash Wednesday, but the char reminding me of my stepmother's recent burning. My father shouting at me when I pulled away from the priest, the racket turning into hacking, blood-spattered coughs, red blending with the purple-dyed linen. But then my sister slipped her hand in mine, and we knelt, together, a prayer on both our lips, not for forgiveness, but for revenge.

Fritzi's palm burns on my chest, as if the ash were smoldering embers, not cold and dead. Although I can feel her, I cannot see her, and the enveloping smoke gives me the impression of solitude. Much like the trials in the Black Forest, the goddesses have separated us.

As I blink away that first memory, the nauseating smell of burned flesh gags me. I try to rip away, to vomit, but I can't move. I can only feel the heat of the fire—not the bonfire, but the stakes, the hundreds of stakes lining the streets of Trier—

I quit fighting it.

I pulled away from the priest when I was a child. I turned away from the stakes when I was a man.

I had not understood the chasm between my father's interpretation of his god and the God I worship. I had not been willing to see the consequences of my too-subtle rebellions, the time it took to plan, the lives lost while I did so.

I will face it now. I will stand, unflinching, before any fire.

And if Fritzi were in that fire, I would stride into it after her.

No one will burn any witch from this moment on without burning me too.

And no one will *ever* hurt Fritzi without answering to my unbridled wrath.

My eyes stare through the smoke.

Fritzi comes back into focus, her palm to my heart, her gaze clear. But she doesn't blink. The fire beside us burns, but the flames do not flicker. The people beyond us dance and sing and drink—all unmoving, impossibly still.

A maiden dressed in white moves behind Fritzi.

"Holda," I say.

"I speak directly to my champion," the goddess answers, touching Fritzi's frozen shoulder. "But right now, as she marks you as hers, I will speak to you as well."

She had spoken to me once before, to give me a trial. My jaw tightens. I'm tired of trials.

But I will face them all for Fritzi.

Holda smiles, as if she can guess my thoughts. "Typically, a warrior of the Well guides the mark they get. Their magic fuels the design, powers the sigil."

I bow my head, aware of my deficiency.

"What do you want, warrior?" Holda asks. She raises an eyebrow, her gaze weighing my worth. "Do you want the strength of ten men? A bear tattoo, one that will grant you the power to fight?"

I shake my head, teeth grinding. I know the legends of men who went berserk. Their strength came at too great a cost. Not even a witch mark would make me want to accept that mantle.

"Cunning, perhaps? A snake then. Coils of scales woven together like elaborate plans, careful precision."

Such a power would have helped me before, when I worked with Hilde to come up with the strategy to let the prisoners in Trier escape. But I have no need for subterfuge and heists now. I will never again wear the cloak of a hexenjäger, not even as a disguise.

"Life. Vitality. The ability to take hits and not fall." Holda speaks softly, but her voice rises when she sees that she finally has my attention, tempting me with a mark that I want. "With a circle, you would have the ability to be within a hair's breadth of dying and yet—" She pauses, tilting her chin up, relishing the anticipation. "And yet you would not die. Your body would heal. You would be nearly impossible to defeat."

I bite my lip, considering. Holda flicks her hand toward the fire, and the flames leap to attention, twining around each other in a woven circle, unbroken. One branch of the flames reaches out to me; the other flickers to Fritzi. The fire doesn't burn, but the implication is clear.

My vitality would come at Fritzi's expense.

How can I ask for my life to be protected when such a protection would come at the expense of magic drawn from Fritzi's reserves?

I shake my head. "I don't want her to protect me," I say to the goddess. "I want to be the one to protect her."

The flames shift back to their normal shape, but they remain utterly still. Holda's gaze softens as she watches me.

"I chose my warrior well," she whispers.

The flames roar to life, and every sensation bursts at once—the bitter smell of smoke, the jarring shouts of laughter, the heat from the fire, the taste of Fritzi's kiss on my lips. My vision goes white, and I stagger back, unable to stop myself from doing so.

Where Fritzi's palm had been is now a black tattoo.

"The Tree," Cornelia whispers, her eyes going wide.

I glance down at my chest. The shape is circular, the top a crown of delicate leaves at the ends of twisting branches, the bottom roots that pool out to form the complete circle. The trunk is made of twisting lines—three dark strokes that weave together to form one tree trunk—but there's symmetry to the chaos, a sense of connection. The palm-sized tattoo is just a little to the left of the center of my chest, right over my heart.

"I—I didn't think of anything," Fritzi says, fear taking hold. "I didn't do that, I didn't have the intention like you talked about—"

"I did." My voice is calm and sure, and it pulls both women's attention to me. "I saw Holda," I say. "She helped me choose the tattoo."

"You chose the tree?" Cornelia asks.

I give her a noncommittal shrug. I wanted to protect Fritzi. It took the form of the tree. I suppose that's the same thing, but I don't want to explain, not to Cornelia, not before I can talk with Fritzi. From the way Cornelia speaks, I can tell that the tree is a powerful symbol, and it must be linked to the mysterious Origin Tree, the one I have yet to even see.

Fritzi's fingers are featherlight as she brushes against the marked skin. I shudder at her touch, but not in pain. I've seen tattoos outside the coven before, and I know they're made with needles and ink and come at the cost of days of pain. This one doesn't hurt. It feels a part of me, as if I'd been born with the design.

"The Tree is the deepest part of our legends," Fritzi whispers. Every witch child knows of its importance, and I feel a little inadequate that I don't.

"Our goddess chose well," Cornelia says when I don't answer, and I'm not sure if she's talking about me or the tattoo. "It's not necessary to show it off to the entire village right now, though, and I have no personal need for your rippling pectorals."

I smirk. "Rippling pectorals?" I ask the priestess. I *cannot* wait to tell Alois that she said that.

Cornelia rolls her eyes, thoroughly done with me. "Do something with your warrior, champion," she tells Fritzi. She picks up my tunic and tosses it to Fritzi.

"Oh, I plan to," Fritzi says, a feral glint in her eyes as she steps closer, leaning up for a kiss as Cornelia strides away.

Fritzi strokes the side of my jaw, drawing my attention back to her, us.

I don't want to think about anyone else. I don't want to feel the burden of peace upon my shoulders.

I only want to feel her.

I lean down, claiming her lips again in a devouring kiss, knowing that no feast around a fire will be enough to satisfy me.

She melts in my arms, and I pull back, sliding my lips down the soft edge of her jaw, nibbling to the shell of her ear. "Not here," I whisper. I can feel her body shiver at my low voice. I take my shirt from her and pull it over my head, looking around for an escape route.

"But this celebration is for us," Fritzi protests weakly as I pull my tunic back over my head.

"Let them celebrate how they want to," I say, biting her just enough to make her gasp. "And let us celebrate how we want to."

She nods against my chest, her arms clinging to me. My hands snake down her body, and she spins away, grabbing my wrist and drawing me away from the fire, into the night.

There is no wall around Baden-Baden, but nature creates its own borders. There is a place where the road merges into a game trail, where the cottages are replaced by trees, where the grasses shift from harvested to wild.

That is where we go.

A clear area of land, under the stars of the night sky. There's a single large oak tree, set away from the edge of the Black Forest.

"You deserve a palace," I say. New daffodils are just starting to peek up from the hard ground, a sign of life and hope. "A soft bed covered in furs. Downy pillows and sumptuous feasts and... You deserve so much more than I can give you, Fritzi."

She sits down gracefully and touches the pale green shoot of an unbloomed flower. It swirls and bursts to life, the yellow trumpet tipping toward the moon, the petals soft as spider silk.

This is the wild magic that she hides from the council, that she shows only me.

"I don't want any of that," she says, looking up, starlight spattering over her skin. "I only want you."

I kneel before her, the only goddess I worship. Over her left shoulder,

I can just see the black smoke of the bonfire, orange specks fading to darkness. To the right is the Black Forest, looming trees full of magic and secrets.

But this meadow is ours. This night is ours.

6

FRITZI

Otto kisses me, his lips soft and caring and full of his usual tender love, and any other night, I would fall into it. Any other time, the intentional palpitation of his mouth on mine would be enough to melt me into compliance, and I would give myself over to his touches and let the weight of him block out all else.

But tonight, I don't want tenderness. I stand again, dragging him up with me, and he complies, eyes pulsing in a brief question before I silence any remarks with my mouth on his, tongue delving deep. I taste him, sweetness from food he'd had earlier, but *him*, some headiness I can never quite name more than that it is the taste of my undoing.

His back hits the oak tree, and he huffs in surprise as I move to his neck, tasting, tasting, pulling the neckline of his tunic aside to lick the contour of his shoulder.

"Fritzi," he gasps, and tries to push me, tries to regain control. "I want to—"

I pull back enough to look into his eyes. I can't hide the tremor of fear beside this need, and so I show it to him, the fear that's driving me, has been driving me.

Holda took over the tattoo. For me, for him. I can see the outline of the tree through the neckline of his tunic, and I have to believe it will keep him safe now. Safer, at least.

But safe enough?

"Let me do this for you," I whisper. "I want to make you feel good tonight."

His eyes flash. Darken. "That is never a concern with you, Liebste." He hooks a strand of hair behind my ear. "But today has been a lot for you, I know. And tomorrow will be too. And I want to make sure you're taken care of—"

I silence him with a kiss. Nothing deep. Nothing suggestive, even, despite the clear intention humming in the air between us.

"Hush now," I whisper into his mouth, "and take what I give you, Jäger."

I know I don't imagine the pulse of heat in Otto's gaze, the flicker of his lips tugging up at the way I grab his wrists and smash them to either side of his body against the bark of the tree. Magic tingles along my arms, and I have vines crawl up the tree, intending to encircle his wrists and keep him pinned.

But before they even touch him, a spasm grabs my lungs, and I halt the spell.

My own wrists burn.

They're long healed, no scars even.

But I still feel the manacles.

The way I'd hung by them in Dieter's room, and then again, attached to the stake. His brand searing into my stomach, my thigh, my collarbone, over and over and—

My palm had been pressed to Otto's chest. The ink and the magic of the tattoo were not a *brand*, not a burning, not something forced on him—he'd chosen this, he'd chosen me, *it's not the same*—

Leaning against Otto, I go rigid, and he feels the change in me, coming out of his own stupor with a sudden inhale.

"Fritzi? What's wrong?"

Nothing. No, *nothing*, nothing here, not now—*please* not now—

I kiss him, but he doesn't return it, doesn't drop back against the tree.

"Fritzi—"

Fritzichen. Oh, sweet sister.

He isn't here. He isn't *here*. He's in a prison in Trier, or dead already, and he's gone, and *he can't hurt me anymore*.

My face ends up buried in Otto's shoulder. The crook of his neck. I take hard, gasping breaths, my whole body shuddering, and Otto's arms come around me, a warm, immovable wall.

"Liebste," he whispers into my hair.

I say something against his skin. Words tumble from my lips, sobbed words, and I hear them coalesce, "I did this to you."

My hand is on the tattoo. Just under his tunic.

Otto holds me closer. "Yes," he says. "We did this. Together."

I lurch back, tears burning my eyes, and then shame matches, burning my throat. I ruined this night. Ruined this moment. My hand fists in his tunic, and I glare at him for being unable to glare at myself.

"You'll get hurt," I tell him, like he doesn't know, like he hasn't foreseen the inevitable ending. "When we go up against the council. When we try to change the way magic is viewed and used outside of the Well. You'll get hurt because of me. Because of this." I put my hand over the tattoo. "Because you're bound to me, and I'm too selfish to push you away."

Is it the same? The brand Dieter put on me, the tattoo I put on Otto?

Otto cups my face in his hands, his focus making no room for me to look anywhere but at him.

"I have *chosen* to be here," he says. "You know me well by now. Do you truly think there is anything I would do if I did not want to do it? You are not the only selfish one. I'm here because I want to be. Because I chose *you*. And yes, I might get hurt—I probably will. But I will do so knowing that it's for a cause I have chosen. For—"

"Damn your honor, Otto." I try to shove back from him, but he keeps my face in his hands, which undercuts me trying to be angry with him. "You're marked by me. Tomorrow, you'll be bound to me. You say you know what you're doing, but what if you want out one day? What if all this destroys you?"

My chest kicks, a sob, and Otto's brows furrow.

"Destroys me? How so?"

"What if your god rejects you because of this?"

What will your kapitän whore think? You, all damaged like this.

"What if your god rejects you," I'm talking too fast, spiraling, "and what if mine one day can't save you? We can't pretend gods haven't betrayed their charges in the past. What will we do when mine leads us to ruin and yours has turned his back on you? What will you do when"—I gasp, but he's still holding my face, catching my tears on his thumbs—"when you realize you've followed me down a path that leads to nowhere but desolation? You say you know what you're doing. But I don't think you do, not truly. Not—"

His turn to kiss me silent.

It isn't a gentle kiss. Not his usual tenderness, love spoken in touch. He kisses me now like he's fighting for dominance; I kiss him like I'm afraid this will be the last time, even though we've had dozens of times now.

He's bruising and vicious, and his aggression throws me back, stumbling across the grass, the foliage of the forest. He lifts me, locks my legs around his hips, spins us both so my back slams to the tree now. I'm aware even more of the lack of cloth in this outfit, legs bare where they belt his waist, shoulders and arms scraping the tree through the gauzy material.

"Friederike Kirch." My name is a reprimand from him that shoots down my spine like lightning, miring me in place between the hard planes of his body and the rough bark of the tree. "If either god, *any* god, abandons us, leaves us to wallow in some abyss or drift through whatever trials alone, then I will be there, with you. Because that is what I have chosen, *that* is what this bonding ceremony means to me: that all the forces of this world could turn their backs on us, but I won't forsake you."

A softer kiss. A promise.

I whimper, a hollow pulse of unraveling.

"I won't leave you," Otto tells me, and he is swearing to me now, trailing featherlight promises across my cheekbone. "I am yours more than I belong to any god or cause."

"And I'm yours," I manage through my tight throat, through the hum rekindling in my blood.

Otto makes a grunt of confirmation. I feel the rumble of it, but I buck against him, and he hisses.

"Say it," I demand.

"You're mine," he says instantly, like the words were there already, pressing against me even more, until there is no air, no space, nothing but him.

"Now, Liebste," he tells me, and that spark in his eyes is back, raging anew, a full bonfire on its own that incinerates me, captivates me. "I will take care of you."

It isn't a question.

I could fight him again. I could push for control, and give instead of take, but taking is giving with him, and I need, on some primal, disastrous level, for him to do this, to be the one to seize control.

I nod. I can't speak. Not anymore. There are no words, no tears; I am hollowed by my admission and my panic, and I think this is what the purification rituals meant to do: scrape away the murkiness so there is only room for light.

Otto grabs me off the tree and lays us both back on the ground, the spring-soft down of the forest cushioning our fall.

All of his earlier tenderness is gone. He seems peeled back, but where my peeling back is in exhausted surrender, his is frantic action, and he moves across me, alternating kisses and bites over my skin until I'm strung taut.

He brings me back to my body. With his fingers, I am only vibrations. With his tongue, I am only goosebumps. With his lips, I am only skin.

He tosses aside my skirts, spreads my thighs, and there is no reverence, just his mouth, hungry and demanding. My head rocks back against the undergrowth, spine bowing off the ground, fingers tearing into the plants, the dirt, until the air smells of new life and greenery.

And then he's there with me, pressing into me without pretense, and I know we both feel the difference tonight. This is no drowsy devotion, no slow build, no worship of skin and noise—it is fast and desperate and exactly what all my mismatched facets need.

I am his, and he is mine, and our lips find each other, sloppy and wet and swollen.

The bonfire was meant to burn the last of our impurities away, and if that's what fire does, then all the nights with him should have turned me to crystal glass by now.

My awareness widens. The little meadow we'd found is now bursting with plants, herbs—thistle and nettle—that have no business growing in early spring, and I feel the remnant of wild magic tingling along my veins.

I'll care about that later. If at all. Let this byproduct linger, let this one bit of magic remain, proof and witness.

Whatever we will have to face—whatever crusade Holda sees fit to shove us into, standing up to the council or changing the world—the one thing I know with certainty is that, at the end, when it's just him and me, I will do everything in my power to make sure he survives.

7

OTTO

It should have been uncomfortable, sleeping in a meadow under the stars. Although God knows we did enough rough sleeping when fleeing Trier. But it's peaceful, and the blooms that are here because of Fritzi's magic wrap us in soft scents and petals.

I wake up near dawn, the sun rising over the mountains, a vivid, fiery red that seems impossibly bright. I don't move. Fritzi is wrapped in my arms and my tunic, but soon enough she stirs and stretches luxuriously.

"I don't remember the last time I slept so well," she says, her eyes still closed. She nuzzles into my chest. My arm tightens around her, and she whispers, "Mine."

"Yours?" I ask, bemused.

"This spot. Right here. This spot on your chest. It was made for my head to rest on. It is mine."

"Yours," I confirm, dropping a kiss on the top of her head. "Good morning, my hexe."

Distantly, I hear a horn, the sound low and melodic but insistent all the same.

"We should go," I say without moving.

"They can't very well do the bonding ceremony without us."

Horse hooves—slow and plodding—thud on the ground near us, and Fritzi and I have just enough time to make ourselves somewhat presentable before Skokse emerges from the Black Forest. The horse blows out a breath of grass-scented air from her nostrils. Atop her bare back sits Liesel, curls perfect, cloak spread out behind her.

"There you are," she says impatiently. "Come on. Everyone's waiting."

"Everyone's waiting?" Fritzi asks. "It's barely dawn."

"Yes, and I've been up for an hour. Rochus said we can't do anything until this ceremony is over, and Hilde said she'd bake me cookies after, and I've run out of parchment, and I have to wait a week until I can get more, and there's nothing left to do, and it's time to go."

I silently vow to never have children.

Liesel scoots up Skokse's withers, and I use a stump to mount before holding my arm out and lifting Fritzi up. It's awkward, but Skokse is a warhorse, trained to carry gear and armor far heavier than me and two girls.

By the time we reach the village, it's well and truly morning, and there's a bustle of excited activity. We separate to freshen up, and Fritzi swaps that gauzy gown for a dress embroidered with every plant imaginable, so decorated that it's almost impossible to see the base of green wool. I find that Brigitta has delivered a week's worth of garments similar to the ones I donned last night, all of them presumably magically enhanced. I select the darkest pair of leggings and a tunic more black than blue.

Fritzi meets me at the base of the tree with Cornelia in tow. "Where are we going?" I ask as Cornelia leads us down a path deeper into the Forest.

"Near the Origin Tree," the priestess says, setting a fast clip. "Something this special, well...we wanted to do it right."

The Origin Tree. My hand goes unconsciously to my chest, feeling the new tattoo on my skin. I need to ask Brigitta what sort of power the Tree sigil on my skin may grant me, how I can use the magic without drawing too much from Fritzi. There are two types of training for me to complete in order to be a suitable warrior for my witch. I must hone my body, but I also need to explore this new magical bond.

With Dieter out of the picture, there are still enemies to face, threats that I must ensure are met. Last night's celebration in Baden-Baden, that unity between two different groups of people who had once been deadly opposed—that's worth fighting for. And I am certain it's the type of peace that can be achieved widely.

How can I not believe we can change the world if Fritzi is by my side?

Cornelia slows as we go along a narrow path skirting the coven. In the Black Forest, there are plenty of trees, but I've yet to see *the* Tree. I know it's southeast from the main coven, set off on a higher peak and, from the way the others have spoken, near a lake. I know also that few in the Well coven visit the Tree. The main priest and priestesses do; Brigitta, as captain of the guard, accompanies them. I think the others have seen the Origin Tree before, but as a special-occasion event, not regularly.

My suspicions on that are confirmed as the village comes alive, a current of excitement zinging through each person as they join us on the path.

I asked once why more didn't visit the Tree. Brigitta tried to explain—much like the Black Forest had helped to protect the Well by keeping others out, forcing Fritzi, Liesel, and me to overcome a test set by the goddesses before we gained entry, the Origin Tree is similarly protected, only allowing people to draw close when they are needed.

"We protect it, of course," Brigitta added after I'd asked. She waved toward the guards who used spells as well as regular patrols. *"But the Tree is sacred. It is the link between magic and mundane, between mortals and goddesses. And so it protects itself."*

I can feel a buzz of excitement as we draw nearer. Some people had already set out before Cornelia collected Fritzi and me. Their mood is infectious—I feel myself practically vibrating with anticipation. But there's a coil of fear tightening inside my stomach as well.

Technically, bonding with Fritzi is going to be nothing more than drinking a highly powerful potion, one that could kill me and destroy her magic if she brewed it incorrectly. But no one has bonded like this in living memory, much less a goddess-chosen champion and warrior, so I guess the Origin Tree approves of a little more pomp and ceremony than usual.

Fritzi, who'd been following Cornelia's quick pace, slows down a little until she's side by side with me. She slips her hand in mine, and I give her fingers a squeeze.

The crowd behind us has grown. Liesel darts in and out of the people, seemingly on a first-name basis with every single witch in the coven. I take a moment to appreciate this new home I've found—because my home is not the room I share with Fritzi in the trees, but instead, it's this. It's Hartung, who wakes before everyone else in the Well to bake bread. It's Alberta, who sharpened my blade for me when she saw me struggling with a whetstone. It's Manegold who teaches the children spells and spelling, and it's Volkwinna who patches their scraped knees. In Bernkastel, I had only the smoke from the fire that consumed my mother. I could never feel a sense of community among those who had done nothing but watch her burn. And in Trier, I was surrounded by enemies. There were the orphans who I helped and who helped me. With a pang, I send a prayer up, hoping they're okay. Trier, though, even with the few friends I could count on, had been a mission.

The Well has become a home.

Our steps slow as we reach a clearing. Hilde stands near Brigitta, both of them beaming at me—they must have arrived here earlier. The other council members—Rochus and Philomena—are behind a table that's been placed in the shallows of a crystal-clear glacial pool.

And behind them—

My eyes grow round. The Origin Tree—for what else could that massive, sprawling tree be?—grows *inside* the center of the pond. And it's not one tree.

It's three.

The roots sprawl out, tangling like vines, knobby knuckles peeking up over the surface of the otherwise still water. The roots are a knotted mess, and so are the branches, woven almost as tightly as a basket. But I can see, even from the distance where we stand, that there are three separate trunks. I stop, shocked, looking up at the way the three trees interlock, the trunks braided together to form one.

It's early spring, but one of the trees already has new growth on it, crisp, pale green leaves still uncurling. In contrast, its branches are tangled with a tree whose leaves are more red and yellow than green. The other tree's branches are bare and spindly.

Fritzi tugs at my arm, and it's only then that I realize I've been awkwardly motionless, gawking at the massive tree. I had heard the legends, of course, the ancient beliefs of Yggdrasil from a Norseman I met in my travels, or the axis mundi, that invisible line between the realms, an astronomer told me about. But seeing *this* tree makes me wonder if there is a seed of truth in the legends, a history that I have not yet uncovered.

I don't really grow aware of my surroundings until I splash into the pool—the same pond the tree grows from—stopping at the table where Rochus and Philomena wait for us. The water laps at our ankles, cool but not cold. Cornelia moves to join the others, with the priest and priestesses on one side, and Fritzi and me on the other.

And between us, a bottle.

The noises of the crowd of onlookers fade. A still silence wraps around us.

Cornelia speaks first, then the others. It is so quiet now that no wind rattles the leaves, no bird breaks into song. The entire world, it seems, hears what Cornelia says.

But not me. Her words fade into the background. I should listen, but...

I'm watching Fritzi's eyes, wide, rimmed in a barely suppressed panic. I hear the thrum of her heartbeat, louder than anything else. I feel the whisper-light tremble in her fingers.

I rub my thumb over her knuckles until she lifts her eyes to mine.

I love you. My words are silent, my lips barely forming the words, but I know she hears the truth of them.

There it is. The shadow of her smile as her gaze focuses on me, her mind focuses on us.

Nothing else.

Cornelia's voice raises, loud and clear. "And now, to seal your fates together, you will both drink of the potion that binds your souls and your powers." She raises the bottle so everyone can see it and then offers it to us.

Fritzi reaches for it first. I watch as her throat muscles work, swallowing half the potion in several big gulps. Her eyes seem to darken; her body grows still.

Is something wrong?

I glance at Cornelia, panic flaring, but the priestess just nods, indicating that I drink next. I pluck the bottle from Fritzi's fingers and down the rest of the potion.

Black.

Cold.

Fierce rage, washing over me—something wanting my head to turn, to look. *At what? My neck muscles twitch. My eyes grow dim. My body is being jerked, pulled, tugged to look at—*

The Tree.

Covetous fury blinds me.

Black.

Cold.

The frigid darkness fades. A connection stretches between us, an invisible tether from Fritzi's soul to mine.

Morning light filters through my eyes. I squeeze Fritzi's fingers again.

Her gaze focuses on me, her eyes full of terror.

8

FRITZI

I keep my gaze on Otto. I focus on him, only on him, because that's what this ceremony is about—bonding with Otto.

But there is something…*wrong*.

In my chest.

In my stomach.

In the brand on my thigh, an itching, a burn, and it rises, aching, *throbbing*—

I ball my hand, the one not clinging to Otto, to keep from tearing at my skin as if I can escape the sensation—and my eyes catch on Cornelia.

She is frowning at me, her head cocked, eyes looking not at me but *through* me, *beyond* me, seeing with magic, not sight.

Her face goes slack. And in that expression, shock and a flash of horror, I feel it all over again, *wrong*, itching, my skin is burning, *burning*—

"Well?" Philomena leans into Cornelia.

Cornelia's specialty lies in the veil, magic beyond our physical plane—Philomena and Rochus have other specialties, which means, of the council, only Cornelia can see if the bonding potion worked.

It *did*, didn't it? Otto isn't dead. I can still feel my connection to wild magic; I haven't been cut off entirely.

But something is *wrong*.

Cornelia nods sharply, but her face is all tension. She turns to the crowd, raises her hands. "They are bonded! Champion and warrior, our mightiest hope made true!"

The crowd cheers, applause that hits me like a thunderclap, and I flinch.

Otto tightens his hold on my hand. "Fritzi? Are you—"

Cornelia dives around the table as the music starts. More dancing. More celebrating. An endless party, this one only for those who live in the Well, everyone basking in the landmark this makes—a goddess chosen champion! A bonded warrior! And our borders open to the non-magical world, hexenjägers driven out—we are a mark of their mightiest hope, indeed.

But I can't get a full breath. My brand scars are throbbing and burning.

Cornelia smiles sweetly at Otto before taking my arm. "You'll get your witch back in a moment, warrior," she tells him, and before he can protest, she hauls me away.

I go, shoes sodden from the pond water, half-aware of her touch on my arm, half-consumed by the pain rising in my brands, in my head, that headache returning tenfold and *banging* on my skull.

Like a knock.

Like something trying to get in.

I wince, nearly collapse, and I feel another hand on my other arm, another firm grip.

Otto.

"What's wrong?" he asks it of Cornelia, who has led me out of the open area around the Origin Tree, behind another cluster of oaks, hidden from sight of the celebration.

I try to lie to him. *I'm fine. Give me a moment.*

But what comes out is a croaked, "It didn't work." I look at Cornelia, pleading, terrified. "Did it?"

Holda? I dare to ask. *What happened?*

She is silent a moment, a thoughtful, tense stillness that seeps over me.

You are bound to Otto, and yet—Holda stops, sounds frustrated by confusion. *This magic is old and powerful. I will follow these lines and figure out what has happened.*

Cornelia pushes me an arm's length back and keeps looking at me how she did after Otto drank the potion. Studious. Frowning, a line between her brows.

"I don't know," she finally says, an echo of Holda's frustration.

"You don't know?" Otto has his arm around my waist, keeping me up. "I'm still alive, so I'd say it did work. How can you not know?"

One hand lifts, Cornelia's fingers tugging at something invisible just beside my head. "The magic is there. You are connected. But—something—"

"Didn't work," I finish.

Cornelia squints. "I can't see it. The magic is murky. I've never seen a bonding ceremony performed before. I have no experience with this type of magic other than in stories. So maybe—" She drops her hand with a scowl. "Maybe this is how it works? The magic merely takes a day or two to truly coalesce? Because it *did* connect you. It's almost like there's something blocking it from fully taking effect, like oil mixed in with water—not truly together, but not apart."

My body goes cold. The brands ache, burn, itch—

But I don't say what I'm thinking.

I can't.

Can't even begin to consider the fact that whatever magic my brother worked on me in Baden-Baden, when I was at his mercy, blocked any chance of me bonding with Otto.

I should feel horrified by this. And I am—Dieter's invasiveness keeps finding new ways to torment me.

But this also means that Otto *can't* be a part of whatever crusade I have to enact on behalf of Holda.

That...might be the only way I can keep him safe.

But if Otto and I are not bonded—if the potion failed, if the ceremony failed—then Rochus and Philomena will have further cause to bar me from the council and any chance I have at enacting change.

Will this mantle be removed from my shoulders?

I am ripped in two. Half with relief, that maybe I won't have to be a champion, won't have to endanger Otto even more and take up the task of undoing centuries of prejudice and belief. Half with...regret. And that regret pierces me in an unexpected burst, that any part of me could look at the possibility of being free of this responsibility and not be elated.

I don't want this burden.

Do I?

Beyond where we linger, the celebration is in full swing, music filling the soft forest. I remember the sight of the Origin Tree, the immensity of this symbol of magic that haunted my dreams and has, for so long, been the constant in our lives.

Holda doesn't just want me to undo the way witches perform magic.

She wants me to show the *world* the truth in our power. That we can help non-magical people instead of being feared by them; that our magic can be used for their good too. That the ways we perform spells will not harm them. Like the people of Baden-Baden, who accepted us with thanks and joy. Like the people of Trier, who still may be trapped under whatever controlling doctrine the hexenjägers adhere to, even without my brother at their helm.

The Origin Tree is both a symbol of hope and a symbol of shackles, and I could change it all.

But can I do all that without Otto?

His grip on me is still tight, reassuring and resolute. Cornelia continues studying me, and Otto just waits by us, patient as ever, effortlessly embodying why he's a warrior. Why he's *my* warrior. Because he's *this*, so easily, so naturally.

I'm still the champion of a goddess without him. I'm still bound to Holda, if not to Otto. But I'll have been a failure at the bonding ceremony, and Philomena and Rochus will dismiss any suggestions I try to make because of my proven weakness here. Whatever change Holda asks of me will have to come with struggle and fight and *war*, because I'll be demanding new beliefs be accepted without any authority to enact them.

A bubbling sensation puddles in my gut. The need to—to *laugh*.

Here I have a way out of what's been terrorizing me for so long, and I'm trying to think of ways to follow it through anyway?

I do laugh. Just once. It pops out of me, and Otto and Cornelia both eye me strangely.

"Do you want to lie down?" Otto asks, thumb moving against my hip.

My body still aches. I gather myself, the back of my hand to my lips.

It's all right.

It's...*right.*

I don't know where that word comes from. But it rings through me again.

Right.

"No," I say and stand upright, out of his grip, pushing all my pain to the back of my mind. "No. We should celebrate, shouldn't we? The potion worked."

Cornelia sips in a breath, hesitates, and I shake my head.

"We'll figure out whatever happened," I tell her, and I don't know where this certainty comes from. A calmness I haven't felt in weeks descends over me. Calm and steady and...*right.*

It's okay.

Whatever happened.

It's *right.*

No—*wrong.* Wrong. Something is...*wrong*...

But I smile up at Otto. I feel it distantly, fogged, but I blink, and my gaze focuses, and he smiles back, cautious, still not sure whether he should sweep me away to bed.

I touch his face. "It's all right," I promise him. "I feel...great."

And, strangely, I find it isn't a lie.

I feel more awake than I have in days. Weeks, maybe. A burden is lifted. Or merely softened. Whatever it is, I find it hard to *care,* and that in and of itself is freeing.

Cornelia doesn't even bother trying to force a smile, staring at me in that abstract studious way like she's trying to see the threads of magic that tether me.

Hm.

They both may be a problem.

Problem?

I shake my head.

There is no—*problem.*

Everything is right now.

9

OTTO

That night, in the privacy of our room, I wake up, and she's gone.

Panic and adrenaline shoot through my veins, and I bolt upright. My shoulders coil with tension.

We're safe here, I tell myself. *Safe.*

We are in the coven of the Well, with Brigitta and the guards patrolling, and Fritzi is a powerful goddess-chosen witch.

Dieter got her in the Well once before.

But Dieter's dead. Or as good as.

We never got confirmation from Johann. The Grenzwache we sent to Trier have not yet returned.

My eyes dart around the room. I note that Fritzi's cloak is gone, her slippers too. And the candleholder.

She's just stepped out. She didn't want to wake me.

I tell myself these things because I want to believe them. I don't want to think about the chance that she had another nightmare and simply doesn't want me around as she deals with it.

I don't want to think about the concern that lingered in her eyes after the bonding ceremony, as if she worried she made a mistake.

Minutes trickle by. More time. It's dark and late, and too much time has passed for her just to be relieving herself, but—

She's done this before. That night when she went to the council room.

Let's keep this our little secret.

I stand, pause. She's fine. I know she's fine. There's no danger here.

But I grab my dagger and slip it into my belt.

I head straight toward the council room. It's unlocked, the door cracked. I step inside, moving slowly.

There are some things—witch things—that I know I don't have the power to help Fritzi with. And while Cornelia is trusted, the others are not. There are politics at play that are beyond my comprehension, but I do know that I'm on Fritzi's side. I'm *always* on Fritzi's side. And so if I can do no more than hold her candle, I'll do that.

Which she knows.

And she knows I can hold her secrets.

Why did you not wake me, Fritzi?

I try to be silent as I head to the council room. I *can* keep her secrets. But the *wrongness* of this all twists my gut. Something claws at the back of my mind. A warning, an instinct that experience has taught me never to ignore.

I haven't felt this way since Trier.

There are no enemies here, I tell myself, but I drop my cloak, feel for the dagger.

I go to the library Fritzi went to before. I never talked to her about it.

Let's keep this our little secret.

But my stomach tightens. I *should* have talked to her about it. In private, I should have asked. Pressed her for information, or at least some sort of confirmation. I let all the ceremonies distract me from what really mattered: her.

The library door is closed but not locked. I turn the handle silently. Step inside.

A figure hunches over the desk, back to me, illuminated only by flickering candles and moonlight. I know instantly it's Fritzi. Her cloak, her hair, her body.

But…

I pad forward silently.

My hand does not leave the dagger hilt.

Books have been tossed about the room, and I step over them carefully, winding around the minefield of literature. Fritzi wouldn't treat books so mercilessly.

She's muttering, her voice low, frantic. Her body moves spasmodically, like…

Like a puppet on a string.

My blood turns to ice.

"Fritzi," I say, my voice flat. The same tone I would use for a rabid dog.

Her body stiffens.

The low laugh that emits from her lips stutters, jarringly unnatural.

"What are you doing?" I ask.

She stands, throwing back the chair so violently that it flies at me. I swat it away, and it hits a shelf and knocks over more books. Fritzi whirls around, her head lolling a fraction behind the rest of her body. Her hair dangles in front of her face, stringy. Her skin is sallow, slicked with sweat.

"Otto," she says in a singsong voice. "Hello, Otto."

She takes a step closer.

My hand grips the dagger.

"Fritzi?" I ask. Tentative. Hopeful.

Her head tilts, and she makes a clucking sound with her tongue. "No-o," she teases. "No, Fritzi's not here right now, mein kapitän."

Her gaze flicks to the blade I hold, and that's when I notice that her eyes are entirely black, no color, no white, just empty, hollow black.

My body washes over with cold, the ghost of all the terror of the last years rising up and strangling my very soul.

"Hello, Dieter," I say, my voice cracking. Shock roots me to the floor.

Fritzi's giggle is high-pitched and manic, and she cuts it off quickly, as if the erratic sound had burst from a whistling kettle that had been whipped away from the stove. "Ot-to, Ot-to," she says, padding forward a single step with each syllable of my name. "Ot-*toe*." That giggle again.

"Let her go," I demand.

Fritzi's body stops. Her head swivels from the left to the right side, eyes on me, hair falling over her face. "Cut me out of her," Dieter snarls fiercely in her voice. A sharp snort. "Oh, but you *can't*, can you, Kapitän?"

One more step closer.

I fumble back, nearly slipping on a book, the spine breaking under my bare foot.

Fritzi's lips twitch in a smile that doesn't quite take hold.

"What if I told you, Otto, *friend*, what if I told you that if you kill her now, if you slide that pretty little dagger through her breast, it would kill me too? What if I told you that I am at my most vulnerable now, sharing a body with my beloved sister, that my life, in this moment, is tied with hers?" His speech is quicker now, so rushed that the words flow together. Fritzi's eyes widen, her lips widen, as if the words are boiling out of her, overflowing. "What if you knew that this, *this*, now, this was the only way to kill me? You tried before. You tried with that poison. It didn't kill me, Otto. It didn't *stop* me, Kapitän. But right now, right now, *RIGHT NOW*"—Dieter screams the words, specks of spittle flying at me—"*right now* if you kill her, you'd kill me too. So do it, *do it*, you verdammt coward, you traitor; stab her heart and kill us both, if you can."

He—she—they are so close that I can feel the heat of Fritzi's breath, can smell the sweet lebkuchen she ate, one last cookie before going to bed. I shove her body away, and Dieter makes Fritzi skitter back, dancing over broken books and cold stone.

"You can't do it!" Dieter cackles. "You could stop it all now; you could end me, but you won't!"

He's right. I won't.

I can't.

I can't kill her even if it would kill him.

I can't even hurt her.

Because even if Dieter is possessing her, it's Fritzi's body. The only one she has. She'll come back to it when he leaves—I pray—but...

Dieter twists Fritzi's head around, black eyes wide, lips stretching into a toothy grin. Without breaking eye contact, he backs up to the desk he had been focused on.

He flicks the candle, toppling it.

An old book alights immediately, flaring high. The orange flames lick up, making the shadows deeper.

Dieter giggles in Fritzi's voice. "Let's keep this our little secret."

Bile rises in my throat. *It had been him all along.* That night—she had acted so strangely because she had not been herself. *Literally.* What had she told me? She'd had a nightmare. She hadn't meant she had a nightmare *before* she left for the library; she meant that the whole time Dieter possessed her and sent her body to the library had seemed like a nightmare to her. She didn't know it had happened.

And I, verdammt fool that I am, did not see the threat even when it kissed me on the lips and whispered for my silence.

"Oh, you're figuring it out!" Dieter crows through Fritzi. "My sister and I, we're *connected*. Not even your little bonding potion can break that."

"Why are you doing this?" I shout, panic blinding me.

"I let you play with my toy long enough."

"Get out of her body!"

"No," he says simply, and he tosses Fritzi onto the flames of the table.

Ashy bits of paper and vivid orange sparks fly up as Fritzi's back hits the burning books, her hair splaying around the flames.

I stare, frozen with horror. There's *no* reaction as the fire licks her skin, singes her hair. There's no reaction—

The smell.

She's burning.

An animal, guttural roar rips out of me, and I throw myself at Fritzi, at the table, grabbing her blistering hands and pulling her away from it.

She laughs. It's *his laugh*. "The irony!" he cackles. "The first witch you ever actually burned, and it's Fritzi! Because make no mistake." All merriment fades in an instant, Fritzi's face falling flat, black eyes narrowed. "This is your fault, traitor. She burns because of you. When you see her scars, know that you gave them to her. The longer you fight, the longer you live, the more pain I will twist through her."

My grip on her goes slack with horror, and as soon as Dieter's words die on her tongue, her lips split open in a huge manic smile. Despite her glee, her hands form into fists, squeezing tight around the burnt skin and slamming into me. I stagger back, and she strikes again, landing a blow to my back with both her fists that sends me stumbling forward. I whirl around, and she jabs stiffened fingers toward my eye, her fingernails clawing down my cheek when I dodge. I scoot away, hitting the wall.

Fritzi throws a punch at my head, and I duck. But Dieter doesn't make Fritzi's body pull back—he lets her fist slam into the stone so hard I wince, blood streaking out of her knuckles. He cannot feel her pain, but she will when she wakes up. *Did she break her hand?*

Her knee goes up, hitting my stomach, and with an *oof*, I bend over double.

Something hard and sharp jabs my back, but the tunic I'm wearing came from Brigitta and was woven magically to be like armor. Dieter, in Fritzi's body, realizes quickly that the attack didn't work, and the blade moves up, stabbing me in the neck. I jerk back, the blade tip sliding behind my clavicle before I wrench free. No major artery was hit, but hot blood spurts up from my wound.

I stand and straighten, positioning myself at an angle so I'm no longer trapped at the wall. My dagger is in her hand, the tip now pressed to her chin. A shining bead of red slides down the blade.

"Which will hurt worse," Dieter asks in Fritzi's voice, "you dying at your lover's hand, or you watching as I carve her pretty face?" The tip of the dagger drags over Fritzi's jawline, leaving a thin red cut.

I cannot fight with a weapon. And he'll kill her in front of me if I try. I shake my head, the futility of it all leaving me breathless.

This is a battle that is being waged with magic, and the only way to defeat Dieter is with magic.

Magic I do not have.

What I need is *Fritzi*. She would know what to do; she would know how to fight. She would have spells and potions and...

And she's the one possessed. I could run, raise an alarm, call witches to aid me, but every second that ticks by is another second the love of my life is trapped inside her own body with her torturer.

"Otto, mein kapitän," Dieter croons. The words lisp as he drags the blade gently from Fritzi's Cupid's bow, over her lips, and down her chin. Blood streaks a crimson red, slicking her pale skin. "Pfennig for your thoughts."

Magic is the only thing keeping Fritzi standing right now, I think. Her body is ravaged—charred skin on her arms and back, blisters over her hands, blood pouring down her face. My heart thuds. I don't have magic of my own. I can neither heal her nor stop Dieter's abuse.

But etched into my chest is a tattoo that links me to Fritzi's magic.

And...

I raise my head, knowing inherently what I need to do. I cannot use magic to fight for her; I don't know how.

But *she* does.

And we're bound.

Which means...could I? Could I use our connection to pull Dieter's dark soul into *me,* and then she could use her magic to banish him?

"Come kiss me, lover!" Dieter says with Fritzi's bloody lips, red spraying out and splattering her teeth, her tattered robe, the floor in front of her. The wound he gave me is nothing compared to what he inflicts on her. Dieter dances, Fritzi's body moving jerkily like a puppet on fraying strings. I think he's trying to mimic the dances from the bonfire night—*was he watching through her eyes even then?*—but it's macabre, eerie in its *wrongness.*

I close my eyes.

I listen to my heartbeat.

This spot, she'd said. *This spot on your chest. It's mine.*

My hand covers that spot. It's where the tree tattoo is, I realize.

It's hers.

And I can feel...something—a magical pull, a *connection*, just like the one I felt when we first bonded.

My heart to hers.

It's a rope that binds us. It's a light that illuminates.

It's a *bridge.*

I look with my mind's eye down the golden connection between us, and I can see a darkness like smoke burning off Fritzi's body. I snort.

"Why are you laughing, Ernst?" Dieter says in her voice. "Is it *funny*?" He stretches her cut lips with his fingers, widening the split, ripping the already severed flesh.

I sober. I was amused because the hold he has on her—and I can see it now—is not that strong. He doesn't have a very good grasp of his magic. No—of *her* magic.

But it was enough to search this library for something, I realize. *Enough to hurt Fritzi.*

I lunge forward—not with my body, but my soul.

And my soul grabs his.

Fritzi crumples to the ground.

I feel his soul, slick like oil, wrestling with me, frantic, manic, stronger than I had given him credit for. He pulls away from my grasp, struggling to get back to her, to torture her.

But I *hold.* His soul squirms away, and I pull him closer. Closer.

Fine, his voice says, the word slinking into me like a snake slithering through my head. *I'll just take* you *instead.*

He quits fighting me.

His soul slams into my body, the blackness overwhelming. I feel my soul shriveling up, cowering, my conscious thoughts receding into a tiny part of my mind, a part that has no control. How did I think his magic weak moments ago? It was only weak compared to her. Against me? Overpowering.

He lifts my hand. I want to fight it, but I have no control over my own body. My fingers do not tremble as he forms a fist. Gone are the jerky movements, the hesitant puppetlike nature of his possession.

He has full control.

You're even more pathetic than her, Dieter says inside my mind.

Images flit through my head. My fingers digging out my own eyes. My teeth biting off my own tongue. My dagger slicing out my own heart.

He's weighing his options gleefully.

And then he settles on a choice.

My hands around her throat, squeezing until she dies.

10

FRITZI

There is a wall of cedar trees. Ancient, wild, with snarled, interlocking branches of green boughs that should be wool-fluffy, alive and vibrant—but they are dense. They are bent in jointed lines like fingers prying at one another, gripping to form a wall, a wall that stretches forever, forever—

Cedar is for protection, I think, woozy. *What are they protecting me from?*

The center of the wall erupts in a single spout of flame, so intense and sudden that I cry out and stagger back, dropping to the forest undergrowth. Pain flares through me—heat from the fire, but something else, burning along my spine and arms, stinging on my lip, my face, a cracking agony in my hand. It leaves me sitting there, limp and mangled, staring up at the fire that eats a hole in the cedar wall.

"Fritzichen," comes Dieter's voice. "Let me in."

No.

No.

It's not him. He's dead. Gone. It isn't—

The fire burns. Burns. *Eats.*

It is hungry.

And he's there, through the gap it makes. Grinning. Manic in his victory.

My ravaged body screams to run, but I can't even stand. I'm held on the ground by my pain and horror as Dieter walks through the cedar trees, their boughs crackling around him.

"No," I manage, and drag myself back. "*No.*"

"Oh, sweet Fritzichen," Dieter coos. "You can't escape me. I told you. You're *mine*. Not his. Not Mama's. Mine." He touches his sternum. "Mine." He touches his stomach. "*Mine.*" He touches his thigh.

All the places he branded me.

What did he do to me? How does he still have magic? How—

Not *his* magic.

Mine. My magic.

He connected himself to *my* magic. With the brands he left on me.

Somehow, perhaps unknowingly, he used wild magic to bond me to him with those brands.

People used to fear witches when wild magic was all we had, when our power was unchecked, before the goddesses capped it with the Origin Tree.

Now, I know why. Intimately.

He shouldn't have been able to do that.

"And, sister..." He crouches in front of me. So close I can see the wrinkles at the edges of his eyes when he grins. "You will get me what I need. They have one of the stones there, in the Well. You will bring it to me."

"A stone?" My breath stutters, and I try, *I try* to be strong, but everything shakes. "I will bring you nothing. You're *dead.*"

He has to be. *Please.*

Dieter giggles. It's high and thin. "No, no, I do not *die,* Fritzichen. Why would you want me dead? Now, my sweet, sweet sister, you will *bring me the stone.*"

"What stone? What are you talking about?"

"The *stone*!" he shrieks, voice shattering in desperation, and he reaches for me. I flail back with a whimper—

But then Dieter *screams.*

He arches, body bowing unnaturally, and the fire behind him snuffs out. The wall of cedar trees vanishes, sucking away in an ear-popping abyss that leaves only me, him, and—

Otto.

Otto, standing with his back to me, Dieter in front of him, his arms up in defense.

Relief chokes me, gives my body permission to feel all this pain even more. He's here. How is he here?

Where is here?

Dieter doesn't hesitate. He lunges, toying amusement gone, all primal fury now as his hands wrap around Otto's throat.

"*Mine!*" Dieter screeches.

Otto fights. Punches and kicks, wrenches to break Dieter's hold, but my brother is a thing beyond now, untethered. His grip on Otto's neck tightens, and Otto's face purples, a sputtering gasp escaping his lips, and I feel that gasp in my own body, a choked release of air.

The word Dieter has been screaming echoes down into me.

Mine.

My warrior. My bonded. *Mine.*

I shove to my feet, wobbling, but I teeter toward them, one hand extended.

"Let," I demand, sweat beading on my forehead, "him"—my body cries out with each movement, each step, each thud of my heart—"go."

I flare my palm at Dieter. The cedar trees launch back up, but there are other things now too, marjoram and nettle and rosemary and *everything*, everything I can think of that protects.

But I don't need these things, do I? I don't need anything but wild magic.

And Otto.

Hands out by my sides, I scream, and everything goes dark.

"Fritzi! *Fritzi—*"

"Don't move—the Three save me, what happened?"

"I didn't—Dieter—"

"*Dieter*? Scheisse, Fritzi, what did I tell you? *Don't move.*" Cornelia. She's talking to me, I think, but all is dark still, dark and—

Pain explodes, bright and consuming, and there's a ringing shriek, like a bell—no, it's me. I'm screaming, and hands are on my shoulders, pushing down.

"Please, Liebste, please," Otto begs, his voice thick. "Please stay still—Cornelia's here, she's here, and we'll help."

"Scheisse," Cornelia curses again. "Why did Holda call me here? She couldn't have woken up the healers, no—*hold still—*"

The air bursts with a smell like lightning, static and ether, and the pain retreats. Not gone, but not overwhelming, and I gasp in air and vault upright.

"Where—" My eyes fly around, expecting Dieter hunched in a corner, wounded and ready to attack again.

But I'm in…the library? The council's library.

And the room is *destroyed.*

Most of the books are off the shelves, scattered across the floor. The table is half burned, charred and blackened, and blood streaks some of the walls.

My focus flares to Otto, panicked, and I sweep him head to toe for injuries. He has a thin cut on his neck, but that's the only wound—so the amount of blood on the walls can't be from him.

It's from me.

I feel it now, wounds here, there, some healing from whatever Cornelia did, but it isn't enough to stop the agony from grabbing me with relentless fists.

"What happened." It comes out as a statement, a demand.

Talking hurts. My throat is rough, and I reach up, touch the skin, feel swelling.

Otto sits next to me, one hand going to my forearm. I wince, and he pulls back, and I see a burn there, barely healed; it leads up my arm and vanishes beyond what I can see. Shock takes over where Cornelia's magic left off, and I go numb.

"Dieter." I answer my own question.

Otto nods.

Cornelia drops back to sit on her heels. She's in a chemise, a robe hastily thrown on, her red hair in a messy braid, and her face wide in shock.

"Dieter possessed you," she clarifies.

"This is the second time he's done it," says Otto, and I whip towards him. "At least."

"What?"

He doesn't look at me as he explains how this isn't the first instance he's followed me to the library. How tonight, when Dieter attacked and tortured me in my own body, Otto used the bonding connection to drag Dieter's consciousness out of me long enough for me to fight him with magic.

Cornelia goes quiet when Otto's voice trails off.

He still won't look at me.

"The Well's barrier wasn't enough to keep him out," Cornelia says. "That's…troubling."

"*That's* what's troubling?" I gag. "My brother is *alive.* And he can still access magic. *My* magic. That's why the bonding potion with Otto didn't fully work. Because Dieter *bonded me to himself* first. He *stole* me—"

I rock forward, body shaking, hurting; I'm a tangle of grief and pain.

Otto leans toward me. "Fritzi, I—"

I throw myself into his arms, pain be damned. "You feel guilty. Stop. There's nothing you could have done to prevent what happened."

Tentatively, Otto returns my hug, wary of the injuries on my back.

He says nothing. But I can *feel* his guilt. It nudges at me, and I'm aware of the thread, warm and sturdy connecting us. It's *there,* whatever bond the potion was able to make against Dieter's influence, the reason Otto was able to pull Dieter out of my body.

I try to tell Otto again. *It wasn't your fault.*

But I don't want to talk more. I don't want to think or *feel* or connect to realize what this means. I'm so tired, inside and out, and I just want—

I want—

Before I can realize that Otto just felt all of that, the same way I can feel his guilt, he pulls me up. "Come. We can deal with this in the morning."

I stand but plant my feet. "No. We really can't."

"I agree."

Philomena is in the doorway. Hands on her hips. Face in a disgusted scowl. At her back is Rochus, who gapes at the library in horrified shock before he shoves around her and drops to his knees over a pile of ravaged books.

"What—" he starts. "What have you *done*?"

Cornelia pushes to her feet. "We had a breach."

Philomena glares at me, sharp with accusation. "A *breach*. From *her*."

"From *Dieter Kirch*." Cornelia steps around us, putting herself between Philomena and me, and as Philomena tries to keep the blame on me, Cornelia explains in an ever more shouting voice what Otto just told her. Rochus half listens, gathering salvageable pieces of books into a pile.

Back through the door, shapes move. Brigitta, members of her guard, all listening, staring in shock.

I'm shaking. I only realize it when Otto touches my shoulder, and his steadiness counters my tremors.

"The hexenjägers didn't kill Dieter," I whisper.

Philomena is yelling. Cornelia too. Their argument gives Otto and me some semblance of privacy, for a moment.

"No," Otto says, his jaw tight. "I don't know why. I was so sure they would."

I don't want to think. I don't want to do this. My body is broken and in agony and all the things I've most feared have just come to light.

But I'm the goddess-chosen champion.

And where were you? I ask Holda. I don't know whether I intend to sound accusatory.

Who do you think was the cedar trees? she asks. *He has hidden his true intent. His lack of magic—I never suspected—I should have. I'm sorry, Friederike.*

You weren't enough to keep Dieter out. Did you know he was bonded to me?

I sensed something connected to you, but I was not sure what it could be. Dieter has no access to magic—or he shouldn't. It did not even occur to me to see if he was the cause.

But he is. He's *bonded* to me. And I underwent the bonding ceremony with Otto, so we're all connected now?

The thought of Dieter having access to me is nauseating.

The thought of Dieter having access to Otto is unbearable.

My body swells with defense, the instinctual lurch that fueled me in the dream-state to push Dieter away—*out*—of Otto. But something comes with this pull now, some weird surge that fills my gut with a sense of effervescence, and I'm hit with a memory so potent I go completely still.

Dieter, in Birresborn, back before Mama and the Elders kicked him out. Before we knew the depth of his insanity, he was training under our healer to be the next caretaker of our village, to tend injuries and illnesses with his affinity for body magic.

I'd fallen out of a tree in a quest for mistletoe. There was a nasty scrape down my calf, and I'd been sobbing into Mama's chest at the pain and the fear, until Dieter knelt by my leg. His hand laid over it, coated in a salve, featherlight, and he whispered a spell as I wept and Mama shushed me.

A sensation wrapped around my leg. Warm and comforting and soft. And when Dieter peeled his hand back, the cut was gone.

That's the feeling I have now. A wave of healing, my mind a jumble of Dieter and Otto and protection, and I try to shake it off, the memory, the *warmth*—

"Fritzi." Otto's voice is thin with wonder and caution.

I glance at him, then follow his gaze down.

The wounds on my knuckles are...gone. The pain I'd felt in my back, from the burns—gone.

All of the injuries Dieter inflicted on me.

Healed.

I gape at the tatters of my nightgown. The only proof of the attack is now the smears of blood in the torn cloth.

"What—" Otto's hands go out, but he doesn't touch me, like he wants to leap to some action but can't figure out what that action should be.

My eyes go to Philomena, Rochus, Brigitta—they are all too locked in their own grief to see what I've done. I need to be more careful with wild magic, but this was an instinctual reaction, a desperate grab at relief.

That came because of a memory of my brother.

I can't focus on this now. I can't linger on anything other than what is in front of me.

"What did Dieter want here?" I ask Otto. "What did he say?"

Otto's face goes briefly emotionless. But I feel the spark of all the things he's fighting to push away—terror, revulsion, anger, remorse, shame.

"He didn't say." Otto's frown deepens, and he turns towards the half-burned table. "He was looking at something, there."

I cross the room. Rochus stares up at me from his pile of books, and he speaks, but it's like I'm in a tunnel.

Most of the materials on the table are destroyed. Books, scrolls. I poke through them—the spine of one book remains, showing a design I recognize immediately.

"He was researching the Origin Tree," I guess.

The flashes I'd had earlier pulse through my mind. The Tree, four elements wrapping around it—

Otto uses the point of his dagger to sort through the ash and debris on the table. "He wanted to break the Well's barrier to corrupt the Origin Tree's magic. Maybe that's what he still wants."

"Did he not know how to do it before, then? Why would he need information on it?"

"Perhaps he realized his original plan wouldn't work now."

"I don't know if—" My eyes catch on something under Otto's blade. "Wait—there."

He stops, picks up a piece of parchment that looks like it was ripped out of a book. It survived the fire and fighting underneath another book, and Otto runs his eyes over it once before extending it to me.

At our backs, Philomena is still yelling. Cornelia glowers at her, shouting back when appropriate. Rochus is instructing Brigitta's guards to start cleaning the library.

I take the parchment, and read.

It shows a picture of the Origin Tree, those three interlocking trees twisting in on each other, boughs reaching for the sky.

Beneath the drawing is a—spell? Or ingredients, maybe?

> Three stones and one spark:
> Water, air, earth,
> And fire in the heart.

I read it over again. Again.

Stones.

Dieter had said I would bring him a stone. That they had one of them here.

What do these stones do?

No, Friederike, comes Holda's voice, a desperate gush. *Destroy this paper.*

Destroy this? What is it?

But if Dieter has already seen it—

She trails off, and I feel her panic. Can Otto feel it now too? I look up at him, but he's watching me with that considering frown.

What is this, Holda? I ask.

Your duty is to show the council and other witches that wild magic is a resource they can use without fear, she says.

Yes, but—

This is not that. The Origin Tree is a cap on magic. It is a dam; this would destroy that dam.

I scowl down at the table. *Isn't that what you want?*

I want our people to know that they don't need the limitations we put on them and that they can access the wild magic that is still outside of the Origin Tree. But this—this would flood the world with all of the magic that has been held back.

This spell, I start, laying each word out slowly, *would destroy the Origin Tree?*

Another of her infuriating pauses. *When we created the Origin Tree, we built in a way to undo it, should it not accomplish what we envisioned. But so much magic is gathered in the Origin Tree that I do not know what the ramifications would be if it were destroyed now. I do not know what a surge of magic would do to the world. The force of the magic being unleashed, for witches and non-magical mortals, could be catastrophic.*

Someone says my name. Shouts it, maybe. Cornelia snaps about letting me see a healer first—she hasn't noticed the absence of my wounds, sees only the smears of blood still on my clothes—but all my concentration is on the goddess.

It's what Dieter wanted originally, though?

No. Her rebuke is sharp and certain. *He wanted to* corrupt *the Tree. A crack in its walls to ruin the magic within. This spell—this spell would obliterate those walls entirely.*

The Origin Tree keeps a cap on magic. Witches access it by adhering to rituals and spells and ways that the goddesses, via the council, instruct.

Wild magic is that same magic but without boundaries. Without requirements. A free flowing brook instead of a walled-off well.

And the Tree is the dam that keeps that well from flooding the world.

My gut roils, discomfort and unease, and behind me, Philomena is still arguing, Cornelia too, and now Rochus. Their noise builds, my frustration builds, and I snap.

I spin around with the paper in hand. "Regardless of what you think of me," I push my voice into a shout, "my brother has the knowledge he needs to destroy the Origin Tree. So maybe you should stop trying to find a way to blame me and let the champion go out to stop him?"

11

OTTO

The council bickers. The Grenzwache argues. Everyone has a different plan, and yet no one seems to know what to do right now.

But what we need to do is obvious.

"I'm going to go back to Trier," I say, "and I am going to kill Dieter myself."

My words silence the room. Fritzi slips her hand in mine. "*We* are."

"Not alone," Cornelia snaps at the same time Brigitta says, "The guard will join you. We already have some in Trier. They should have reported back by now, but regardless, we'll reconvene and come up with a tactical plan."

"We have to move fast," I say. I can feel the years of training upon me. I was a Kapitän in more than just name. I glance at Brigitta, who nods, allowing me to take charge. "Dieter knows a way to...compromise Fritzi."

"I know of some guarding spells that will help," Cornelia interjects.

"But..." Her eyes go to the other council members. Rochus ignores her, taking the page from Fritzi's fingers and scowling at it.

I don't know how much I trust simple spells against Dieter, and I don't want Fritzi to have to guard her body and her mind from her abuser.

"Regardless," I continue, "we cannot let Dieter go on. He *must* be stopped."

"You have no idea." Rochus's voice is hollow and dark. Everyone else watches him, but he is zeroed in on the parchment, barely glancing up from it as he turns to Philomena. "He can't do anything if he doesn't have them all."

What does that mean? I wonder.

"He can do much," Philomena says to Rochus, her voice a razor edge of warning. Her gaze shifts from Rochus to the rest of us. She looks around the room, finally settling on Brigitta. "What is your purpose?"

"To protect the magic that protects my people," Brigitta answers immediately, speaking the words like the mantra they are.

"And it is magic itself that is at stake now." Philomena's voice rings with authority. "This is no longer just about one girl and her demented brother."

Fritzi flinches, and I squeeze her hand, glaring at the pompous priestess.

"This is about a grasping witch who wants to break the magic of this world," she concludes.

Outside, the wind is howling, branches scraping against the windows and walls of this sanctuary built into the trees. But, while vast, this tree is not *the* Tree, the Origin Tree that's hidden even in the Well.

Cornelia shifts closer to Rochus, reading the words etched on the scorched page. Her face goes pale, her mouth slack in horror.

"What aren't you telling us?" I demand, whipping my furious gaze out at the members of the council, the priest and priestesses.

Fritzi takes a shaking breath. That's what kills me. The fear she's trying to hide. She repeats the words she read on the page before: "'Three stones and one spark: water, air, earth, and fire in the heart.'"

"Please," Cornelia whispers, "don't." Her eyes are downcast, as if the words themselves hurt her. Philomena and Rochus glower behind her.

But none of them steps forward with an explanation. Whatever it is Fritzi's read—a spell of some sort—it's the key to all of this, and still, *still*, they cling to their secrets.

"Is that a picture of the Tree?" Brigitta asks, looking at the page in Fritzi's hand. She turns to the council. "Is this a spell to *burn* the Tree?"

Cornelia steps forward, and Philomena grabs her elbow.

"Is it really better for you to keep us all in the dark when Dieter knows more than us?" I snarl. "Secrets will kill us as surely as he will."

Cornelia's jaw clenches. "You're right," she says, ripping her arm free of Philomena's grasp. "The Origin Tree is the connection between our world and the goddesses. It is through the Tree that all magic flows."

"Why is there a spell to destroy it?" Brigitta asks. She's moved even closer to us, and so have several of the Watch. Her eyes narrow in rage. "And why was I never informed? How am I supposed to fulfill my oaths to protect magic if you do not even tell me about this potential danger?"

We're drawing battle lines.

"Because magic is a gift." Cornelia's shoulders sag. "And a gift can be refused. If there was ever a time when magic was causing more harm than good, the goddesses gave us a...a fail-safe. A way to sever our world from theirs."

"Water...air...earth..." Brigitta says, reading the paper Fritzi holds. "The elements?"

"Each goddess used a key—a stone—to create the Tree," Cornelia explains. "And each goddess worked with one of her champions to hide or protect those stones. The Tree is otherwise indestructible. But if you bring all three stones back to the Origin Tree, it can be burned with witch fire."

"That's what Dieter wants to do," Fritzi whispers, but everyone hears her.

"Why?" Brigitta gapes at her. "Wouldn't destroying the Tree destroy magic?"

"The Tree is like a dam. Burning it down will open the floodgates. All the magic will pour out—likely into him." Fritzi's voice is hollow, monotone, and I realize it's because she's so deeply aware of how horrific this situation is, in a way no one else in the room grasps.

Her brother, her *brother*, would let the entire world crumble just so he could have more power. And he is willing to burn up his sister's soul to do it.

"It is cataclysmic," Philomena states, tilting her chin up. "Abnoba gave her stone to the council. We protect it here."

Brigitta makes a noise in the back of her throat, a growl of frustration. I'm not sure if she's mad at the council for having kept this secret from her or if she's worried that whatever protections they've cast aren't enough.

"Where is it?" I ask. "Because whatever you're doing to keep it safe is probably not enough."

"Don't tell me!" Fritzi screeches, her face draining of color. She looks wildly around at Cornelia, Rochus, and Philomena. "Don't let me know. Don't—" Her voice breaks in a sob. "You can't trust me with secrets, not with Dieter able to..."

Bile rises in my throat, and I wrap Fritzi in my arms.

"It is safe," Philomena says, and for the first time ever, I think I hear some actual human emotion in the cold witch's voice.

But Dieter has found ways to break through the protections around the Black Forest before.

I glance at Fritzi, who looks more terrified than ever. We can't talk about this in front of her, not when she fears her mind is being spied on. I want to know where the other stones are, but I have to trust that they are safe—at least for now. From what I know of the goddesses, I doubt they just tossed the stones into the sea or something like that. If this is truly about a choice, the means to destroy magic have to still be accessible to someone determined to do so.

Someone like Dieter.

"We have to get to Trier," Fritzi says. Her eyes take a moment to focus on the room, and I realize she'd been talking to her goddess, Holda, while everyone else has been wondering how much she can safely hear.

"That's exactly what I want to do," I say. Go to Trier and eliminate the threat of Dieter.

"No, you don't understand." Fritzi clutches my hands. "Dieter *is* in Trier, Holda says, but so is her stone."

"What?!" I shout as the room erupts in chaos.

Fritzi's voice rises above the commotion. "She's been watching the city carefully. She says he didn't know about the stone before." Her face settles into grim worry. "He knows now."

Birresborn isn't far from Trier; going from the village to the city would have been a logical step for Dieter. But if Holda's stone is in that city already, and he now knows that it's there...

"Does he already have the stone?" Cornelia asks, blanching.

Fritzi shakes her head. "Holda tells me it's still safe. But..." She frowns, concentrating on the voice only she can hear. "She can't see Dieter. He's blocking her, so she can't tell if he's close—but she does know the stone, at least, is untouched. For now." It makes sense that the goddess doesn't say exactly where it is, but it's still frustrating to have to dance around knowledge.

"We will have to send troops to the city," Rochus says grimly.

Now they care about Trier. They watched the city fall to darkness and a reign of terror, watched the innocents burn. But since the people burned had not been actual witches, just innocent humans who'd been accused by corrupt people in power, they...just had done nothing.

Fritzi leans in closer to me. I know she knows what I'm thinking, not because of our bonding, but because she shares my rage at the council's apathy.

"The council will focus on the protection of the stone we hold here," Philomena insists, her tone ringing with authority. "Even if Dieter claims Holda's stone in Trier, he cannot possibly find Perchta's, and the third will be protected. We must concentrate all forces *here* in order to ensure that protection."

Rochus nods with her. But I can tell that Cornelia, Brigitta, the rest of the guards...

We doubt.

We doubt the safety of the council's stone. We doubt the security of the goddesses' stones.

We doubt that the Tree—and all magic, all the world—is safe.

What we do not doubt is that Dieter will find a way to get what he wants.

"We have to kill him," I say again, even more certain now.

Brigitta nods, understanding me. The stones are not safe because the council guards one in the Well and the other two are hidden, especially if one of the hidden stones is already so close to where Dieter is. The only way the stones will be safe is if Dieter is dead.

"Trier," Brigitta says, the word an order. We all ignore the way Philomena sputters at her.

"Trier," I say. "Best case, Dieter's not found the stone, and we kill him. Worst case, he's found the stone, and we still kill him."

"He may not be in Trier," Cornelia reminds us.

But the stone is. "New best case," I say, "we find the stone first, take it back here for protection, and then kill Dieter."

"I will lead another contingent of Grenzwache," Brigitta states, turning to the priest and priestesses in the room.

"I believe that may be a bit...too obvious," Cornelia says. "Baden-Baden may have been swayed to tolerate us, but marching a militant branch of our coven through the principalities may not go over so well with the rest of the Holy Empire."

"So we operate undercover," I offer. "We can appear as...nomadic merchants. Pilgrims. Something."

"You're not assassins!" Philomena says. "You cannot just leave your posts at the Well! If we protect the stone we have, and—"

"No, they're right," Rochus says, touching her shoulder. "Even if he never gets the earth stone, the water and air stones are powerful in their own right. He could cause such destruction..."

"On the lands of the people who would burn us," Philomena snarls. "They wanted the hexenjägers. Let them deal with the monster they created."

Cornelia and Rochus both gape at the priestess.

"Perchta is the Mother," Fritzi says quietly. "Does she love the children without magic less than the ones with it? Is your goddess truly willing to let children die just because they are not in the Black Forest with us?"

Nothing could have silenced the priestess more.

"I may be the Maid's champion," Fritzi adds, "but I don't think the Mother easily forgets her children. Any of them."

I hold Fritzi tighter. I know without a doubt that she's not thinking of the Mother goddess Perchta; she's thinking of her own mother, who loved Dieter too much to kill him. Her mother could only banish him, because even when she knew he had become something twisted, something dark...

She still loved him.

"I'm sorry," I whisper to Fritzi while the council starts planning with Brigitta. "I know he's your brother."

She swallows, her eyes sliding away. "He's not. At least...he's not the brother I thought I knew. Not the brother I remember. Whatever he is now, he's...twisted."

And beyond saving.

I'm not sure if it's her thought or mine.

The quiet certainty in my heart that I must kill Dieter is like a stone weighing down the bridge between us. This mess happened because I did not see it through in Baden-Baden. I must be the one to assure Fritzi she is safe, and the only way I can do that is...

Our dual intent is held between us by grief and sorrow, by guilt and regret. But that concept—*Dieter must die*—has no doubt attached to it. From either of us.

I squeeze her hand, then turn to the others in the room, even if they're so lost in their plans they barely notice us. "You may all figure out what you want to do, who will come with us. But at dawn, Fritzi and I are riding to Trier."

"You are not," Philomena snaps. "The stone the council holds here needs to be protected. Fritzi is our champion, and you are her warrior, and—"

"I am not your champion," Fritzi says, her voice low and monotone and terrifying. "I am Holda's champion. I do not answer to you, and you would do best not to think you can command me."

Silence weaves around the room. Fritzi stands strong, glaring at everyone, daring them all to try to object.

And then a tiny voice cuts through the awkward quiet. "Me too."

Everyone's attention whips to the door, where little Liesel stands wearing nothing but her long chemise, her blond curls shining in the candlelight. "Is it true?" she asks, stepping fully inside. "I heard... Fritzi, is he back?"

Her eyes are red rimmed and wide; her face is splotchy. When she looks up at me, I'm sure she can see the weariness in my body, the aftermath of my fight with Dieter as he possessed Fritzi, the blood on the walls, the destruction. She can smell the smoke that clings to my hair, and this little girl with an affinity for fire and a background of her own abuse at Dieter's hand must also smell the different sort of smoke, the burning smell of Fritzi's skin. Her lips tremble; her eyes water.

"I'm so sorry," Fritzi says, her voice breaking into a sob as she drops to her knees. Liesel rushes to her, wrapping her arms around her.

"Careful!" Cornelia says, unaware that Fritzi has been healing on her own. Her blisters are gone, the thin cut around her jaw no more than a shadow. Even her split lip is a narrow scab that belies the severity of the cut before. *Magic*, I think, shaking my head.

Liesel pulls away from Fritzi and glares at me so fiercely that I flinch. "You were *supposed* to kill him before," she accuses.

"I thought I had." The poison in Baden-Baden rendered him powerless, and the hexenjägers had finished the job. I'd thought. I'm the planner, though, the warrior who should be prepared for every threat. I should have known; I should have finished the job myself; I should have...

Fritzi's hand taps my knuckles, and I look up and see her watching me. Our connection isn't clear, but it's enough for her to not let me spiral into a dark hole of guilt.

"Catholic," she accuses gently.

"Guilty," I answer, aware of the irony.

"You're going to do it now, right?" Liesel asks, her little voice brooking no argument. "You're going to make sure he stops?"

I look her right in the eyes. "I swear."

"I'm going to help," Liesel declares.

There's immediate uproar, from the captain of the guards all the way to the high priest and priestesses. I see the hard set in Liesel's jaw, the way her tiny fingers curl into fists. Before she can say anything, I raise my arm.

Miraculously, the others quiet.

"Liesel, I need your help," I say, my attention solely on the little girl.

Her fists relax. She raises one hand up, sparks flickering on her fingertips. "I will help you. He hurt Fritzi. He needs to be stopped."

I shake my head. "I don't mean help like that."

She stomps her foot. "I can help! I'm a champion too! Abnoba chose me!"

"I know," I say before anyone can interrupt. I can feel Fritzi's eyes on me, the trust she has for me. "I know," I tell Liesel again. "But we don't know where Dieter is."

"He's in Trier, you said."

"I *guessed*," I answer quickly. "But I don't *know*. And if he comes here, we need a champion to be here to help protect the Well. How much did you hear? There's a stone the council has, and—"

I can see the rebellion rising in Liesel's eyes. The Well is not a place Dieter can easily breach. This is the safe option for Liesel, and she knows it. But she also knows the gravity of the situation. The stone the council has must be kept safe. This isn't a distraction, but an important task.

"Please, Liesel," Fritzi whispers.

Emotion wars on the little girl's face. Liesel is far too clever to not see how we're manipulating her with this. But she is, no matter what she says, still a child. One I've sworn to protect.

I lean closer to her. "And can you stay with Hilde?" I ask. "Protect her if..." It's a low blow, and I know it. Liesel is keenly aware of what it's like to have only one family member left alive.

"Do you promise to kill him right this time?" she grumbles, glaring at me.

"I swear."

Liesel huffs a sigh. "Fine."

She turns to Fritzi, giving her another hug, and I'm reminded again that Dieter may be related to them both, but he hurt them in a way that can never be forgotten. And whatever chance of forgiveness and family he may have had left, he long ago burned it as surely as he burned both girls.

Still wrapped in Fritzi's arms, I hear Liesel whisper, "You have to tell me *everything* so I can write it down for my epic, and I mean it, Fritzi, you have to tell me *everything.*"

When they pull apart, Liesel's eyes are redder than before as she looks up at her cousin. "Promise to come back."

"I promise."

Liesel turns. The three of us had all forgotten about the others, but when Liesel looks at Rochus, Philomena, Cornelia, Brigitta, and all the rest, she commands their attention. "Well, that's all settled then," she says firmly. "Fritzi and Otto are going. And you guys can figure out the rest without us." Liesel takes Fritzi's hand and starts to lead her away. I hear some of the others muttering protests, but Liesel glowers so fiercely that the way parts before us.

She's right. Fritzi and I need rest. Because at dawn, we leave.

Liesel doesn't relax until we're back outside. She holds Fritzi's hand as we cross the bridges to Fritzi's home, and then the cousins hug again.

When they pull apart and Fritzi steps inside, Liesel glances at me, blocking my entrance. She looks mad, but I know her well enough to see that she's frightened.

I give the girl a carefree smile. "Don't you want me to promise to come back too?" I ask.

Liesel shrugs, refusing to make eye contact. "Come back if you want to, I guess."

She steps aside, and I enter Fritzi's room.

Before I can close the door, Liesel grabs my arm, pulls me closer, and hugs me around the waist.

I can feel her tears, hot and wet, soaking through my tunic. I drop a kiss on the top of her head. "I promise," I tell her.

Once the door closes, I turn to Fritzi. She pulls down the shoulder of her chemise, exposing her clavicle and the brand Dieter put on her. The scar is perfectly shaped, a clear letter *D.*

The hexenjägers used that brand. It meant *Dämon.*

But I realized after Fritzi escaped her brother the first time that the brand was a torture that *he* came up with, not the archbishop. And it was a way of labeling his own handiwork.

D for *Dieter.*

He wanted to claim her—her magic, her self—as *his.*

"Here is what I know, Liebste," I say gently, calling her focus back to me. "What he did to you does not define you. Dieter runs about this world claiming possession of anything he wants. But I am yours because I give myself to you. It is a choice I make with every breath I take. He may have bound you to him by force..."

Her hand flutters to the scarred brand.

"...but he has no concept of how much stronger a bond is when it is a gift."

She looks at the floor, but I can still see the worry and fear etched on her brow. I put my finger under her chin and tilt her face up, waiting until she focuses on me. I want to say something that will ease the anxiety clenching her heart; I want to have the right words to make her see herself as I see her, to have as much faith in her as I do. But when she looks at me, I find I can say nothing more than, "I love you."

And perhaps that is enough. She wraps her arms around me, pulling herself up to my lips, our kiss a promise more powerful than any fear.

The next morning, we gather outside of Hilde's house. Brigitta obviously spent the night with my sister, something we all tacitly ignore as the Grenzwache arrives separately. Brigitta has selected five fighters to join us, and Hilde passes out brown cloaks that are intended to be a part of our disguise as pilgrims to pay respect to the remains of Saint Simeon. The chosen soldiers are all grim about the mission, all but Alois, who bounces like a colt.

"I can't believe I missed all the action last night," Alois mutters, but he shuts up pretty fast when he catches the look on my face.

I ignore him and head over to my sister. "Do you mind keeping an eye on Liesel?"

"Of course not," Hilde says. "Liesel is a dear."

"You do know she has the ability to burn this entire village to the ground if she has a temper tantrum, right?"

"She would never!" Hilde gasps.

"Yeah, I would never." Liesel pops out from around the corner, Hilde's cat trailing behind her, mewing for more attention.

"Honestly, how could you even suggest something like that from such a sweetheart?" Hilde says, glaring at me as she stoops to give Liesel a hug.

While my sister's back is to me, arms around her, Liesel sticks out her tongue at me, a tiny flicker of flame dancing on the tip. She giggles innocently and goes inside Hilde's house. My sister follows her, and I can already hear her promising Liesel more cookies.

When I turn around, I see Cornelia approaching. Rochus and Philomena are wildly opposed to a priestess taking up arms, but they cannot control her.

The priestess goes straight to Fritzi. When I reach them, Cornelia gives Fritzi a silver charm on a leather thong. "I do not know how powerful Dieter's magic has become, or what the nature of his cursed connection is," she says, "but this should keep your mind and body safe from possession."

Fritzi slips the necklace over her head, tugging her blond curls free. "He can't get in my head anymore?" The tremble in her voice blinds me with rage.

"You're safe," Cornelia confirms. "The bond between you and Otto has already proven effective. Now that you know Dieter's formed this horrid connection, you'll be able to fight it. And this will help." Cornelia leans in, giving Fritzi a hug. "You're safe," she repeats.

INTERLUDE

DIETER

Ha! Safe.

No, my sister.

Nothing is further from the truth.

As if a *charm* could protect you from *me.*

I watch her draw closer. I should be flattered, really.

My little sister needs a whole brigade with her just to face me. Does she think that will be enough to kill me?

She will fail.

How *delightful* that she is delivering herself to me, though! The anticipation! Such fun. A little game for us to play until she offers me her magic on a platter.

I shall suck that magic from the marrow of her bones.

And then I will use it to break the walls that hold all magic back. I will *burn* their precious Tree, and the magic of the world will flood into *me.*

They have tried for so long to hide so much from me. All of them. All of them liars. Everyone lies. *Everyone* lies. The only thing real is power.

My mother told me when I was young that she loved me, no matter what. But then I realized there were conditions to her love, just as there were conditions to wield magic.

"I will always love you, my only son," she whispered to me just before she banished me from the coven. *"But I cannot allow you to put your sister in danger."* It was *so obvious* she cared more about Fritzi than me. My sister and I are special. I knew Fritzi was powerful even before the goddess chose her. Had my mother truly loved me, she would have let me drain Fritzi oh so long ago.

Holda lied to me, too, when I was a child. She regaled me with the delights of wild magic, and told me the limitations were not real, but when I dared to believe her, when I had the *audacity* to truly believe the rules of magic were nothing more than false restraints, when I tried to test those rules she claimed not to care about...

She quit speaking to me. A goddess can lie as well as a man, better even. It didn't take me long to realize the stories she whispered in my head were only half-truths. Because if I was a witch with wild magic, how much more powerful could I be if I were a god with the powers she tried to pretend she could not share with me?

Holda whispers to my sister now.

Good little *obedient* Fritzi. Trusting little sister.

Who could have possibly guessed that *Fritzi* would lie to me the most, would nearly *kill* me and strip me—*me!*—of my power.

Now, the only lies my sister tells are to herself.
That she is loved.
That she matters.
That she is safe.

Safe. How amusing the thought.

Nothing fun is safe.

12

FRITZI

The journey we take to Trier is a stark contrast to my desperate escape months ago with Otto and Liesel.

This time, we do not travel on the barest dregs of resources, scrounging for rations in markets, Otto, Liesel, and I posing as a family to avoid scrutiny. Now, it is clear to all we pass that, though we are pretending to be pilgrims, we are not to be trifled with. No one dares to intercept us, and we travel well stocked, taking crowded barges up the rivers instead of a rowboat. The size of our party means we do not have to duck to hide from hexenjägers—in fact, there *are* no hexenjägers, not in any of the towns we pass through, and at first it is a relief. Everyone gives us a wide berth, eyeing Brigitta and her guards, clearly wondering how so many muscled people became seemingly pious worshippers traveling to Trier, but we are, ultimately, untroubled.

I feel the difference between these two trips like a lifting of a weight. The responsibility to stop Dieter is mine—he is my brother, from my coven. But it is no longer just *me* standing against him, and I cannot pretend that the guilt and burden of stopping him is only on my shoulders now. I have support, I have aid, I have a whole contingent of Grenzwache guards at my back.

And I have Otto at my side. Always.

Though the guards' support becomes mildly less reassuring when their faces go from the focused glower of a serious mission to utter enchantment with each town and landmark we come across.

This is the first time they have left the Well, I realize, the first they have set foot farther than Baden-Baden, and for a few unguarded seconds whenever we arrive somewhere new, these hulking, vicious witch guards become delighted, wide-eyed children. Alois is the most terrible at hiding his blatant wonder for the surrounding world, gawking at markets and little village taverns as though he's popped into a story being sung over a fire. Brigitta chastises him, but the wonder is refreshing, an innocent break from the purpose of our journey.

I cling to that wonder. Smiling at the guards as they point at the spires of a cathedral we pass from the river and one of them mutters something that sounds like, "Why are they all so *phallic* shaped?"

Their jesting and awe is far, far better to focus on than the days that pass without issue. The ease of travel.

The closer we get to Trier, the more worrying that ease becomes.

We get off the barge a few miles outside of Trier, preferring to approach on foot. The barge would take us directly into the docks with no time to scout or get a lay of the city; this way, we approach on our own terms, able to retreat if needed.

"Let me make sure I understand your concern," Alois says as he drops a pile of kindling on the ground of our makeshift campsite. "You're *upset* that we haven't been attacked by soldiers or jägers?"

"Not upset," I say. "Suspicious. The hexenjäger influence stretched beyond Trier only a season ago, and now—"

I spread my hand in a show of *Where are they?*

Brigitta, sharpening a sword across from me, grunts in agreement. "Perhaps Dieter's fall disbanded them, and wherever he is, he's got fewer supporters than he used to have, so he'll be easily overpowered."

The crackling fire between us catches my attention briefly. Was that—a flash of green? I stare at it, but nothing coalesces. Perhaps a bit of grime was caught on a log and burned oddly.

I shake my head and refocus on Brigitta. "That sounds unlikely. Particularly considering we still have not heard from the original guards sent to investigate Trier."

Cornelia has tried to track them as much as we have been trying to track Dieter, to no avail. Which could either mean their presence is masked. Or they are dead.

Alois drops to a crouch next to the flames, orange playing off his attempt at a smile. "Worst case, his possession of you was the last remnants of Dieter's dying breath, his spirit clinging to yours as he was swept into the afterlife, and we'll scout Trier and find this whole trip was a waste, and that the first contingent of guards are merely blackout drunk in a tavern."

My eyebrows go up. "That's the *worst* case? How so?"

Alois grins. Highlighted by the fire, backlit by twilight's darkness, it's feral. "We won't get to kill Dieter ourselves."

Brigitta thwacks Alois on the back of the head. He winces and gives her an offended frown.

"Her *brother*," Brigitta says with a pointed look at me.

But Alois is undeterred. "I think our dear champion will be first in line to do him off."

My chest catches. A stalled breath. A twinge that could be pain, could be anxiety.

I can't figure out where my resistance lies. *He is not my brother*, I want to say, much as I said to Otto. But also, *Yes, I do want vengeance*, and deeper, harder, carved from grief and pain, *I will be the one to kill him. I should have killed him in Baden-Baden.*

I should have killed him in Birresborn.

His fate is your choice, Friederike, Holda says. *Do not let anyone else influence what you know in your heart to be right.*

I barely restrain myself from laughing, not wanting to be too crazed, sitting here, suddenly chuckling at a voice only I can hear.

In my heart? I scoff at her. *What I want or what is right is hardly important. The only thing that matters is stopping him.*

Holda's uneasiness is potent. *We created the Tree, we hid the stones, we did all of this to protect our people. I am limited from interfering in the mortal world. My sisters are as well. It is part of the pact we made when we created the Origin Tree—limiting magic, limiting our interactions. It is why we depend so heavily on our champions. We intended this scaling back to keep our people safe, but... I am sorry, Fritzi.*

She never calls me that. Only ever *Friederike*, an echo of Mama, of something maternal. My throat thickens with unexpected tenderness, and I swallow, chin dipping to my chest.

Has Dieter found your stone? I ask, changing the subject.

No. I still cannot see him. But he has not accessed it yet.

He's using his access to *my* magic to block Holda's sight.

Anger surges up through me, vicious and vile.

I weigh her words, weigh my own thoughts. She knows where her previous champion hid the stone. The most direct route would be to have her tell me its location so we can go into Trier and find it. But I can't risk Dieter accessing that information through me. Not yet.

Not until we have no other choice.

In my silence, footsteps crunch through spring undergrowth near this clearing, and Otto emerges, trailed by two of Brigitta's other guards and Cornelia.

"Perimeter set, wards up." Cornelia sinks against an oak tree near the fire. "We left two of the Grenzwache to take the first rotation. We move at sunrise?"

"No," Otto and I say simultaneously, and I blink up at him. The invisible ribbon stretches between us, connecting our intent. His eyes meet mine, and a whole conversation passes through us without words, without thought, and I see my awe reflected in his eyes.

If this is how the bond is when it's been manipulated by Dieter, I cannot fathom how it will be when Dieter is disconnected from us.

"We're an hour outside Trier," Brigitta says, sheathing her blade. "The sooner we can get to the city and scout his location, the better. We are not even sure if he is in Trier—he could be anywhere in the country chasing after these stones now."

Otto lowers to the ground next to me, and I lean into him, absorbing his warmth as he faces Brigitta. "I don't argue that," he says. "But the city is too dangerous for all of us. You"—he eyes Brigitta, Alois, Cornelia, and the two present guards—"especially. We have been lucky with the lack of hexenjägers on our route. But if they are not spread across the countryside anymore, then it is most likely that they have all been recalled to Trier, and if that city is now beset with them, it would be beyond foolish to bring you lot in there, looking as you do. Our cover as pilgrims will only hold so far."

Alois leans over to Cornelia and whispers loudly, "He's saying we're too good-looking to pass as pilgrims."

She scowls at him, but her eyes glint.

"You propose that you and Fritzi go alone?" Brigitta asks, her brows lowering. "I do not like that idea."

"We'll only scout," I say quickly. "Just see if that is where Dieter even is, or if it is safe for all of us to go in. It's for the best."

"And you two won't be recognized?" It's odd for Alois to voice objection. But he's frowning at Otto, then at me, and I have half a mind to tease him for caring, but his serious tone puts pressure on the situation, pushes and pushes until I feel the heaviness of it anew.

Otto cuts a smirk that doesn't reach his eyes. "I know Trier better than anyone. We won't be caught or seen unless I want us to be."

"So you'll scout in the morning and return with a report," Brigitta tells us. "If you aren't back by nightfall, we'll come in for you."

"Can Holda pass messages, do you think?" Cornelia leans forward. "She woke me when you needed me nights ago. It was simple, an undefined urge to get to the library, but if you fall into trouble in Trier, do you think she could do something like that again?"

Yes, Holda says instantly.

I nod, eyes slipping from Cornelia, fixing on the dirt beneath my fingers, the few strands of vegetation trampled soft and broken over the course of this site being used by travelers.

If we get to Trier. And Dieter is there.

If he has taken the city and holed up in it with his hexenjägers, then...

I see Baden-Baden, overrun with witch hunters. I see my brother, sneering in the dark, telling me how it wouldn't matter if I ran this time; none of his soldiers could be coerced into helping me. They all wanted me to die. To *suffer*.

The way Dieter made me suffer.

The way he made Mama suffer. Our whole coven.

Otto's hand closes around my shoulders, yanking me out of the encroaching dread, and he pulls me into his chest. I release a breath, coming back to the present with Alois laughing at something Cornelia said.

It'll be different this time. My brother doesn't have access to his magic anymore, and whatever he can use of mine, it will be paltry in comparison. He can't affect the minds of everyone beneath him to be just as consumed by hatred as he is. Whatever we meet in Trier, *whoever* we meet, will not be under his control.

It isn't as comforting a thought as I want it to be.

Otto squeezes my shoulder again. "Come. Let's get some sleep."

"You two take the full night," Brigitta says as we stand. "We'll cover the watches. You'll be doing the hard work tomorrow."

Otto leads me to bedrolls near the edge of the clearing, close enough to the fire for warmth but far enough to have some darkness. He arranges himself in his, and I drape myself over his chest and nestle into his arms.

I feel the rumble of his huffed laughter where my cheek rests on his chest, but he says nothing, merely shifts onto his side and curls his body around me.

"A far cry from our first night of sleeping in the woods together," I murmur into him.

He hums in thought. "Quite. The food is much better than hexenjäger rations."

"And I'm not tied to a tree."

It's meant as a joke. A way to add levity to this, the way Alois does, the way I used to, so easily, sarcasm and humor to buoy against the darkness.

But joking about that now, being restrained, kicks into my stomach like a booted foot. I can feel shackles on my wrists. I can feel the rub of blisters. The stench of burned flesh.

I burrow into Otto, wanting to press close, closer, until my body stops remembering all this pain and only feels *him.*

Otto presses his lips to my forehead and breathes, one hand lifting to stroke my hair back from my face. He's quiet for a moment, fingers in my hair, and the whole act serves to make me feel like something precious. It counteracts the rising tide of panic enough that I relax, and I do only feel him, the swell of his chest as he inhales, the dip of his waist under my arm.

"I think I knew, even then," he whispers into my skin.

"Knew what?" I whisper.

"That you would be important to me."

My grip on him tightens.

I want to ask him to stay tomorrow. To not put himself at risk by going into Trier. But I know he'd refuse, just like I'd refuse if he asked me to stay behind; and so we're trapped in this, both at risk, both fearing it.

Three stones and one spark:
Water, air, earth,
And fire in the heart.

My brother knows how to destroy the Origin Tree, and destroying the Origin Tree may destroy the world. Stopping him, once and for all, is the only thing that matters.

More than my fear.

More than my desire to lie here with Otto and never get up again.

More than whatever bond links us together.

The walls of Trier are unchanged. I don't know why I expected the city to look different, but it should. If Dieter is alive in there, plotting how he'll get into the Well and break the Origin Tree, then the high gray walls of stone protecting him now should be black with corruption. They should give some clue as to what awaits us within, some way of admitting what they hold.

A line of travelers slowly enters through the eastern gate. Otto and I fall in with them, bundled in cloaks and scarves against the lingering spring chill. The guards are slow to allow entry into the city, and the length of the line stretches around the wall, all the way to the old Roman arena.

The moment it comes into view for us, my body goes rigid. Otto follows my gaze, an unspoken pull, and he stiffens too.

We can just see past the high stones that mark the entrance to the old arena. And there, the door where Otto and his jägers dragged me into the aqueduct tunnels beneath Trier when we were enemies.

Now, a handful of hexenjägers, their black cloaks dark and intense, oversee workers hauling rocks out of the doorway.

"We collapsed the tunnels," Otto says quietly.

"And they are trying to reopen them?" I guess.

He shrugs, but his face is set in a contemplative scowl. "It was a useful way in and out of the city, unseen. I can't imagine the tunnels are secure now, though. It is an odd project for your brother to prioritize."

"If he's still in charge," I say. I have to. My hope is brittle.

Otto finally turns away from the workers to give me a soft look. "If," he echoes.

But Dieter survived the justice that the hexenjägers had every right to dole out. What other impossible things has he done? Reclaiming his elevated position likely wouldn't be hard.

The line of travelers moves, and we soon find ourselves just under the gate of Trier. Hexenjägers alone stand watch—where are the town guards?—and they throw judgmental eyes over the travelers.

Occasionally, they'll yank someone aside, demanding to search a cart or bag; I can't tell what reason they have for the people they choose to search, but I hold my breath as we draw closer to them.

I eye Otto, wondering if he recognizes any of the jägers close to us, but I barely have to think the question before I notice the way he keeps his head lowered under his cloak's hood.

I have a panicked second of wishing I truly had made him stay in the forest.

I dip my own gaze. We amble through the gate, and I don't think either of us breathes until we pass the final hexenjäger, who is already focused on a cart coming through, one laden with barrels of ale. He calls out to the driver to stop and pay a tithe, and Otto and I duck away, vanishing into the winding streets of Trier.

For a moment, I'm so overcome with relief that we made it in that nothing else matters.

Then we take a turn, another, Otto's hand in mine leading me deeper into the city, and my mind fights to reconcile my memories of Trier with what I see around us now.

Last I was here, the city at least had the Christkindlmarkt to add flickers of joy. Ivy and holly draped across buildings and music lit the air, tinny and pitchy but celebrating the season. There was still an oppressive feeling of solemnity, but it was offset by attempts at happiness.

Now, Trier is every bit a city of fear and prejudice. The dirty streets snake between towering plaster-and-wood buildings, the cathedral dominating the skyline. The air is ripe with refuse and body odor, and everywhere, *everywhere*, is an oppressive, invisible scratch of *wrong*. Something is wrong. An enemy lurks in the shadows. The people who had crowded anxiously through the gate scatter immediately, peeling off into stores or homes or down narrow alleys, no relief in being through the city walls;

just trying to get *hidden*, everyone keeping their eyes to themselves, moving like they're being hunted.

"The streets are practically empty," Otto says, breathless. He's slowed us to a determined walk, not running, but not wanting to draw attention by lingering, and his eyes cut around, spotting faces in windows and people slamming doors as we pass. He looks down at me, brows pinching. "Are you comfortable asking Holda where we should go? We could try to head for the main hexenjäger buildings to scout if Dieter is there, but if she can tell you where the stone is hidden, that may be a better starting place."

His face is all soft, not wanting to push me to ask Holda. He can likely sense my spike of discomfort at having this information, wondering if Dieter could overcome me in spite of the steps I have taken to keep him out.

But we need to do this.

I close my eyes briefly, letting Otto guide me through the streets. *Holda? Where is your stone?*

Her pause twines with my hesitation, and I know she fears telling me too, fears that she cannot stop my brother's grip on even the barest power.

After a long beat, she says only, *Beneath you.*

I frown, eyes splitting open. *The aqueducts?*

Confirmation comes in a settling of certainty. And I can't help it—I laugh.

Otto glances at me oddly, half his lips lifting inadvertently. "What?"

"Holda had her stone hidden in the aqueducts," I whisper. "The whole time you were routing people to safety and mapping the tunnels—"

"There was an ancient, powerful witch relic lodged somewhere nearby," he finishes, and the same humor flashing in his eyes. "Where in the aqueducts?"

But I slam my mind against Holda telling me more. "Let's get down there first. Step by step. Just in case."

Otto nods. "This way. The fastest access is through the—"

We make another turn, Otto bent on a destination, but he stops up short.

The market square. The place where he took me shopping for food and supplies before we enacted his plan to free the prisoners in the basilica. Here is the starkest reminder that the Christkindlmarkt has passed; what was once the epicenter of festivity is now a wide expanse of dirty gray stones. Everything has been cleared out of this square.

Except for stakes.

Standing tall amid piles of burnt kindling are bodies bound in chains. Each corpse is blackened, shriveled into unrecognizable horror with their mouths agape in last, permanent screams of agony.

My hand goes to my stomach, pushing hard, unconsciously trying to dislodge the rising rush of nausea.

There are more than a dozen people on these stakes. Some still smoking. And there are unused stakes too, set up and ready, but no hexenjägers are currently here, no one being dragged to their deaths.

Most of the bodies are too burned to be recognized. But I know, in a sudden punch of instinct, that this is what happened to the other Grenzwache guards. This is why we couldn't track them. This is why we didn't hear from them.

Sorrow falls over me in a staggering wave. Otto's fingers clamp on mine, holding tight, and I think he's comforting me until I get hit with a wash of his emotions through our bond: Horror. Agony. Guilt.

I look at the side of his face again.

He's gone pale, lips in a thin line, eyes wide and inert. He takes a frantic breath in. Gasping.

I heave him to the side, into an alley, away from any prying eyes. Though there *aren't* any eyes, not in that square; no one is here. No one is looking. Everyone has been chased inside by of the fear that rolls through these streets like fog.

Out of sight, I cup Otto's face in my hands and make him look at me.

He worked so hard to free Trier. That was his one consolation upon running away with Liesel and me, that he had instigated sparks of change. Johann, one of Otto's former jägers, had dared to tell us that the city had begun to buck off the oppression of the witch hunters after the prison break.

Any fragments of that change have been swept away. All the work Otto did, all the things he sacrificed to free this city, have been undone.

"We will fix this," I promise him. My voice comes out stronger than I thought it would. I'm just as broken, just as terrified and trembling, but seeing Otto on the edge of collapse, I find some deeper well of strength I didn't know I still had. It's him, for him and from him, and I lower his forehead to mine. "We will *fix* this, Otto, I swear to you."

He licks his lips, trembles against me, his hands coming up to encircle my wrists.

"We cannot stay out here," I whisper. "We need to get to the aqueducts. Are you all right to do that?"

I don't want to push him. But at the same time, I know this man. I know how his mind works, how best to distract him:

Ask for a plan.

Otto loves his plans.

I would torment him for it, but it works.

Almost instantly, he peels back from me. Some of his panic recedes, and I catch the moment where he comes through it. Is that how I look when he drags me out of my pain? Like I'd forgotten how it felt to fill my lungs all the way.

He dives in and kisses me hard, rough lips and his hand on my jaw.

"Come on, hexe," he whispers, and drags me off into Trier.

13

OTTO

It's already so much worse than I expected.

There had been a glimmer of hope, I realize now, a faint belief that perhaps our fears were unrealized. That maybe Dieter wasn't as strong as he'd been before, that Fritzi's possession was no more than a dying gasp from a withering man.

But no.

He has consolidated all of his power and strengthened his grip, choking the city in an iron-tight fist. The murders have continued. The terror has continued.

Focus.

I can grieve, or I can act. And Fritzi needs me to act.

We need to get to the aqueducts. The passages the hexenjägers know about—such as the one outside the arena or under the Porta Nigra—are too risky. I don't love the idea of returning to the housefort I used before. Our stunt to free the prisoners in Trier last year will no doubt have caused Dieter to take a closer look at the old tunnels that remained, and the routes that were once secret may be compromised. But it's still the best option.

By which I mean, it's the only option.

I pull Fritzi under the arched entryway of the narrow alley leading to the Judengasse. I'm on edge, intently focused on every detail, looking for the swish of a black cloak, the flash of a silver brooch.

A pebble bounces off my shoulder.

I suck in a breath, my heart hammering. I want to whirl around, but I can't cause a scene. I don't see anyone else on this street, but hidden eyes may watch me from covered windows. My fingers tighten around Fritzi's, and we both pause. I look casually over my shoulder...

There.

A mass of dirty rags huddles in the corner, shadowed. The lump almost looks like refuse, but I see bright eyes shining in the darkness.

Mia, an orphan who lived with her brother in the Judengasse and watched over my housefort when I was away. She's better than any spy; no one looks twice at an orphan, not in a city with so many mothers burnt.

The bundle of cloth shifts, and Mia stands up. Ignoring me completely, she steps deeper into the alley, behind another building. I wait a beat, then follow, Fritzi breathless with anticipation beside me.

Mia leads us into a tiny shack leaning against one of the buildings, chickens rooting among the muck behind sticks woven into a crude pen.

"You came back," Mia says when Fritzi and I round the corner. I cannot tell if there is relief or accusation in her sharp tone.

"I thought—I thought it would be over," I say. Emotion chokes my voice. Can she tell how sorry I am? I should have come back so much sooner. I should have made sure Trier was safe. I should have made sure *she* was safe, and her brother, and the other orphans and destitute people.

There was so much more work to do, and I let myself celebrate a false victory instead, I let myself revel in joy when there was still so much grief left in the wake of the city I abandoned—

Fritzi presses her weight against my shoulder, grounding me. I can almost sense her admonishment to not feel guilty through the touch.

"It's not safe for you here," Mia tells me.

"Where is your brother?" I ask.

Mia shakes her head. "Not here. He found work on a farm past the city walls and—"

My shoulders sag in relief. Mia and her brother were among the first I saved; their father had wanted to make way for a new wife, and Mia's brother had been born with one arm much shorter than the other, something his ass of a father considered a flaw. The witch trials had given their father an easy way to start a new life, and while I'd been able to save them from the stake, I had not been able to find them the home they deserved.

"Why didn't you go with him to the farm?"

She rolls her eyes as if to say, *Because obviously there's still work here to do.* "What do you need help with?"

"Is the housefort safe? I need to get to the aqueducts, and—"

"He told me to give you a message, if you ever came back."

Her words stop me, redirect my thoughts. "Who?" I ask. I exchange a look with Fritzi. Mia can't mean Dieter, can she?

"Johann," she says.

Johann. The young hexenjäger who dared to warn me about Dieter's approach. The one who escorted Dieter back to Trier with the promise to oversee his execution. Johann—perhaps the only ally I have in the hexenjäger units now.

"He's alive?" Fritzi asks, hope sparking in her voice.

"He's been helping us since you left," Mia tells me, and guilt twists around my gut again. I know Mia means more than just her brother and herself; the *us* in her statement refers to all the victims.

Johann stepped up to help when I left the city behind.

"We do what we can. There's a..." Mia flaps her hands, looking for the word. "A group of us? We don't all know each other, just the signs. We try to warn the people the hexenjägers target, free prisoners, undermine the Kommandant..."

Johann isn't just helping.

He's started an underground network of rebels.

"He told us that you may come back," Mia said. "If you found out that things were bad, still."

I kneel, ignoring the disgruntled hen that flaps against my leg as whatever muck it sought seeps into my trouser leg. "I am so sorry I left you, Mia."

She glares at me. "We don't have time for your apologies."

"I like her," Fritzi says.

"He told us to tell you to go to the church."

I shake my head, confused. "Which church?" There are dozens, from the grand cathedral to the church of Porta Nigra, from the chapels attached to the monastery in honor of Saint Simeon to the little parishes scattered around.

"He just said that you need to find the star before you can see everything."

I suck in a breath.

"What does that mean?" Fritzi said.

Mia shrugs. "It wasn't safe to be too obvious. If one of the jägers caught us and found out what we were doing..."

Coded messages.

"I think I know where to go." I say, then turn to Fritzi. "Johann knows the aqueducts too, and if he's been tracking Dieter, he can point us in the direction we need to go."

Fritzi nods tightly, and I'm aware that the direction we need to go gets us one step closer to confronting her brother.

To killing him.

Before I leave the little girl, I dump the contents of my purse into her hands. "Get out of the city," I tell her. "This will buy you and your brother passage south." I tell her about Baden-Baden, and that there are friends in the Black Forest.

She takes the money, but I can see she's not happy with me. "I'm not leaving," she says sullenly. "Why would I?"

I gape at her. "To be safe."

A smirk twists her lips. "I don't care about that."

I feel awe as I stand before her. Maybe Fritzi's right, and I'm too noble, too guilty, too everything. I want to save everyone. But Mia reminds me that not everyone wants–or needs–to be saved.

And I'm not alone in my fight.

"So, where are we headed first?" Fritzi asks me as I lead her back out of the Judengasse. I don't want to pass through the square, but it's the most direct route. The Porta Nigra looms to my left; the burnt corpses of Dieter's most recent victims smolder to my right. Fritzi and I rush past, turning up a street before Fritzi stops in her tracks, her eyes wide.

"The cathedral?" she gasps. The seat of the archbishop is there, the man who signed off on all of Dieter's evil. *Likely no more than a puppet of that demon*, I think sourly.

I shake my head, pulling her to the side as a man with a cart full of hay lumbers past. "There's another church, beside the cathedral, but separate. The Church of Our Lady."

Fritzi frowns, still unclear, but she follows as I lead her closer.

"I can show you better than I can tell you."

We both pull our hoods up as we approach the church square. The cathedral rises up more like a fortress than a holy place. But, just to the right of it, another little church rests in the shadow of the main cathedral. Our Lady was built by the French—Trier is close enough to the border—and it was often ignored despite its beauty in favor of the archbishop's seat. The buildings are a stark contrast to each other—one a brute, the other delicate; one made of stocky, solid stone blocks, the other with stained glass and carved arching designs that make the rock look like lace.

No one stops us as we go inside the smaller church, even though most pilgrims go to the cathedral to see the relics there.

We are not here for relics.

It's still early enough for the stained glass windows to cast nothing more than flickers of blue and red over the pale floor. I lead Fritzi to the center of the building.

"A star," she gasps.

A gold-colored star with twelve points is inlaid on the stone floor.

"What does it mean?" Fritzi asks me. Her voice is hushed, but sound carries. I raise my finger to my lips, warning her that others could hear us across the room, even if we whisper. There aren't many here, but a church is never empty. And this building was designed to amplify sound in the center.

Standing on the star, I point to each of the twelve pillars holding up the soaring roof of the church. Pictures are painted on the columns, but it's impossible to see all of them lined up unless we stand atop the star. It is an optical illusion, a brilliant use of the building's structure to force worshippers to pause and contemplate the heart of the church if they want to clearly see each image. Moving just a little to the left or right would throw the whole effect off; only when standing in the exact center of the church, marked by the star, can the entire series of paintings be seen.

I pull Fritzi to the side of the building, where the acoustics are not quite so echoing. "This has to be what Johann meant—the church with the star where you can see everything."

Fritzi nods. The clue makes sense. "But where is Johann?"

I cross over to one of the pillars. In addition to a portrait—each pillar showcases a different apostle—there are lines of text painted onto the stones. "The Apostles' Creed," I tell Fritzi.

She squints at the text. "In Latin?"

I nod. "But look." I point to a line that reads, *Creatorem caeli et terrae.* "Creator of heaven and earth," I translate, but as I do, I trace the chalky line someone faintly sketched under the word *terrae.*

"A clue?" Fritzi says. "We're looking for earth?"

"Let's see if there are more."

We split up, each of us going to a different pillar. I find another chalky line under the word *sub,* which means *under.* Fritzi motions for me to come to her, and she points out a third word underlined: *mortuos. The dead.*

"Earth, under, dead," I whisper to her. "We need to find the dead who are under the earth."

Her eyes grow round. The clues all point to one place.

The crypt.

Fritzi looks around the small church, scanning for steps that will take us down to a crypt. I grab her hand. No one would know this route unless they were deeply entrenched in the Church, someone who studied the maps and knew the passages. Someone like me. Or Johann.

I take her through a back door, into the courtyard connecting Our Lady to the archbishop's cathedral. A priest I don't recognize has his head bowed in the cloister, but a light rain has kept the courtyard otherwise clear. I pull Fritzi down another passage and to a dark stone staircase and the filigree door at the base, quickly entering. There's no light here beyond the guttering candles. The scent of petrichor and damp rises up to greet us.

"Could this be a trap?" Fritzi asks, her voice a trembling whisper.

I step deeper into the crypt. I know, only because I have studied the tunnels and maps, that there is a passage from here to the Roman aqueducts, but it collapsed long ago, a century before now. The only entrance to and exit from this part of the crypt is by the stairs Fritzi and I just descended. If hexenjägers stormed the crypt, we'd be trapped.

I'm just about to grab Fritzi and run to the stairs when I hear footsteps—not from the door, but from deeper in the crypt, in the dark shadows.

"You're here," a voice says. One dying candle flickers at the speaker's breath.

Johann straightens, looking from me to Fritzi and back again.

In the space of a few short months, the boy has aged a decade. Pale scruffy hairs scratch at his chin, the barest markings of a man that seem reluctant to catch up with the boy's age. His face is gaunt, his skin sallow. Johann squints up at us, and I think he must doubt we are real.

"I'm back," I say. *God, forgive me for leaving. For not finishing what I began.*

Johann swallows, the lump in his throat rising and falling against the thin corded muscles. "We must pray it's not too late."

"What's been going on?" Fritzi asks, stepping closer. Johan motions for us to follow him deeper into the crypt. I grab a candle, the wax soft and cheap, denting under my grip, and go with him.

"Dieter's mad," Johann says. "But he somehow...he has sway over people. The archbishop is like a..."

"A puppet?" Fritzi guesses.

Johann nods. "He speaks, and it is his voice, but he says things that he would never say, does things he would never do. He rarely leaves his office, but the decrees he's given... Dieter holds all the power now."

I curse. I had thought Dieter powerless when we overtook him at Christmas, but he's been drawing on Fritzi as a magical source and using that to manipulate those around him. And there are other sorts of power than magic, like the power of control over a diocese.

"I've been in hiding for more than a month now," Johan continues. This is an ancient part of the crypt, deeper than I've ever been before. Rocks are scattered, and Fritzi and I have to go slower, picking our way around them so we don't fall.

This hiding place is brilliant, I have to give him credit. Not only is it unlikely that anyone would look for a rebel within the church complex itself, but the crypt here is rarely used. Unless the archbishop himself died, no one would come down here. The cathedral's crypt is reserved for the most illustrious members of the church; the regular parishioners who die—at least the ones not burned—rot in an ossuary before being packed into graves. They're not given their own chamber beneath the holy floors. Pilgrims to the cathedral worship at the altar, kissing the reliquaries, those elaborate gilded boxes that hold holy relics. The archbishop sits on his throne, and the priest's robes brush the smooth floor above, all without knowing that the one human living in the shadowed crypt beneath their feet plots to free the city of their tyranny.

The only problem is...

"How do you leave the crypt unnoticed?" I ask.

"Dieter has been focused on the tunnels," Johann says. "But he hasn't found this one."

Johann sweeps his arm aside, and I gasp. The old tunnel, the one that had caved in, has been cleared. The rocks piled up around the tombs are debris from the excavation.

"You did this?" I ask, looking into the depths of the tunnel. A thin pile of stones separates this from the main aqueduct; no one in the aqueducts would think the tunnel was open.

"I've had help." Johann turns to me. "It wasn't just you, you know. Lots of people hated the regime of terror. Lots of people have been fighting back, even in little ways."

"And you have united them." I swallow down the emotion welling in my eyes. I should have done what Johann has done. I should have trusted others, formed a rebellion, not a heist. I should have unified the people.

I never had to fight alone.

How different would this all have been had I sought allies instead of plots? Working with more than just my sister and later Fritzi, perhaps we could have toppled Dieter before he ever had the chance to be what he became. Perhaps Fritzi's coven would have been spared; perhaps more stakes would have been unburnt; perhaps...

A world of possibilities is heaped like broken rubble in the corner.

I made this life from my past actions. I can only move forward and attempt to change the future into one that does not bring me shame.

"I saw you," Johann says. "Before. It took me a while to realize what you'd done, how you'd worked. That time you hit me in front of the others, told me I couldn't talk the way I did...you meant that. Not because you wanted me to believe in what the hexenjägers said, but because I really couldn't talk that way...not if I wanted to stay alive. Not if I wanted to find ways to fight back."

I remember that hit. I hadn't held back. Not only would talk of mercy for the prisoners have gotten Johann killed, but if I had been lenient, it might have blown my cover.

"I started seeing the other people who didn't talk in the same way you didn't talk." Johann takes a step forward, grabs my shoulder, and gives it a comforting squeeze. "I started finding friends and allies. But only because I saw you first."

"Thanks," I mutter.

"I'm glad you're here now," Johann continues. "Because Dieter has been searching for something. At first, I thought he was just trying to reopen the tunnels, but the Kommandant has maps and books and notes. He sifts through the aqueducts. He's seeking...something."

"A stone," Fritzi interjects. "He's trying to find a stone."

Johann shoots her a confused look and casts his eyes around the crypt and all the rocks scattered on the ground.

"A specific stone," Fritzi adds, offering a weak smile.

"What does it look like?" Johann asks. "Is it a gem, or perhaps cut in a certain shape...?"

"We don't know," I say, knowing how unhelpful that is. But part of the security of the stones is how little is known about them.

"It may make him stronger," Fritzi said. "The stone he's looking for... it could give him...powers."

Johann blanches, clearly horrified at the thought of an even stronger Kommandant. "All I know is that he started in the Porta Nigra, going through the tunnels and excavating them from there. And he's ramped it up. Day and night. I can hear them sometimes."

He indicates the pile of rocks used as a barrier to hide his secret tunnel. "Dieter will tear the city apart to get what he wants."

No, I think. *You're wrong. He'll tear apart the whole world.*

14

FRITZI

Otto bends closer to Johann, the two of them talking quietly in the shadowed tunnel. Our candlelight turns everything a pale, flickering yellow, and as their voices drop to a low murmur, I let my mind drift.

Hesitation is tart and uncomfortable. I don't want to ask. I don't want to know.

But if Dieter is already looking. If he already knows...

Otto gets a look on his face. Something pensive, something severe, his brows set in a deepening frown. "Dieter is underground at this moment?"

Johann shrugs. "It's likely. He's been overseeing the excavations personally, but sometimes he goes up into the city to oversee the—" He stops. Swallows. "The burnings."

"If he's in the tunnels now," Otto continues, and I can see the willpower it takes to move on from any mention of burnings, "that gives us an advantage."

"How so?" I ask.

Otto smiles with half of his mouth, a cold, calculating smile. "We've collapsed these tunnels before."

My eyes widen. "You want to bury him."

Otto nods. "Then find the stone in the aftermath."

We told Brigitta we'd be back by nightfall. This was meant to be a scouting mission only, to reconvene and plan for how to take him out together.

My chest tightens. "Can we even access enough explosives in time, or—"

A scream rips through the tunnels. A bright, terrified cry, and I drop in half, hands over my ears, body tensing, ready to flee, ready to fight.

But Otto and Johann only dive toward me, Johann with one hand out like I might fall over, Otto seizing my arms.

"Fritzi?" Otto demands "What's wrong?"

"You didn't hear—" But a warbling cry thuds across my mind again.

Friederike! Holda shouts. *He's found it; he's found the stone—*

Her voice devolves into shattering wails, so beset with terror and grief and *guilt* that I stumble again, nearly going to my knees.

"He's—he's found it, he's—" I can only mumble, consumed by Holda's increasing panic, and then I'm scrambling forward, tearing through the thin stone barrier Johann set up to hide his tunnel. The stones clatter all around, but I don't care about the noise, desperation funneling into every limb as I start sprinting blindly through the tunnels.

"Fritzi!" Otto tears after me, and I think Johann does, too, but I'm beyond myself, no thought, only drive.

I see the turns laid out, side routes to take as Holda unfurls the path to me. I don't know if she's meant to; I don't know if this strains the limits of what she can do, but she is panicked, and so I go. Candlelight barely illuminates me from where Otto and Johann bring their flames, but I don't trip, racing into narrowing darkness like I know this path. Another turn, the tunnel slopes downward, going and going, down and down—

The tunnel widens. Opens into a massive circular chamber with stone columns holding the ceiling high above us. The space is lit by torches set into the walls, the floor is covered in an inch of water that makes the space smell of mildew and rot.

And in that space are a dozen hexenjägers and my brother.

Otto and Johann patter to a stop behind me at the very edge where the hall opens into the room. Otto curses. Johann is silent, his anxiety a tremble in the air.

The jägers have their backs to us, which is the only thing that saves us for the moment; they're all transfixed on Dieter.

He stands at the far end of the chamber, half inside a massive hole that has been gouged into the wall. Within that hole, I can barely make out a stone table holding up a golden box. Even from this distance, I can see it's encrusted with gems, untouched by dust or grime despite being hidden away. It gleams in the torchlight, sapphires and rubies.

"A reliquary?" Otto whispers, seemingly unaware he's even spoken.

I want to ask him what he means—a reliquary? But I have seen items such as this in cathedrals and churches, one of the many types of treasures Catholics display on their altars.

This Catholic relic cannot be Holda's stone…can it?

Dieter throws back the golden lid and peers inside. He looks so like a character from one of Liesel's stories, uncovering a great treasure, that I'm hit with a pang of wanting to tell her, of wanting this to be a simple story—just a villain finding buried gems, easily defeated.

Then Dieter smiles. Even in the low light, I watch his lips curve as he reaches into the box.

And comes up with a stone the size of his fist, cradled in his palm.

"I'm glad you could make it, Fritzichen," he says to the stone.

He turns and throws his smile at me across the room.

That yanks the attention of the hexenjägers, who whirl, some dropping construction tools to reach for weapons.

"Ah-ah," Dieter says, staying them. "That is no way to treat my guest."

Another lurch. He's using my magic to control them. A dozen armed soldiers, all held by my brother's control.

Disgust tinges my throat, rises up across my tongue like bile.

I cut Dieter off from overtaking me. There has to be a way to block him from my magic completely—how? How do I break the bond he made?

His face drops into a scowl. "Though you should not have brought *company*, Fritzichen."

He looks past me, glancing once at Johann, then at Otto.

"Give me that stone," I demand. I know it's useless. I just want his attention back on me and off Otto.

Dieter cocks his head. "Why did you push me out of your mind all those nights ago? We were working so well together. Did you at least do what I asked you to do? Do you have the stone?"

He doesn't wait for me to confirm or deny any of his questions—I feel his grasping fingers of magic, my own magic doubled back on me, picking at my brain, cold, boney fingers that pluck a headache across my forehead.

He's trying to overtake me again.

Panic overwhelms me. A surge of terror, and I grasp for the connection with Otto, for the amulet Cornelia gave me.

Dieter can't get me.

He can't overtake me again.

He seems to realize it at the same moment I do. That scowl grows darker as he heaves himself out of the opening with the gold box, boots sloshing in the water that coats the floor of this wide chamber.

"You shut me out, sister?" Dieter cradles the stone to his chest. "You didn't bring me the stone from the Well, did you?"

"Give me that stone," I say again, though I know it's hopeless.

Dieter grins. He tosses the stone in the air. Catches it.

"No," he says. "No, I don't think I will." He turns to the nearest hexenjäger. "Kill those two. Bring my sister to me."

"*No!*" The scream tears out of me at the same moment two hexenjägers lift crossbows and fire.

There are no plants here, nothing connected to what magic is most instinctual for me, so I'm acting on will only, will and horror, and so I grab at wild magic and pull, up and over, thinking only *shield*.

The water responds.

In a great lurching wave, the inch of old stagnant water rips from the floor and covers the opening between this tunnel and the chamber in a wall of protection. The arrows thud off it, clattering to the ground on the other side, and through the waving, distorted wall of water, I see my brother take a jerky step forward.

"Unfair, Fritzichen! *Play nice!*"

More arrows fire, ricocheting harmlessly off the wall of water I hold up, hands splayed.

Next to me, Otto touches my shoulder. "Are you all right?"

"Am *I* all right? He just tried to kill you!"

"Fritzi. You're controlling *water*." He says it with wonder. As though we have time for wonder. As though hexenjägers aren't currently hacking at this protective wall with swords.

But it is something awe-inspiring.

I haven't gotten to see the bounds of wild magic while hiding my abilities in the Well. I haven't practiced what I'm capable of.

This is the first time I've used magic that isn't associated with plants, the first time I haven't depended on the teachings instilled in me.

I gasp, throat welling, and somehow manage a smile.

"This is all real, then?" comes Johann's still, small voice.

We both turn to him. His gaunt face is gray, and I see in his wide eyes that some part of him had still hoped there was a simple explanation for Dieter's takeover. To what happened in Baden-Baden. The battle in that village was chaos, things that could have been explained away; but seeing a wall of water hold off arrows and swords is undeniable.

"Yes," I tell him. "But we're not all like Dieter."

"I know," Johann says. He quickly crosses himself. "I know. How do we stop him?"

Otto is already pulling weapons out of scabbards at his waist, focus jumping between the soldiers beyond the water and me. "You can manipulate water—what do you think you can do with the rock that makes up the chamber?"

"I don't know," I admit. Sweat starts to bead on my forehead despite the chill of the tunnels, muscles along my back cramping with the effort of holding up the water. A particularly strong hit from an ax makes me stagger; Johann catches me, steadies me upright. "What do you want to do?"

"Our original plan," Otto says, his eyes glinting. "Bury the bastard."

Can I do that? Collapse the room. We can dig out the water stone from the rubble.

I nod, shaking with anger and fear and growing fatigue.

"I think—" I waver again. "I think I'll have to drop the water to focus on the stone."

Otto holds up his knives. Johann has weapons in hand now, too, a short sword he removes from his back and a knife from his waist.

"Do it," Otto says.

We'll have seconds. Maybe less before the jägers are on us.

Drop the water. Reach for the stones in the ceiling. Bring the room down on my brother without burying us alive.

Holda, I pray, beg, though what guidance can she give me? Her panic is only feeding into mine, and so I close my eyes in one steadying moment and drop the water wall.

The soldiers are right there, weapons midswing to hit the wall again.

Behind them, Dieter laughs.

Laughs.

I look up, reaching for the ceiling, ignoring his cackle and whatever it might mean—

A growl resonates through the chamber.

The hexenjägers, weapons up, go rigid, frozen by Dieter's will, and that growl rises, rises, thunders like horse hooves.

Dieter's laughter turns to manic glee. He bounces on his feet and looks down at the stone in his hands. "Oh, *yes*," he coos. "Fritzichen! Can you feel it? Oh this will be *fun*."

Not growling.

Not horse hooves.

Each stone the goddesses hid is connected to an element. Bring all three together, and the Tree can be burned with the final element, fire.

The stone bound to earth is safely in the Well. Abnoba's stone.

The stone bound to air is hidden. Perchta's stone.

But this stone. Holda's stone.

Otto grabs my arm. "*Water*," he shouts a beat before a wave rushes up the tunnel behind us and slams into our backs.

We go sprawling into the room, thrown into torment and tumult with the hexenjägers. Water sweeps up over me, yanking me down and around, flipping me and letting me break the surface only to tug me under again. The torches on the walls snuff out, plunging us into darkness.

I lose Otto in the chaos; Johann cries out, but it's gone; there is nothing other than that growl of water rushing in single-minded focus and my brother's echoing laughter.

It is the summation of every nightmare I've had. Just darkness and Dieter and no escape.

Terror sweeps up over me. It could eat me alive. It will—

I slam my arms out.

No.

He has no power over me now. Not ever again.

NO.

The water around me stops, holds me upright, and I break the surface with a desperate gasp. The lack of light makes it impossible to see where the water's taken me, how full the room is now, and I scream, "Otto!"

The roar is too loud. My brother is too frenzied. The darkness is too potent.

I throw my hand up and light the first thing my magic can latch onto—a stone in the ceiling. Witchlight is an easy spell, one most children learn, and the soft white glow illuminates the chamber.

Water is filling the room, raising us closer and closer to the ceiling. The only free space left is around Dieter, who stands in the middle of a whirlpool, juggling the water stone from hand to hand.

Fury overwhelms my terror.

He's only able to use that stone because of *me*. Because of *my* magic.

So I should be able to use it too.

I scream and throw every ounce of my power at my brother. Invisible tendrils like thorny vines latch onto what he's using, his own connection to the water stone.

He falters, dropping to one knee, and his laughter breaks in a startled cry.

"*Fritzichen, stop*!" he screams, but *no*, I am not his, *I am not his*.

The water stone reacts to me. I can feel the moment it separates from Dieter's control and connects with my magic, the element Holda secreted away in this relic.

I sever Dieter's commands. His intentions, vile and dark and twisted, though he still holds onto the stone, grips it in his now magicless hands.

The whirlpool in the room stops. There's a pause, then the water surges into the space Dieter occupies, the only free part he kept dry.

He's hit by a wave and goes down in a gurgling shout.

"Fritzi!" Otto's voice rings out, and I whirl to him, treading water as the chamber levels, but it's still too full, and now the current reverses. Where Dieter had dragged water in, its natural flow is to go *out*, and so it surges back for the tunnel, carrying us with it.

I struggle to stop the current, to swim to Otto. He's dragged past one of the stone pillars and grabs on, sinking below the surface once before breaking free again. I haul myself toward him, and he reaches out, trying to catch me as the increasing current of water hauls me toward the tunnel.

"*Fritzi!*" Otto stretches, *reaches*, arm extended, the other snaked around the pillar.

My mind centers enough that I make the water shove me in his direction, a rocking surge that sends me hurtling into his arms. He snatches me to him and the two of us slam into the pillar, gasping, drenched in the beating waves.

"Where's Johann?" Otto asks.

We turn, eyes scanning the chamber—

Across the room, the current trapping him against the wall by the tunnel opening, is Dieter. He's caught between fighting to keep his head above the surface and trying to regain control of the stone, but I redouble my hold on it, on him, straining with everything I have.

I start to slip out of Otto's arm. He clings to me, but my focus teeters enough that Dieter tries to force his way back into control of the stone.

"I can't hold him!" I shout. "Otto—"

The water level is lowering, fast and determined, but not fast enough. I can barely think in the churning water, the pulsing glow of the witchlight I made over us, the threads connecting me to Dieter, to the water stone—

"Johann!" Otto shouts. He tries to point but can't with both his arms keeping us from being swept away.

I spot a head pop above the surface across from us. The current drags him forward, and he surfaces again, this time with something in his hand: a knife.

The current is hauling him directly at Dieter.

I can't breathe. Can't blink or move or think how to help him in the second between spotting his knife and his body smacking into my brother.

There's a shout. A warbled cry.

The water lowers, lowers, rushing and roaring, a caged, angry beast.

Johann detaches from Dieter. He floats backward for a moment.

He doesn't turn to us. Doesn't move away at all until Dieter pushes again and dislodges the knife that he'd managed to wrest away and drive into Johann's chest.

"*Johann!*" Otto screams, and I think he might dive to help him, but he stays against the pillar, body strung taut. "*Johann!*"

Dieter shoves Johann's body again. The current sucks it down, out, leaving a red trail in the water as he's dragged up the tunnel.

The water drops enough that we can stand on the floor.

My knees give out, and I hit the stones, coughing, sputtering. Instinct pushes me to move—I reach out, fighting to do something, bring my brother to the ground—

Otto staggers to his feet. He has no weapons now, grief heavy in his eyes, and he gets one step before he makes a brittle, fractured cry.

I look up across the waterlogged room, hand extended, magic pooling in my chest.

Dieter is gone.

15

OTTO

Water drips into my eyes, blurring my vision.

Johann...

I know I should care about Dieter—and I *do*—but he's gone, and I don't have any magic to find him. I may be able to find Johann, he may still be alive, and—

I rush to the tunnel, Fritzi on my heels, where his body was swept with the flow of water. How far could the current have carried him? These aqueducts lead out to the Moselle; could he already be drifting in the river, injured and flailing? He needs help; he needs—

I trip over something big and soft and wet. When I look down, Johann's eyes stare up at me.

I know without touching his cold skin that it's too late. The knife is gone from his chest, but the hole is still there. It doesn't pump with blood. The wound doesn't gush because his heart isn't beating.

He's dead.

I drop to my knees beside him. I killed him. This is the price he paid for following in my footsteps.

I feel Fritzi beside me, the sorrow radiating off her.

"He was good," she says in a soft voice.

My head is bowed so low that the ends of my hair touch the murky water. *He was good.* It's so simple, but what truer, better thing could be said about someone, at the end, beyond that?

"He was here to help Trier when I abandoned it," I say.

"Stop that." Fritzi's low, barely audible words are for me, but her eyes are on his body. "He is not another mark in the ledger of your guilt."

She's wrong.

I am not a priest, but I murmur the de profundis prayer for Johann's soul. Someone should.

When I stop, Fritzi touches my arm. "Do you think he would mind...?" Her fingers splay, and I can almost envision the magic within them. I shake my head, and Fritzi focuses, the stones of the tunnel opening up and enclosing Johann's body in a makeshift tomb. At least he will not rot, bloated and stinking, among the corpses of the jägers.

Something glints in the pool nearby, and I pull up the heavy golden box Dieter had ripped from the wall. The history-lover in me recognizes the symbols etched into the metal. I was right; this is a reliquary.

I gesture to Fritzi as I place the box atop the makeshift barrow. Johann deserves gold. Fritzi has more stone wrap around the reliquary, allowing a glimpse of the shining metal to serve as a marker.

"This is ancient," I mutter, running my hand over the gold. Christianity was still young when this box was made. It could even be as old as Trier itself, or Saint Simeon.

Holda isn't my god, but I still shoot off a quick thought to her: *Good hiding place. Putting the pagan rock inside a Christian box. Not bad.*

Water sloshes along Johann's grave. Water...the water Fritzi summoned, the water Dieter pulled... Did both the siblings have such strong powers with water because of the water stone Holda hid here?

"We have to go," Fritzi says, tugging on my arm. I shake myself, blinking away the burning in my eyes.

I must stop Dieter, I tell myself. *I must stop him, and then I must come back and complete the work I started, and that Johann continued.*

Swallowing down my emotion, I nod at her. "I'm ready."

While earlier Fritzi ran through the tunnels as if she knew them, she pauses now. I realize it was her magical connection—to Holda, the stone, or her brother, I'm not sure which—that had led her so assuredly through the dark. Without that beacon, she's lost.

But I know this darkness well.

"This way," I say, the map of the aqueducts already unfurling in my mind. We're too close to the basilica, where the debris will be the worst and the tunnels the most unsteady, to venture that way. North, toward the Porta Nigra, is out of the question. The third gate, closer to the amphitheater, is crawling with hexenjägers and still at least partially collapsed.

I lead us west, following the tunnels as they grow narrower and narrower. There's a drain under the Roman bridge, one that dumps into the Moselle river. We slosh through the crisp water, both of us shivering. The cold and the shock vibrates through us, ricocheting against our bones. Keep moving. If I keep moving forward, we will make progress.

If I stop, I'll only see Johann's unblinking eyes.

We emerge at an opening under the old Roman bridge. The aqueduct flows directly into the river so that we have to swim the last bit, following the current until we pour out into the Moselle. The concrete and stone pillars holding the Roman road up are spaced out all the way across the river, creating a dangerous blockade. The surface teems with boats. And...bodies?

"Help!" someone nearby screams, and I whip around. At the same time, Fritzi surfaces behind me, gulping air. She meets my eyes, nods—*she's okay*—and I spin to see a man shouting, pointing to the water where a young girl a little older than Liesel thrashes. I grab her by her braids so her flailing arms don't pull me back under and swim one-handed toward the man, who helps me haul up the panicked girl. All around me, there are more boats tipped over, people screaming or swimming, chaos reigning.

"What's going on?" Fritzi asks, her skin flushed with exhaustion. Her teeth are chattering in the cold as we tread water.

"That pull of water Dieter did," I guess. "The water had to come from somewhere. He pulled the river through the tunnels, then it all got pushed back..." The resulting waves and flooding sent the small boats tipping and the large barges banging into each other or the waves. Barrels of wine bob nearby, caught against the pillars, and there are looters throwing ropes down, trying to steal the goods that have fallen overboard.

"Can you swim?" I ask. Fritzi nods and, together, we weave our way through the debris toward the shore.

The only good thing about this is that we are merely two more drenched rats among dozens as we claw our way up the shore. Near the bridge, the crane that lifts cargo from ships swings out, and the workers there scramble down, helping get people up. Water and mud make the banks even slipperier, and the crane operator swings the arms around, dropping a rope to help us pull ourselves closer to the road.

Once we're up, Fritzi leans against the white plaster of the round crane hut, her hands on her knees as she catches her breath. I cast an eye at the river, where things are still chaotic.

"What are the odds Cornelia, Brigitta, and the others didn't notice this and are waiting for us at camp?" I say.

"I can ask Holda," Fritzi starts.

"Don't bother."

I jump at the deep male voice and whirl around, heart thudding, in time to see Alois, brown cloak pulled up, his face mostly hidden by the hood. His eyes are dark, and his expression is more furious than I've ever seen it, but as he rakes his gaze over us, a smile cuts across his glower.

"Thank the Three you're both safe," he says, pulling me into a hug and clapping my back so hard I cough up some water on his cloak.

He whips off his cloak and wraps it around Fritzi, whose teeth are chattering, then leads us away from the main bridge.

"We all felt the magic surge," he says, setting a quick pace. "But Cornelia already had us racing this way. She said Holda was..."

"Screaming at her?" Fritzi guessed.

"Something like that."

"But—" Fritzi starts.

"We're reconvening at a new camp. And we got horses."

He leads us off the road to a place where some horses are hidden among the trees. Alois mounts, and I pull myself atop a brown gelding as Fritzi clambers up a black mare. I watch her carefully, but she's as strong as ever, no sign of exhaustion or sorrow, even if I feel it exuding from her. She won't break. She won't allow herself to.

Alois takes us about an hour east, into the woods. When we stop, he hobbles the horses and we make our way to the fire, where the others are waiting for us.

I let Fritzi tell the tale, filling in only as needed. I keep my eyes on the flames, which sizzle and pop almost as if they were trying to join the conversation.

"So," Cornelia says as soon as Fritzi stops. "Dieter has one stone."

"He knows the location of another," Brigitta adds.

"There's only one left," Fritzi says.

"Jesus, what the *hell*?" I shout, leaping back, spraying forest litter and pebbles into the crackling fire.

The crackling fire that very distinctly looks like *Liesel.*

Fritzi's eyes are wide and fearful, but all I can do is point. Alois is already laughing as Cornelia peers closer. Fritzi's face shifts from panicked to confused as she follows their gaze.

"Liesel?" she asks, dropping to her knees and scooting closer.

"Hi, Fritzi!" The flames flicker, forming Liesel's face, beaming with joy. "Abnoba taught me a new trick!"

My heart refuses to calm down, and adrenaline surges through me as I gape at the fire.

"I've been trying to find you for ages; this spell is so tricky," Liesel complains. Her ember eyes flit to me. "And then when I am just trying to say hello, Otto *curses* at me."

"Very rude, Otto." Alois smirks.

Fritzi swats my leg. "Come closer."

Witches. They're going to be the death of me. All of them.

Still, I kneel beside Fritzi in front of the flames. "Is all well at the Forest?" I ask. "Is Hilde"

At the mention of my sister's name, Brigitta's head snaps up, eyes zeroed in on Liesel, speaking to us from the campfire.

"Everyone's *fine*," Liesel says, as if my question was impertinent. "Abnoba told me that Holda's stone was taken."

"Does the council know?" Cornelia asks.

Liesel nods, sparks flying. "We all felt…I don't know, a sort of pull? Like something in magic is off-balance." Before any of us can ask more, Liesel rounds on me. "You were supposed to stab him, Otto. You *promised.*"

Fritzi shoots me a sympathetic look.

"I'm working on it," I say, because what else are you supposed to say when you swear to an angelic little girl that you will cut the heart out of her cousin?

Liesel makes a doubtful face, as if she's a little disgusted that she has to rely on me to get the job done.

"So where is he?" she asks, looking from me to Fritzi.

Fritzi stares at the fire so intently that her eyes start to water. "He *disappeared*. That sort of power..." Her face drops, and we all take her meaning. While Fritzi disrupted his connection to magic long enough to stop the whirlpool and flooding, Dieter likely regained it. And he's more powerful now than ever.

"Well, let's take the stone Dieter has back," Brigitta snarls. "There's enough of us to mount an offense, and Otto can tell us about what defense he may have—"

"Where is he?" Fritzi asks. She raises her eyes to meet each of ours. "We couldn't track him before, and now he has the water stone. He vanished before my eyes. How do you intend on finding him now?"

Brigitta's jaw works. "We'll send scouts. We'll use a pendulum. We'll—"

I look at Liesel, watching us from the flames. "Is the council capable of finding Dieter?"

She shakes her head. "They've been trying all their magic. He's hidden."

Cornelia puts her hand on Brigitta's arm. "We have to be smart about this. If we can't track him, and he could be anywhere..."

"We have to *try*!" Brigitta says, her voice cracking on the last word. It breaks us all. The futility of it.

"I'll get Philomena to pester Perchta," Liesel offers brightly. "That's the thing with the goddesses—they'll eventually just give you what you want, you just have to—"

"Drive them mad with questioning?" I offer.

"Be persistent," Liesel says, sticking her tongue out at me, flames spurting in my direction.

Dieter has more power than any of the witches here. He's already ahead of us.

We can only hope to find the next stone before him.

After filling our bellies, Fritzi and I fall into an exhausted sleep early. When I open my eyes again, it's not quite dawn. The light between the trees is paler than before, but not bright enough to see beyond our camp.

Fritzi's already awake.

"Good morning, hexe," I whisper.

She kisses my nose, then lets out a heavy sigh and curls into the curve of my body. My arms tighten around her.

"I'm sorry about Johann," she whispers to my chest. A crack of pain jolts through me, but I force my body to still, to not let her see how deeply wounded his loss has left me. She knows anyway. I can feel it in the way her body tenses even when mine doesn't, in the soft touch of her hand over my heart.

My chin drops to the top of her head. I almost think she's fallen asleep again when Fritzi pushes against me, lifting her head to meet my gaze. "How can we find the third stone?" Her voice breaks in desperation. "We only knew to come to Trier because Holda left her stone here. But we don't know where Perchta hid hers."

"On the bright side, Dieter probably doesn't know either."

Fritzi frowns. "But out of all the tunnels in the aqueducts of Trier,

Dieter *did* find the stone. Holda wasn't helping him. And even if he knew it was in Trier, how did he know to look in the aqueducts?"

I can sense the question she's not asking—was it magic? Did he pull power from her and use it to find the stone that a goddess's champion hid centuries ago?

"He didn't know where it was," I remind her. "Remember what Johann said? Dieter's been tearing apart the aqueducts for months. If he *knew,* he would have gone straight there."

"But then how—"

I snort bitterly, no amusement in the sound. "History."

Fritzi's brow furrows, but everyone in Trier knows Saint Simeon locked himself up in the Porta Nigra and became a hermit, imprisoning himself so that he could dedicate his life to prayer. Soon after, Trier flooded, and the citizens blamed him, calling him a witch who sent the rising waters to curse the people.

"Dieter knew of Saint Simeon. He knew the legend of the floods. Perhaps he connected that to the water stone. Maybe there was something in the books he read in the council's library that helped, but... I think he knew about this one. Perhaps for a long time. Perhaps that's the reason why he settled in Trier in the first place, because he knew there was an important relic in the city."

"Abnoba's stone in the council represents the element of earth; Holda's is water. We just need to find Perchta's before Dieter does. You don't happen to know of any historical connection with a city of wind, do you?" Fritzi asks sardonically. "Or some temple full of air?"

Perchta, the Mother. The most severe of the goddesses, the one who adhered to the rules more than the others. Holda was the somewhat rebellious Maid, much like Fritzi herself. Abnoba had chosen Liesel as her warrior, and had trusted the council to hide the earth stone.

I think, judging from what I have learned of Perchta, if the goddess had any choice in the matter, she would have kept the stone or hidden it herself. But she had to have a champion do it.

I sit up, pulling Fritzi into my lap, and see that some of the others are starting to wake up as well. I stroke Fritzi's hair, thinking. Holda seemed to have entrusted a champion who used Catholicism to hide the water stone, adding a sacred reliquary as additional protection. Dieter had tossed it aside, but had a Christian stumbled across the golden box, I have little doubt the artifact would have been brought into the cathedral and worshipped, even if the archbishop couldn't have known what it was.

Perchta, I guess, would not have wanted to ally herself with the Catholics, not even for a level of protection.

I lean forward, drawing the rough shape of the Holy Roman Empire on the forest floor. Cornelia, now awake, shifts closer to us. "The Romans brought Christianity, but they were terrified of the Celts," I say.

"As they should be," Fritzi murmurs. I snort.

"They didn't breach the Black Forest, as we know," I add, nodding to Cornelia. "But they also set up walls to the east. Places where they basically gave up, ceding the land to the Celts and not bothering to push deeper."

Cornelia frowns, looking at my crude diagram as I draw a squiggly line to indicate the Limes, the fortified border that the Romans believed separated them from the barbarous Germanic tribes.

"If I had to guess," I say slowly, "I would think Perchta would hide her stone somewhere like this, in lands that her people kept out of the Roman's hands."

Fritzi sits up straighter. "And if Abnoba already has one stone in the forest..." She brushes the right-hand side of my map. "That's still a lot of ground to cover, but it does narrow things down."

If I'm right, I think.

But Cornelia's staring at my squiggled lines with fierce intensity. "There's weight to this," she mutters. "Brigitta!" she calls sharply, and the captain gets up from her bedroll so quickly that I'm certain she was already awake.

"What's this?" Brigitta asks, looking down.

Cornelia taps a spot near the line that represents the Roman border, then traces it back. "Our location," Cornelia says, glancing at me.

"Roughly."

She draws back over the line, due east, tapping another spot. She turns to Brigitta. "You know the legends of this area?"

"The Alamanni," Brigitta gasps, squatting down by the map.

"Alamanni?" Fritzi looks from one woman to the next. "What is that?"

"Who is that," Cornelia corrects. "A tribe that fought the Romans. Alamanni means 'all man.' The tribe was a conglomeration of different people from different tribes. And they built a huge fort here."

"I've never heard of such a tribe," Fritzi says.

"Because they're nothing but ghosts now." Cornelia's voice is dark. She looks up at us. "They were the ones who led the battles against the invading Romans. While some of us hid—going back to the Tree, the Well—the Alamanni fought."

Brigitta touches the map I made, bouncing her finger from one spot in the east across the squiggling line I drew to show the Rhine. "And according to legend, one of the ways they fought was by flying over the Rhine. The frozen river couldn't be crossed by boat, and the ice was thin and dangerous. But the goddesses carried them over the river so they could push back the Roman forces."

"Maybe it wasn't the goddesses," I say. "Maybe it was the air stone."

16

FRITZI

I didn't know the stories of the Alamanni—so it is likely Dieter doesn't know either. Unless it is something he discovered while using me to research in the Well's library.

I think that and manage not to shudder. The resistance doesn't come from how I usually just ignore the pain; it comes from flashes of memory in the tunnels. The wall of water bending to *my* magic, then the enhanced power of the water from the stone. The way I kept Dieter out of my head, even with the chaos and destruction of the water thrashing around us.

My bond with Otto, the tattoo strengthening his own fortitude, my now seemingly unlimited abilities with wild magic—it can all *work*. I've seen it now.

"We can do this," I whisper to my palms, stretching and closing my fingers.

Cornelia, Brigitta, and Otto look at me, but I sniff away the flare of... of *thrill*. I cannot bear to let Otto, especially, see the spark of hope on my face, not so soon after losing Johann. I can't let him feel that errant emotion from me, and I try to shield it from our connection. Part of what happened under Trier may have felt like a victory to me, but it was a loss in so many ways.

"Do we know if Dieter has left the city?" I ask. "We can still take him out without having to risk going to—"

"He isn't in Trier," Brigitta says, her voice going to iron, the tone I've heard her take with those under her command. Like she expects pushback.

I frown. "How do you know?"

"People are buzzing with news that Dieter left almost immediately after the flood and took most of his hexenjägers with him. Alois and Ignatz scouted the city while you were resting."

"They—*what*?" The breath kicks out of me, all lingering specks of hope evaporating in a lurch of concern. My eyes snap around our forested campsite and there, I spot Alois, with another of Brigitta's guards, packing their supplies. They made it back, but still, fear swarms me.

It's Otto who says, "You sent them into Trier? Without talking with us?"

"They came to rescue you, if you'll remember." Brigitta's tone doesn't change. "And you are not the sole deciders of these events, warrior. We appreciate what you two are doing, but you cannot, *will not*, be the only ones who take risks."

I want to argue. But all of my arguments stem from exactly that place: that Otto and I *should be* the only ones to take risks, because we have been given the greatest responsibility. But if we fail in this mission to stop my brother, everyone will suffer.

We came on this mission with friends, with support.

We have to trust in them.

It would be far easier to believe they have a chance at being safe if they could access wild magic, too, I think. The idea springs fully formed into the midst of my struggle. I pause, expecting a wash of...something. A reason to dismiss the idea. Even a comment from Holda, but that is what she wants, and I realize the thing I am imagining is not other witches deciding to sever from the Well and open up to wild magic, like I did. I am imagining there being no need to sever at all. I am, in one errant, unexpected flash, imagining a world where all magic is wild and free, and we do not have to worry about rules holding us back at all.

A world where no matter what horrors are thrown into our path, everyone has the power to face them.

I prod at my mental defenses. I'm still wearing the charm Cornelia gave me, so none of this is Dieter. And it doesn't *feel* like him, slimy and self-serving. It feels...hopeful.

But it is too close to what he wants.

We do not know what would happen if the Tree broke, if that dam opened.

But...what would the world look like if it was saturated in magic again, as it was before the goddesses funneled magic into the Origin Tree and told witches *wild magic* was bad? What could witches do with that kind of power?

"...has abandoned the city," Brigitta is saying. "A handful of hexenjägers remain, but most of his numbers are gone, and we heard that their arch-bishop is dead. With the flash flood now too, Trier is in shambles. But—"

Otto flies to his feet.

I stagger in the absence of him and follow him up, but I'm hit with the wash of his feelings before I even need to ask.

Guilt. Fear. Such fear, intense and choking, and his eyes snap to the west, toward Trier.

But he hesitates. His indecision is an iron chain tugging him one way, another. He wants to help his city; he will stay with me and see this through.

"No one remains to help the people there," he says. "We cannot linger, I know. But Johann—and I—"

He stops. His lips thin, and I grab his shoulder.

Brigitta stands, too, and her eyes are holding on Otto, her tone and posture still that of a commander. "The city may have no leadership now, but Dieter's form of leadership was cruelty. They are better off without him; we can all agree on that. And with his influence gone, whoever remains highest in power—some clergy, likely?—will be able to wake up from whatever fog he put them under. The city may be suffering the aftermath of his madness, but they are far better off now."

Otto's shoulders relax. I hadn't noticed how stiff he had gotten. So much of him is still tied to Trier's fate.

I'm hit with that image again. Of a world saturated in wild magic, so ripe with it that anyone—*anyone*? Even non-witches?—could tap into it.

Otto wouldn't have to worry about Trier anymore. He wouldn't have to stretch himself thin with trying to protect everyone.

The image is spiraling out, my heart racing at the idea of a world that doesn't have to *fear*.

But for every innocent person who could access magic, there would be someone with ill intent too. And before all of that, *we do not know what breaking the Origin Tree would do*. It could destroy everything, the whole of the Well and Black Forest flattened; it could obliterate all magic, or something far worse.

These fantasies are just that—*fantasies*.

But Otto's fear is a potent instigator, and I want nothing more than to make real a world where he never has to fear again.

Otto nods at Brigitta, eyes dipping to the ground in deference.

"So Dieter has left Trier with the water stone," I say.

What if we are wrong about the Alamanni lands? What if we go to this ancient, long-dead settlement, and not only is Dieter not there, but the air stone isn't as well?

Holda? What can you tell me of the air stone, of the Alamanni, of—

Nothing, she cuts in. She has barely spoken to me since yesterday and has been so consumed in her grief that she didn't even react to my thoughts about destroying the Origin Tree.

I get a wash of her sorrow through our connection. Between her emotions and Otto's, I hardly have room for my own.

Perchta hid the air stone, says Holda. *I was kept out of it, as she was kept out of mine.*

Perchta does not like me, I say. *But will she understand why we are seeking her stone? Will she help us?*

It's a futile ask. I remember all too well my few interactions with the Mother goddess. Her disgust of me and my refusal to adhere to the rules she oversees. I am the antithesis of everything she commands, order and rules and tradition.

But Dieter is a threat far larger than Perchta's distaste for me.

I will try to speak with her, Holda says, and I feel the finality in it.

"Our best guess is to go to this fort," I say, rubbing my forehead. "How far?"

"It's Glauberg," Cornelia says. "A few days' travel."

I nod. We've only just awoken but exhaustion settles over me, and I nod again, as though affirmation will take the uncertainty away.

Otto takes my hand. Squeezes hard.

"To Glauberg," he tells me. His own roiling emotions give me something to anchor to. We did what we could for Johann, and Trier *is* safer without Dieter, but there is nothing else I can do to comfort Otto now, and it breaks my heart.

All this magic. All this power.

There has to be *something* I can do.

Because otherwise, what is the point of being a goddess-chosen champion?

"To Glauberg," I whisper.

We stick to the land this time, not wanting to forgo horses and unable to take a river the entire way, although we pay heavily for both us and our mounts to be ferried across the Rhine.

The cost has increased, it seems, due to the unexpected flooding in the area.

All rivers we pass, offshoots and brooks, are swollen with water. Villages on the riverbanks are flooded, people rushing around to salvage belongings, rescue missions well underway. As we leave the valley behind, I voice aloud my concern.

"The excess water is Dieter," I say.

Brigitta, from her mount next to me, only grunts.

"We could track him based on the flooding," I try. "Follow it back to wherever he originates."

"How long would that take, to figure out which direction the waters started? They wouldn't have to follow the normal current of the river, so we couldn't assume he's upstream. What if we pick the wrong direction?"

I start to respond. But find I have nothing to say.

Brigitta gives a soft smile. "There are many paths to take in war," she tells me. "Learning to trust your commitment to one direction is what sculpts a soldier. Indecision could cost lives."

"The wrong decision could cost lives too."

She nods and kicks her horse on, and I watch her push ahead in silence.

It's only a two-day journey across the rolling hills and thick forests of the Empire, the sky alternating between crisp blue and clouded early spring.

If Dieter took this path with his hexenjägers, we see no sign of it. There are less waterways, so signs of his flooding destruction, if there are any, are fewer. They could have taken more populous roads; we stick with a direct route, charging our own trails through dense woodlands with Brigitta at the lead. I try hard not to worry about whether Dieter is on our same path. I try not to worry about whether he's already found the air stone, and this is all futile. I try not to worry about how *not* seeing him means we may have misinterpreted the next stone's location, and Dieter has already found it elsewhere.

I think of none of those things.

Instead, I think about the town we arrive in near dusk the second night of travel, and how we'll reach Glauberg before noon the next day.

And I announce to our group that we'll be staying at the little village's inn.

Brigitta gives me a look of abject horror, as though the mere fact that we are on a mission of utmost importance means we *have* to sleep on the hard-packed earth of the forest.

Cornelia doesn't give her a chance to interject. She squeals her agreement and throws her head back, red hair tumbling out of her cloak's hood. "*Yes*. You can continue on for a campsite if you like, Brigitta. Take your guards with you. But I'm sleeping in a *bed*."

At least two of the Grenzwache eye each other and look torn between protesting for comfort and duty to Brigitta.

But Brigitta sighs. "Fine," she relents, and if there's a flicker of relief on her face, she hides it quickly.

The inn has a stable where we leave our horses with eager stable hands who grow even more willing to help when Alois pulls out a satchel of coins.

He dumps a mound of gold into his palm. "Is this enough to feed and house our horses for the night?" he asks me.

The two stable hands are practically salivating. By their gaunt faces and gangly limbs, and the brightness in their eyes at the prospect of customers, I can easily guess that they do not see much business, let alone profit, so for Alois to flaunt money like this will either get us robbed or have them build a statue to him in the town square.

"It's perfect," I tell him, and he hands over the coins. The stable hands take the money like they're being handed soap bubbles.

I catch the eye of the one who looks the oldest, not far off from my age. "Have you seen any soldiers come through? Ones in black?"

We crossed out of the Trier diocese and into Protestant lands, but my brother has never cared for subtlety among political or religious struggles. He would barrel through with his forces regardless of who owned what land.

The stable hand shakes his head. "None but our own lord's fighters. Nothing unusual." He hesitates, hands fisting on his share of the coins, and he looks between his treasure and my eyes with a sudden wariness. "Is there trouble about, Fräulein?"

My instinct is to tell him no. To lie, to spare them.

But I bite the inside of my cheek. "There may be. Have you noticed any flooding?"

The stable hand's eyes go momentarily sullen. "Aye. A farm flooded on the outskirts of the village not a day ago. Bit unusual for the time of year. Why, Fräulein?"

It could be nothing. A single farm flooding is hardly the same power as the whole of the Moselle devastating Trier.

I shake my head. "Never mind."

He nods, wariness trading for practicality. I have seen faces like his before, set with determination; he has seen struggle, has lived through it, and knows he will face more yet to come.

My throat closes.

What if magic was everywhere? What if, what if…?

These thoughts are consuming me. As though I opened my own internal floodgates, and I'm buoyant in possibilities now.

The inn is as empty as the stable suggested, and the innkeeper is just as eager for our business. Brigitta arranges accommodations with her usual efficiency, putting guards on patrol while we ferry ourselves into rooms. The innkeeper offers to make us supper; the hour is late, but Alois and Cornelia jump at the chance to eat a warm meal.

Otto starts to open his mouth, but I snatch his hand and haul him to the stairs.

He stumbles after me, his surprised laugh a cooling breeze. "You're not hungry?"

"Later," I tell him and drag him into the room we've been given.

The inn is all sturdy wood carved from the surrounding forest, dense and earthy and baked in with years of travelers. The room itself is simple, a threadbare straw mattress on a lifted frame, a pitcher of water on a table by a banked fire. The single window is shuttered, darkness pervasive when I close the door behind us.

Otto's brief spell of levity starts to fade as I make my way to the fire and rouse it. "Liebste…"

Flames catch, casting him in orange as he eyes me, a question hanging in his silence.

I brush ash from my skirt and face him. "Banish your debauched thoughts, Jäger. I didn't bring you up here so you could have your way with me in a roadside inn."

He barks a laugh and scratches a hand through his hair, the dark strands coming loose around his face. "Scheisse. You do know how to seduce a man."

"I'm *not* seducing you. That's the point." I nod at the mattress. "Shirt off. Lie down on your stomach."

He blinks at me. "Pardon?"

"Shirt *off*. Lie down." I undo my cloak and hold my hands out to the fire, trying to warm them, glad for the smallness of the room. It's heating fast and so when Otto opens his mouth to question me again, I know it isn't because of the chill.

"Please," I cut him off. I turn, the fire at my back, and cross to stand in his space. The bond is so much more intense the closer we are, the emotions from him mingling with the weight of his presence and the warmth of his body.

"Fritzi, I—"

"FRITZI!"

We both jump at the shriek that comes from the flames. I whirl around to see my cousin's face wreathed in orange and yellow, sculpted of gilded fire.

"*Liesel!*" I snap, hand to my chest. "The Three save me, *you have to stop doing that*." But my shock twists sharply into worry. "Wait—what's wrong? Why are you contacting us again?"

Liesel smiles, so my worry ebbs, but it only makes room for that initial shocked annoyance to rage back up.

"We're fine!" she chirps. "Hilde just made me contact Brigitta for her, and they were *so* gross with all their *looooove* talk—I really don't think Abnoba meant for this spell to be used for *that*."

A voice behind Liesel goes, "I told you not to listen."

Liesel makes a face over her shoulder. "I don't think the magic will stay up if I'm not here!" she says, but her overly innocent tone tells me she knows exactly that the magic will stay up, she's just nosey. "*Anyway*," she refocuses on me, "Brigitta told us you were fine, but I wanted to check in on you because we haven't heard anything about Dieter, and Philomena and Rochus are still trying to track him, but they aren't getting *anything*, and I'm so *bored* because Hilde made me go back to school lessons yesterday, and I—"

"Liesel." I kneel down by the fire. Her flame-sculpted face twists to me, wide eyes showing a brush of fear before she forces a cheeky smile.

My annoyance disintegrates.

"I miss you too," I tell her.

Otto crouches next to me. "We'll be back soon, I promise."

Liesel looks between us. "And...you're okay?" she asks, her voice softer, smaller than it was before.

I smile. True and gentle. "We are. We're at an inn now. We get to sleep on a real bed tonight."

Her face screws up. "I did *not* like that part of traveling. I like *real beds* all the time."

Otto chuckles. "Don't let her know I told you, but I think Brigitta does too. Our tough kapitän likes sleeping on the hard ground as much as you do."

Liesel laughs, the sound high and bright, and it makes me beam at Otto.

"Oh, I *have* to tell her!" Liesel laughs again. "She was *just* telling Hilde how wasteful it is to not be camping out."

Hilde's voice comes through, "Do not mock my delicate love."

Through my smile, I lean closer to the flames. "Go to bed now, Liesel. It's late. We can talk in a day or two."

She hums, seeming lighter, less concerned, than her manic energy when she'd first appeared. "Okay. You too." A pause. "I love you, Fritzi."

"I love you too."

Another pause. Her face in the flames starts to fade.

"*IloveyoutooOtto.*"

Then she's gone in a wisp of smoke.

"She put out my fire," I pout to the embers.

Otto, next to me, wheezes. "Did she—" He grins when I look up at him. "She said she loves me."

His cheeks are red, happiness shining deep in his eyes, and it warms me more thoroughly than any flame.

I touch his chin. "What's not to love?"

He stands, beaming joy. "Perhaps there's a market in this town," he says, searching along his belt until he finds the money purse attached to it. "I can buy some wood to whittle her a new animal. Or would they have toys to buy, do you think? Or—"

"Otto." I stand and grab his arm in a huff of laughter. "It's the middle of the night."

He wilts, but he's still smiling softly, and he rolls his eyes at himself. "You're right. I'm just—" A low hum of delight. "I really want her to like me."

My chest swells, warmth and happiness overflowing, and I wonder if it's possible to combust from seeing the man I love so smitten over my cousin.

"Tomorrow," I say, "you can buy out all the toys this little village has. I'll help you."

He rolls his eyes again and sets aside his money pouch. "It sounds a bit ridiculous now. I'll control myself."

"Perish the thought."

Otto hesitates, then his lips pucker in a suppressed smile.

"You had mentioned something about me taking my shirt off?" he asks.

I step closer to him and rest my hands on his chest. "And *not* seducing you, as you'll recall."

"Hm. Definitely not."

My gaze on him goes serious, intent. "There is very little I can do to help you deal with what happened to Johann, what is happening in Trier. Let me do this."

"You don't need to help me," he says. "You're struggling too, I know you are."

"So you can alleviate one of my struggles by allowing me to do this for you."

"Do *what*?"

"Take your shirt off and find out."

"Fritzi."

"Otto."

He sighs. I haven't heard that in a while. His sigh of exasperation, of me vexing him, and I grin.

I haven't grinned in a while either. Haven't wanted to, or been able to. Bogged down by fear and memories and worry. And while all of that is still here, I feel like I can *move* under it. Like the weight of it has lifted, just enough that I can stretch and work feeling back into numb limbs and *breathe.*

I undo the clasp of his cloak and remove it. He doesn't protest.

"It may be cool in here, but I'm not restarting the fire," I tell him. "Just in case."

"I thought you *weren't* seducing me."

"Do you think of anything else? I am capable of other delights."

"You're having me take my clothes off in a private room, Liebste. What else should I be thinking of?"

"Innocent things. Angelic things. I am a virtuous, saintly woman, Otto Ernst, and I am appalled you would assume otherwise."

He laughs, rich and hearty, and I hook my fingers under the edge of his shirt and tug. He lifts his arms and lets me strip it off of him.

My breath snags in my lungs at the sight of his bare chest. I hope I never get used to it. I hope he always fills me with longing.

There's a beat of separation, of disconnected thought where all the scars I still carry fight through, but I push past them, I'm *able* to push past them, and I widen my grin to give Otto a suggestive leer.

"I've changed my mind," I tell him. "I do want to seduce you. Defile me, jäger."

His gasp is dramatic. "What happened to my saintly hexe?"

"Those two words have no business being used together."

My grin holds on his, and he seems to realize what I have—that we haven't done this, teasing and *fun*, in far too long.

I push on his shoulder. "Lie down."

This time he obeys, resting his cheek on his folded hands as he stretches out on his stomach.

I straddle his hips and take a small jar out of my pocket, an ointment typically used for healing, beeswax laced with mint and lavender. The smell of it permeates the air with floral and heady mint, and I take some on my fingers and work it between my hands until it warms.

"We haven't yet talked about what you did with water in the chamber under Trier," Otto says, his voice half-muffled in the bedding.

"We haven't," I agree and rub my hands from his neck straight down his spine.

He hisses, more in surprise than anything, his muscles going tense at the contact. But I do it again, more firmly, working my thumbs in circles down his back, and after another repetition, he starts to relax into the mattress. Two more swipes, and he emits a low groan.

I want to talk about what I did in the chamber. How I controlled water and stones to encase Johann, and how those simple acts have cracked open something in my chest so that now I feel like part of me is slipping through that crack. How I can see the world that Holda wants, a world of wild magic and infinite possibilities.

But as wonderful and miraculous as it could be, wild magic wasn't enough to save Johann, and I'm so sorry, so unspeakably sorry, because I don't know if this kind of magic will ever be enough to save everyone.

I want to talk to Otto, I do. But all we've been doing is talking, and planning, and worrying, and this moment feels simplified, the way our travels did when it was just him and Liesel and me. The fact that *that* time suddenly feels *simple* elicits a chuckle from me.

Otto flicks an eye open but doesn't turn to look back at me. I push the pad of my hands into a muscle on his shoulder, and instead of asking why I laughed, he keens, long and low and ending on his own chuckle.

"Why haven't we been doing this the whole time?" he mumble-whimpers into his arm.

"There were far many other things I wanted to do with your body," I say.

"So this is you being bored of me, is that it?"

"Excruciatingly. Can't you tell?" I find another knot and work it with my thumbs and the noise he makes is sinful, so deep that my stomach tightens.

"I missed it," he says softly.

I frown down at him. He doesn't see, but he answers my unspoken question anyway.

"Your laugh," he whispers.

My hands still.

It's the barest pause, but he flips beneath me, and I lurch up with a squeal. He catches me and resets me on his hips, only with him facing me now, and he yanks me down, capturing my mouth with his.

17

OTTO

When she starts to pull away, I follow her, my lips unwilling to part from hers. She giggles, swatting at me, but I do not relent until we've shifted positions. Her hair splays on the bed, golden curls unfurling over white linens as my arms frame her shoulders. She watches me languidly, eyelids hooded, mouth slightly parted, as if she is merely waiting for me to draw a gasp from her lips. The heady aroma of the salve she used weaves around us, drawing us together.

I drop my face closer to hers, the end of my hair tickling her upturned cheeks. When I lift my hand to her face, my fingers tremble.

There is fear in love.

That was something I knew from an early age, because love can always be lost. It can be twisted, bent until it's broken. It can sour, or poison, or kill.

There is fear in love, because love is so deeply powerful, and anything powerful can hurt. It's like a flame, casting light even as it burns.

And our love is worth burning for.

She looks up at me through her lashes, and I know she can feel what I feel, understand me even without words. And it's not because of magic.

Only love.

I lower my lips to hers. We have kissed with passion, with urgency. On the night before we bonded, when Fritzi made the meadow burst in blooms, there was a frantic nature to our mutual claiming, a desire to drown out all the noise and exist only within each other. But now, even though the world is chaos and turmoil, even though we don't know what tomorrow will bring, or the next day, or the next, even though nothing is settled—

I take my time.

I savor the taste of her. The softness. I draw the gasps from her lips, and I make her eyes widen with desire, and I relish in the warmth of her wrapped around me.

Even when she begs, her body and her lips both calling for release, I take my time. My eyes don't leave hers, and when she falls, shattering, I am there to cradle her in my arms and make her whole again.

We avoided the city of Frankfurt as we traveled, but there's no denying that the deeper we go into the state of Hesse, the fewer people we see. We near the ancient Roman fortification limes and skirt the town of Altenstadt. Literally named "old city," this area was built upon Roman ruins.

On the other side there's...nothing. Open fields—some plowed, some fallow—give way to groves of trees, the forests thickening as we venture farther past the limes. These verdant lands are bursting with the promise of spring, the trees young and nothing at all like the ancient wonders of the Black Forest so many days away to the south.

"The Roman campaigns against the Germanic tribes happened in the decade or so before and after Christ's birth," I tell Fritzi as our horses weave through the trees. "This was the dawn of Christianity, really, but also the dawn of Germany as a nation. The two are linked."

"Mmhm," she mumbles, only half paying attention.

"It was all strategy. The Romans wanted to hold Gaul—which is basically France, now—but the Germanic tribes were pressing in from the east, helping Gallic tribes. But the thing about the Romans is, they didn't just try to conquer. They tried to convert."

"Sounds familiar," Fritzi mutters, and I give her a little nod of acknowledgment. The way the Romans worked was insidious and ingenious. Converting former tribe members to Roman citizenship and giving them a stake in the Empire meant that the conquered had a reason to not rebel and establish a new status quo.

"But they couldn't get much past the Rhine," I continue. "Romans didn't expect the Germanic tribes to team up. They'd been used to dividing and conquering, but they couldn't divide the Germanic tribes. So they set up forts and towns and invented a border so they could pretend they weren't defeated. Just consider for a moment the Battle of Teutoburg Forest!" I laugh, despite myself. "It took the Romans more than a hundred years before they dared try to attack again after that battle!"

I glance up and meet Fritzi's eyes. I can tell she has no idea what battle I'm speaking of and could care less what I'm saying, but it's still sweet to see her endearing smile as I ramble.

"My point is, it's not just that the Romans stopped invading the Celtic lands here," I say, waving my hand toward this new forest. "It's as if all of civilization vanished."

She frowns, thinking, her brow furrowing in little lines under the shadow of her hood. "If the ancient tribes couldn't hold the land, perhaps Perchta is ensuring that no one does."

Wind whistles through the trees, early daffodils poking up through the undergrowth, but little else. Brigitta calls us to a halt when we crest a small hill, the trees clearing out to more open land. She points silently as I draw my horse up to hers.

Scattered at the base of another hill are the remains of houses and other small buildings. Crumbling stone foundations support a few rotting timbers, and there's clearly a worn path connecting the homes in the small village to one another, but it's been abandoned for at least a century, I suspect.

"Looks like someone tried to live here," Fritzi says, her voice hushed. "What happened to them?"

Cornelia, on the other side of Brigitta, shrugs. "Could have been a plague. Could have just been a small village that died out. It happens."

"Could have been the goddess," Brigitta growls.

"Or ghosts," Alois chimes in cheerily.

Cornelia rolls her eyes. "It's not ghosts."

"You don't know that. It *could* be." Alois tilts his chin defiantly.

I glance at Fritzi, who shares my concerned look. There's a feeling to this area that reminds me of the first time we entered the Black Forest together. The goddesses tested us then, ultimately granting us entry to their domain.

This land feels the same. A goddess's chosen land, one we are not yet proven worthy to enter.

"Give me a moment," Fritzi says, wheeling her horse around and heading back to the trees nearby. She has to stand up in her stirrups to reach the low-hanging mistletoe adorning the oaks, but she grabs several bunches and tosses them to me to hold before she dismounts.

"Good idea," Cornelia says. "Let's break here."

Everyone gathers, hobbling the horses. Alois and I share some dried meat while Fritzi and Cornelia weave mistletoe crowns for us all. Cornelia recites a blessing as she crowns Brigitta, but Fritzi tucks the mistletoe on my head silently. She doesn't need spells to tap into wild magic, and while none of the others know this, I do. She leans closer to me, standing on her tiptoes, and it must look like she's chanting the poem into my ear, but her lips remain silent as she brushes the tip of her tongue along the shell of my ear, nearly undoing me right there among the trees in front of them all.

My body stiffens, and she huffs a little laugh at me, her breath warm and sweet and deliciously cascading over my skin, and I have to bite back a growl, bunch my fingers into fists so that I don't grab her and carry her into the dark forest and do things I'm certain none of our gods would approve of.

Once everyone has the protection of mistletoe in their hair, we remount and head past the abandoned village and toward the hill beyond, the area Cornelia and Brigitta agree has to be where the ancient tribal people rebuked the Romans. We stop at a low round hill at the base of a ridgeline.

"There's nothing here," Fritzi says. "I thought..."

I nod, agreeing with her. I'd expected ruins. Living in Trier, I was surrounded by the mark of the Romans—the Porta Nigra and the basilica both were centuries old, built when Christianity was still new. Builders occasionally found stores of Roman coins in the earth—immediately donated to the church, of course, unless no one saw—and there were still a few Latin graffiti marks on stones that had been pilfered from the baths and reused to build new homes.

But this?

This is nothing. Just a hill.

A perfectly circular hill rising from the flat meadow before it.

I lean back on my horse, looking up at the enormous mound of dirt. There is a higher ridge behind the mound, but this hill is separate, too evenly shaped compared to the natural chaos of the nearby plateau. I dismount, digging my boot into the soil. Packed earth but not rocky.

"This is man-made," I say, peering up at the hill. Even though it's nearly noon, there doesn't seem to be any warmth from the sun in the cloudless sky.

"It's not man-made; it's too big," Brigitta starts, but Cornelia grabs her arm, staring at the hill.

"It *is*," she mutters. "It's a barrow."

"A grave?" Alois snorts. "That hill is big enough to build a house on. It's huge. That's not a grave, it's—"

"It's a grave," Fritzi says, eyeing me and then looking back up the hill. "That's all that remains of the ancient tribes. A grave. A huge barrow mound marking the deaths of the people who stood against all of the Roman Empire."

"But…" Alois's voice dies off.

Once we've said it, there's no denying it. All around are softly rolling hills, but this one is too perfect, too tall, too round.

"Are we supposed to dig it up and hope we find the stone?" Alois grumbles.

Fritzi slips her hand in mine as I walk back to her. "Does Holda" I start.

She shakes her head. "This is Perchta's stone to hide. And Perchta will not make this easy."

Brigitta's voice carries as she speaks with Cornelia. "I think past this mound—that was the city proper. Up on the ridge. The maps showed it expanding that way, using the plateau for defense."

"And then this grave here, on the southern end." Cornelia frowns at the hill. "Outside the city."

"Protecting the city," Fritzi mutters.

I cast an evaluating eye at the topography. Barrows are graves of important people, the earth mounded high over bodies and treasure. It is a mark of Perchta's protection that this obvious mound has not been looted—much like the abandoned village to the west, I can only assume that grave robbers looking for treasure have been *dissuaded* from digging the earth up. And that certainly gives me hope that we're in the right place.

If that plateau ahead was the location of the city, then this slope along the edge could be trace remains of what may have been an ancient road. And to reach it, we have to cross by the imposing barrow.

This isn't just a settlement. There's purpose here. This is a city, and it was designed to point us to this barrow.

"I think you're right," I tell Fritzi. "This barrow is not just a grave. The location has to mean something—a warning, perhaps, to invaders, or..."

Fritzi shivers, and I wrap my arm around her, still puzzling through the odd geography. If the ditches nearby really do indicate a road, is there such a clear route southeast from this city? Glauberg once took up the entire plateau, a massive city. And a road southeast would lead to...

The Black Forest.

I shake my head. No, that's unlikely. The Black Forest is a long way from here. But...

"Why is it so misty?" Fritzi mutters, taking a few steps forward.

I turn, following her line of sight. Rather than burn away the morning mists, the rising sun is even more obscured now than it was minutes ago.

Fritzi and I instinctively reach for each other. "Cornelia!" Fritzi's voice is a sharp crack as she shouts for the priestess. Already, the mist is so thick that we can barely see the outlines of the others. When did they wander so far away?

"Don't let go," Fritzi murmurs, her grip tightening.

"Brigitta!" I call. One of the forms seems to turn, but I hear nothing. Is no one else shouting for us?

Fritzi pulls me closer to her. "This remind you of the Black Forest?" she asks.

The mists that separated us, the trials the goddesses gave us.

Our grip on one another is iron strong.

In the fog, a figure runs toward us, *fast.* A man, I think, with broad shoulders. Tall. Too tall to be Alois—

The gait is off. Loping, the head bobbing in the thick fog, an unnatural pace, as if the creature in the mist runs on four legs instead of two, despite the humanlike outline.

I reach for my short sword, drawing it out silently. I feel a crackle in my skin, starting at the hand that grips Fritzi's, and I know she's calling up her magic.

The creature races through the mist, swirls of dense, cloudy air rippling around it.

It passes in a blur, and I catch only the barest hints of a humanoid face, of darkness, of streaming white hair. Fritzi and I circle, keeping the racing creature in sight. Why didn't it attack us? It's almost like the... *thing*, whatever it is, ignored us entirely.

Fritzi moves so that she's at my back, facing the mound, and I look down the path, our hands gripped tight. We may have a better chance at fighting if we let go, but neither of us is willing to do that.

The mists roil, surge forward. The creature is racing back toward us. *Ah,* I think. *It scouted around before it picked us as its target.*

"Something coming down," Fritzi chokes out, her voice tight. I glance over my shoulder, past her head, and see something else, bobbing and weaving through the fog, as if it were on a sailboat in rocky water.

I turn and stagger back, choking on my own horror. The fast-moving too-large shape of the creature that had been racing toward me is *here.* Right in front of me.

What I thought was hair is fur, white and tawny, cascading in a long frame over a monstrous skull. The creature watches me through yellow eyes speckled with black pupils. Its lower jaw is wider than its upper face, as if someone removed the creature's bottom teeth, stretched them disproportionately, and then jammed the bloody jaw back onto its skull. A long orange and black tongue flops out of the uneven mouth, stinking drool hot enough to steam, mingling with the heavy mist.

The creature pants, watching me, its yellow eyes narrowed. Its whole chest heaves, and that's when I notice the horns—six of them. Two are long and straight, like a young roe deer's antlers protruding from its ridged and furry forehead. Two more curl like rams' horns around each floppy ear, and then there is another set, sharp as scythe blades, sticking out of the back of the monster's head.

The front arms of the creature point out and down, like two sharp walking sticks that help the odd beast remain upright. The creature watches me, panting heavily, its body rocking, the sharp ends of its forearms tapping so they don't sink into the ground.

What is strangest of all, though, is that the creature's teeth look *human.* Teeth on a monster should be fanged like a bear's or pointed like a goat's. They should be black or bloody; they should foam; they shouldn't be so *normal.* The creature's protruding lower jaw is lined with teeth that are straight and white and boxy. Unbidden, I run my tongue over my own teeth.

The creature mimics me, its long, snakelike orange tongue whipping out, slithering over the white molars as if to emphasize how alien the creature is in all ways except its teeth.

The monster slobbers, its tongue lolling as it makes some sort of gurgling sound, some attempt at speech through such a mismatched jaw.

"What do we do?" I gasp at Fritzi, unable to take my eyes off the monster standing in the fog in front of us.

"I've got two in front of me; how many do you have?" she asks, her voice tight.

"One, but it's big. And fast."

I can feel her magic seething around us, through us, but the creatures do not attack. And we are not willing to make the first blow.

"What are they doing?" I hiss through clenched teeth. I dare a glance behind me. There are two creatures in front of Fritzi, one of which seems to be nothing more than a floating head, pale, ghostly, and almost beautiful, with exaggerated feminine features, white-blond hair that disappears into the fog. The other is short and stubby, with one set of horns that would seem large except they sit atop a face that seems to have been melted and stretched grotesquely long, a sharp chin sticking out at a curve like a crescent moon.

"I think..." Fritzi swallows. "I think these are Perchta's guardians."

I turn back, eyeing the one facing me. It vibrates in constant short motions, like a fighter ready to throw a punch, but it doesn't move closer to me.

"At the end of the year, some of the old covens celebrate Perchtenlauf," she tells me, her voice coming out strangled. "My mother told me about it. Villagers wear masks to scare off winter."

"These are more than masks."

"I *know*." Stress makes her snap. "And we are not in winter."

I've never heard of such a tradition, but as a Christian, there are Karneval masks worn during Lent, wooden things that are meant to scare away the devil. And despite the archbishop decrying the tradition, some mothers still tell their children about Krampus, and some fathers don scary masks and pretend to steal their misbehaving children while Saint Nicholas gives gifts to the good ones.

I have a feeling that no mask could compare to these monsters.

And while these beings are terrifying, they still aren't attacking. I tug Fritzi's hand, and she takes my meaning, stepping with me as we shift left. The creatures watch us, but do not attack. They do, however, close ranks, the three of them forming a semicircle with the mound behind us.

"Do they want us to go up the barrow hill?" Fritzi asks.

"I think so." We take another step closer. The circle of monsters tightens. We take a tentative step away, to the south, and the large one with the uneven jaw growls until we are another step nearer the barrow.

"The mistletoe," Fritzi says, leaning against me. "They don't attack us because of the protection of the mistletoe."

I wonder if Fritzi's crown of green leaves and white berries is different from the ones Cornelia made. Perhaps Fritzi using wild magic did something to separate us from the others, or perhaps they are all being herded by monsters toward the barrow.

We take several steps away from the monsters. The ground underfoot is uneven now as we are herded sideways up the hill.

More monsters join, all of them pushing us higher, higher...

We reach the top of the barrow, Fritzi and I at the very apex, surrounded by more than a dozen monsters, each more hideous than the last.

And then the ground gives way, and we fall straight down into the grave.

18

FRITZI

A scream rips out of me, the noise cut off by the jarring impact of my body slamming into something dense and moist. Darkness permeates the space, the single hole above giving only barest gray-white light, and I scramble to my feet, immediately swinging around, terrified that losing my grip on Otto's hand means we're separated now.

But he's there, picking himself up from the fall. A spongy layer of moss coats the ground, pieces of it sticking to our clothes, and Otto bats chunks of it off as he looks up at the hole above our heads. It's at least twice my height over us, too far to jump, but the distance tells me we haven't fallen all the way through the barrow.

I start to shout for Cornelia, for Alois, when shapes appear over the hole.

Perchta's creatures.

I lurch back into the shadows instinctively. A dozen grotesque faces gather around the hole, backlit by the lowlight so they become horned silhouettes peering down at us. I can feel their empty eyes on my skin, but they make no move to pursue us; they simply stare, standing watch. Standing guard.

"Does this mean Perchta *wants* us to be here," Otto whispers, "or is this her way of killing and entombing us?"

"I don't give a damn what Perchta wants," I say. "There has to be another way out of this barrow. If there isn't, we'll make one."

"The stone could be here," Otto notes. "In which case, she led us to it. Or her guardians did."

I turn around, trying to get a better look at where we are, and I prod the connection with Holda in my mind.

Unsurprisingly, there is resistance. Like I have fallen not only into a barrow, but into a cage that bars me from her. Panic flares in me, and I look down at the moss beneath my feet, using one quick pull at wild magic to make a bundle of wildflowers grow. They launch up without hesitation, and I exhale.

I'm cut off from Holda, but not wild magic. Perchta can control access to her sister in this space, but that is all.

Resolve settles over me, and I squint, willing my eyes to adjust. We're in a circular space, moss spreading out across the floor and up over the walls, a muted green blanket that cakes the air in smells of earthiness and sealed growth.

"There." Otto points. In the far part of this space is a darker shadow—an opening.

He takes a step forward, but I stop him with a hand on his arm. "This is a tomb."

Otto's brows go up. "Yes. We knew that."

"No, I—" I spin again, looking at what I can see of this chamber, willfully ignoring the masked creatures still looming over us. "This isn't how barrows are laid out. We don't bury our dead this way anymore, but barrows are only one chamber, not—"

I wave at the doorway.

Otto's face screws up in thought. "This could *not* be a tomb. It could have been made to look like one to keep out interlopers. But if this is where she hid the stone, maybe it is laid out differently."

Something scratches at me. A creeping, shuddering sense of wrong.

Perchta is the goddess of rules and tradition.

She wouldn't create a barrow that didn't follow the norm. Would she?

I take a breath, fighting to level my concern. Otto is right. If this is the stone's hiding place, she could have had her champion build it in a unique way.

I rub at my temple, glaring at the doorway. The anger and certainty that swells in my chest stuns me. I'd gotten so used to feeling afraid, exhausted. But this kick of surety and righteous fury temporarily yanks me away from the reality of what we're facing. This is invigorating, and I feel more in control than I have in weeks. Months, maybe.

A quick rummage in my satchel reveals a small jar half-empty of balm. I make a witchlight of it, and the steady glow creates a bubble of light around Otto and me.

"Stay behind me," I tell him as I walk forward.

His arm swings out, his sword already bare in his other hand. "I don't think—"

"Otto, this place is steeped in Perchta's magic. There may be things you can slice at, but for now, let me go first in case there are spells to counter."

His face sets. He wants to argue, and I love him for it, but he relents and falls in step behind me.

I enter the doorway, and a long hall twists downward, the floor giving way from moss to smooth dirt. The walls change, too, becoming stacked stones, man-made, and the hall twists, down and down, each bend making my chest wrench tighter.

How far beneath the ground are we now? And what happened to Brigitta, Cornelia, and our group? Perchta wouldn't let her guardians harm them, would she?

I shake my head. We'll find out if the stone is here. We'll get the damn thing and make our way out of this accursed place, and I'll deal with whatever Perchta did to my friends.

The hall continues down, and one more turn shows the floor leveling. I come up short, back to the wall, and peer around the corner.

I let the witchlight go out.

Otto starts to hiss, "Why—" but he stops when a yellow glow takes the space of the witchlight, coming from farther down the hall.

"There's a wider chamber," I whisper. "Lit torches. It looks like a burial room."

"So this *is* a tomb?"

I shrug.

"Who lit the torches?" Otto asks.

Another shrug. I meet his gaze and mimic throwing spells.

Ready? I mouth.

He adjusts his grip on his sword and nods.

I don't count down, don't warn him further; I dive around the corner and hurl myself into the burial chamber.

Torches rim the stacked stone walls, flames dancing orange and yellow off the piles of goods around me. Tables are strewn with gold jewelry, pieces of armor, fine leather and wool clothes. Another table is set for a banquet feast, platters and serving trays holding long-rotted food and herbs kept almost preserved by the moisture of the tomb, wine flagons and drinking horns and goblets set at places like guests are moments from coming. At the back of the room, lit by the largest torches in the space, is a bronze couch attached to a gold-plated wagon. The wall behind it has four concave dips each taller than I am, alcoves that nestle around four identical clay statues. The wagon, the torches, the statues all stand guard over a body wrapped in white linen laid in repose on the couch.

I stop, eyes waiting for any stray movement, but the only motion comes from the snapping of the torch flames. I can feel Otto next to me, just as wound, and after a beat of nothing, we both straighten.

He doesn't sheath his sword, but he takes a step toward the closest table, the one piled with jewelry. He lets out a low whistle. "How this place hasn't been robbed is a testament to Perchta's guardians."

"Don't touch anything," I say quickly.

Otto gives me a look that says, *Do you think I'm that foolish?*

I wave my hand. "Sorry. This place just has me on edge. We're at Perchta's mercy. And I—"

No. I won't panic.

Otto puts his hand on my shoulder. "Let's do a survey of the room—without touching anything." He smiles. "We need to know what we're dealing with."

I nod. Nod again. "All right. I'll go—"

A shout jerks me around.

Something's rushing at us, fast.

I scramble to grow a plant, or even grab at stone, but the shape moving at me is quick and determined and so I settle for flinging my hands forward.

Wind answers my call, grabs onto my wild magic surge and *pushes*—

—just as I realize who is flinging himself at me.

"Alois?"

But he goes hurtling through the air on my gust of wind and slams into the stones across from me with a startled cry.

He sinks to the floor, eyes wide on me—not in pain. In mixed fear and confusion and *awe*.

"What spell was *that*?" he chirps.

"I—" My hands are still out.

I used wild magic. In front of Alois. No attempt at murmuring a spell to cover me, no way to explain it off. And it wasn't something I'm known for using, not plants or herbs.

Uncertainty and dread pin me in place.

Otto takes one of my outstretched wrists in his hand and looks at Alois. "A bonded ability we've been working on. For use against an enemy who tries to *attack my witch*."

His last words end in an accusatory, expectant glare. It redirects the focus, and Alois rolls his eyes.

"To be fair," Alois says, "I thought you were one of those goddess-damned horned monsters. Not that I'm not glad you're alive, but how in the Three goddesses did you get down here?"

I lower my hands and grip them into fists against the relieved tremble that rushes through me. Otto throws me a quick reassuring look, and I smile gratefully at him.

He ducks around me and helps Alois to his feet. "How did *you* get down here? We were corralled down a hole by Perchta's terrors."

Alois pulls back, scowling in confusion. "So were we. I didn't see you—"

"We?" I cut in.

"We," comes another voice. Cornelia moves in from the hall, a knife in one hand. She throws me a relieved *you're alive* smile. "We got separated from you and the rest. Those masked creatures pushed us up the barrow hill, and we fell into a room—"

"—covered in moss?" I finish.

Cornelia's frown deepens.

Alois groans. "Perchta's messing with us. Fantastic." He sheaths the knife he'd tried to attack me with, and I start to say something about it when Otto juts his chin at the weapon.

"Don't put it away."

Alois takes it back out, but he gives Otto a searching look. "We haven't seen any of those creatures down here. No one else, really, except you."

And in an instant, his confusion turns to suspicion.

"How do we know you *are* you?" he asks.

Alois's usual banter makes me want to dismiss it as a joke, but his question grows roots and settles in my brain, and I clench my jaw tight.

"How do we know *you're* you?" I return. "And not some figment of Perchta meant to stick a blade in our backs? You already tried to attack me."

Alois's suspicion holds on me. "Say something only Fritzi would know." He blanches. "*Not* about Otto, I beg of you."

I can't help it. I snort. It draws a smile across Alois's face, and Otto shakes his head, but one corner of his mouth lifts.

"*He* has to be himself, at least," Otto says. Alois bows.

"Where's everyone else?" I ask. "Brigitta, Ignatz, the rest of—"

Alois shrugs. His face goes a bit gray, and he settles, humor sliding off. His silence hangs, and my own uncertainty wells up in it.

We don't know. The creatures could have corralled them elsewhere, or—

No. Thoughts like that won't help.

But why are the four of us down here, then? Why not the rest?

"If you're quite finished," Cornelia says, "I'd rather like to get out of here."

"Were there any teachings about how to escape a goddess-created barrow in your journey to become a priestess?" I ask.

She grunts. "If only. I'm beginning to wonder what in my teachings and position *was* actually useful, outside of falling in line."

My eyebrows smooth out. She's always been the closest to believing the things Holda speaks of, but I haven't heard Cornelia outright say anything of that sort before.

I manage a shaky smile. *You have no idea*, I want to say.

"Any god that expects obedience may do well to not be so damned obscure," Otto mutters, which makes my eyebrows shoot up.

Cornelia steps deeper into the room, moving gracefully around the tables, her focus set on the back wall.

I cross with her and stare up at the four statues.

"They're unsettling," I say.

She folds her arms. "There's something...off about them. Isn't there?"

I cock my head as Otto and Alois join us, and we stand in stillness for a moment, mimicking the statues in front of us. Each one is massive, at least six feet tall, with mistletoe headdresses, armor, a sword, and a shield all carved of the same stone. They *look* identical, scowling faces set for all eternity—but it isn't that there's something off about all of them. It's that there's something off about *one* of them.

I take a step closer. Three of the statues are a terracotta orange-red, and their texture looks rough, like sand. But one is not quite orange, not quite red. And the texture is broken up by almost minuscule pieces of something lighter, strips of—is that straw?

The moment I think that, I'm hit with memories. Mama threatening my brother and me that if we didn't behave, Perchta would come and slice open our bellies and stuff us full of straw. She threatened Dieter far more than me, but those were the tales always, haunted whispers that the goddess of rules exacted her punishment with a knife and straw. That was how Perchta threatened me, too, when she was testing me in the Black Forest before I gained entry to the Well.

"This statue," I point at the one second from the left. "The stone is in this statue."

Cornelia comes closer. "Are you sure?"

I laugh. It's humorless. "No. But there's straw in this one. It could be intentional. It *has* to be intentional. Right?"

No one responds. I glance at Otto, who has his sword in one hand, his eyes scanning the room, and I can see his brain working hard to figure out something else, *anything* else.

We don't know what the game is here. What Perchta wants with us, if the stone is even *in* this statue, or if this one is stuffed full of straw for another reason. It could be important to Perchta for some other purpose, something to do with this barrow, this chamber, whoever's final resting place this is.

I wish I could talk with Holda. And that thought has me grateful that she was the goddess who chose me, not the manic, unhelpful, rule-obsessed Mother.

Rules.

Perchta is the goddess of rules.

What will happen if I use wild magic on her statue? Had she planned for that in whatever traps she's set down here? I used it to fend off Alois, and nothing happened.

I can't keep speculating. *Indecision could cost lives*, Brigitta had said.

I shake out my hands and take a step back.

"Give me space," I say.

Cornelia and Alois back up.

They're here. They'll see me use wild magic.

I'm not sure I care anymore.

Unlike Cornelia and Alois, Otto comes closer.

I cock an eyebrow at him, and he readies his sword, but he makes no move to obey me, and I nudge him with my shoulder.

"All right, Perchta," I snarl as I face the statue. "Let's see what's so special about this statue."

I grab for the same thing I used to push away Alois: air. This is—hopefully—the resting place of the air stone, so it's only fitting. I can feel particles dancing through this space, stagnant for too long in this locked-away tomb. Air winds around the statue—it isn't set into the wall, merely cradled in this alcove, and there's enough space between the body on the couch and this wall that I can knock the statue out onto the floor.

Hands clenched, I tug, harnessing the air to pull the statue forward.

It rocks and resettles against the alcove.

Again. Again. The statue teeters in wider arcs, and part of me unwinds when it doesn't leap out to fight us like the masked creatures had. It just wobbles like any stone statue would, and sweat beads down my face with every tug, but finally, *finally*, the statue pitches all the way forward.

I back up as it falls. Otto plants his hand on my back and steps with me, the two of us braced for a shatter, a crack at least.

What we are not braced for is the statue's arm snapping out and catching itself before it crashes to the ground.

19

OTTO

Maybe it won't attack.

That's my only thought as the enormous, larger than life-sized sandstone statue pushes up from the ground. The monsters didn't attack. They just herded us here. And Fritzi and I are both goddess-chosen, and—

My thoughts come to a crashing halt as the statue touches its side. A sheathed blade is etched into it, but as soon as the moving statue's fingers touch it, the sword becomes very real, shining sharp metal.

In front of me, Fritzi fumbles, too shocked, I think, to call up a spell quickly. I shoulder past her, putting her behind me, and throw up my own blade just in time to feel the strength of the blow, to stop the sword as it swings down toward us.

As soon as our blades meet, sparks flying as the metal grinds against metal, I know—I'm in trouble. Strong as I am as a warrior, my muscles are not made of stone, my flesh is not solid, my body is not as big. I dig my heels into the packed earth at the bottom of the barrow, eyes glaring. I may not be able to fully fight this statue come to life, but I will not relent.

Heat burns in my chest, over my heart.

The tattoo, I think, remembering the way the tree engraved itself upon my skin at Fritzi's touch, the visual reminder of our connection. The tattoo has been dormant—I almost forgot about it, because drawing from its power would mean siphoning magic from Fritzi. But our bond seems even stronger now, and when I reach for the magic, I know—I *feel*—Fritzi not just allowing me to take some, but shoving it at me, eagerly giving me more strength.

Her power rushes into me. The Tree tattoo is one of protection, and *that* is my only thought as I slide my blade along the statue's.

Protect Fritzi.

Our hilts catch, and power rushes from my chest into my arms, and I throw my force against my sword so strongly that the statue stumbles back, his sword glancing off mine. Rather than swing his blade again, the statue raises both arms.

For the first time, I notice three sharp spikes against the statue's throat—a metal collar known as a torque. The neck ring had been engraved in the statue's sandstone, tight, with the three spikes pointing down, but then the statue makes a resonant, hollow sound. The torque glows with golden light, and, like the statue's blade turned real, the neck ring becomes solid gold metal.

My eyes are pinned on the statue, my arms tense and ready to strike in case it attacks again. It does not move.

Instead, the other three do.

Each of the other statues in the alcoves shuffles forward. Each reaches for their engraved blade, and, when they pull it out—the stone transmuting into razor-sharp metal—each prepares himself in a fighting position.

"Get ready," I call, panic raising my voice. Out of the corner of my eye, I see Alois, already standing like a soldier, weapon drawn. Cornelia faces the third statue, and I'm reminded that she may be a priestess, but she's spent her life defending the Well.

The statue I've been battling is motionless, but even if its eyes are nothing but orange-red rock, I feel them watching me. It lowers its sword and gestures with its other arm, as if to say, *You are welcome to try.*

And then the other three strike at once.

I lunge to the right, Fritzi staying close to me, slamming my sword into the nearest statue. It is only because I have the strength of Fritzi's magic steeling my muscles that I do not crumble at the force of the statue's returning blow.

I spare a glance at the first statue, the one Fritzi pointed out, the one that seems to have straw stuck in its stone. It still watches, its head turning from me to Cornelia and Alois, each of them fighting their own battle.

Fighting...and losing.

Alois and Cornelia aren't bonded, and they don't have any extra goddess-blessed strengths. Alois has power-enhancing tattoos from being in the Grenzwache, and Cornelia's a priestess, which—I hope—grants her something extra in the battle, but I can see that we're in a grim position. And if the straw statue decides to join the fray, we'll be even more outnumbered.

"We've got to end this. Quick," I snarl, using my weight to parry another blow from the statue in front of me.

"Got any ideas?" Fritzi has opened her magic to me, but being Holda's champion means she has a deeper internal well than others. From her position, she's using her magic to lift treasure—gold chains, heavy gems, polished weapons—from one of the tables and add to the assault against the statues Alois and Cornelia fight.

I catch her when she stumbles back and push her upright. She's divided too much, funneling magic into me, using it for the others... The longer this battle takes, the more I'll drain her.

The statue in front of me swings up, and I lunge forward, hacking at its side. The sandstone breaks.

They're hollow inside.

My attacker folds a little to the left as its torso cracks, but it doesn't fall. The blow is enough to make it lower its arm, though, and as soon as it does, I whack my blade against its shoulder. One arm drops off. The thing doesn't stop, though, so I grind my teeth, aiming for the neck.

It blocks, using its one remaining arm. I think about the way the torque on the straw statue glowed, and I feel more certain than ever. Before the statue in front of me has a chance to recover, I rear back, leaving myself wide open for a hit but taking the chance anyway, and use the momentum to swing hard, driving the tip of my blade through the statue's neck.

It crumbles to the ground in shattered pieces.

"Little help?" Alois cries, high-pitched and exhausted.

"Aim for the neck!" I shout as I lunge across the room, Fritzi at my heels.

Before I can get to him, a blast of magic bursts out—Cornelia threw some sort of spell at the statue fighting Alois. "Nice," I mutter as fractures appear along the statue's neck.

It doesn't break, though. It slams a stone arm down at Alois, who rolls out of the way, closer to Cornelia, just as the statue Cornelia is fighting strikes her. Alois leaps up, blocking it, sparks and stone chips flying.

I want to help them, but I have to stop the statue Alois had been fighting first, even the odds.

I throw a leg up on the bench, kicking off the table of rotting food.

I can feel Fritzi's magic pushing me, driving me with more force as I soar across the room, my sword aimed at the statue's back as it lumbers closer to help its brother fight Alois and Cornelia. I break through the sandstone with a hollow cracking sound, and rather than pull my short sword out, I pull it *up*, driving the steel through what would have been the spine, yanking the blade out at its neck and then smashing it back down. Thanks to the cracks Cornelia already gave it, I can behead the statue and watch it crumble all in one fell swoop.

I leap to the other side of the room, aided by Fritzi's magic. It was like a tap before, a steady flow of power, but it's like a raging flood now, magic driving through all my muscles, the strength so intense that it's dizzying.

Is this what Dieter wants? Because this is—

Intoxicating.

The thought almost makes me stumble, but it's Fritzi, her calm, true connection to magic that keeps me going. This power washing over me, it's good, but it's good because it's *hers*, and it's good because she *gives* it.

Taking it?

Acid roils in my throat at the thought.

It is the gift, the consent, the shared nature of the magic that makes it valuable. It is not the magic itself. It's that it's *hers* and that she gives it freely.

I feel her presence as I fight, even though she's moved to the far wall; she's leaning against it as if out of breath. I'm draining her. I cannot let her sacrifice of strength be in vain.

Alois looks at me from behind his statue. He and Cornelia are working together, his sword and her magic in perfect harmony as they parry every blow. I had hoped to attack from behind, but the statue turns, deflecting the blow with such power that I slam back into the table, my head cracking in a teeth-jarring slam. Alois shouts, lunging forward, but the statue pivots, throwing him back as well. I push up, knowing that it's only Fritzi's strength that helps me stand now, none of mine.

I can't force the statue back; I can't do more than parry and dodge its blows, an onslaught of attacks. It swings its free arm wide, knocking Alois on the head, and the man crumples. I hear Cornelia scream his name, and I pray he's only knocked out, not dead. I cannot turn to check; already, the statue is driving down on me, walloping me with its sword, stroke after stroke, giving me no room to advance.

And then it deftly swings up, twists, catches my hilt despite the curve, and my sword goes flying, clattering useless against the table with the banquet feast, knocking over goblets of dried-up wine and skidding through mold-covered platters that splatter stinking rot.

I feel for my jacket, my sleeves, but no weapon is within reach, not now, not as the statue drives me farther and farther against the wall in the tightly contained space.

My eyes flick to the first statue, the one that only watches. His golden torque had three spikes. Two are now sandstone orange; only one still glows golden.

The statue I'm fighting slams a fist, and I duck only just in time, dirt and pebbles cascading over me.

I have no weapon. My enemy knows no pain and will never stop.

Unless I force him to.

I reach for Fritzi, feel her reaching back to me.

If I fail, I have drained her of her magic, and I have left her without protection.

I. Will. *Not.* Fail.

My back's against the wall. I kick up with both feet, slamming my boots into the statue's torso. It doesn't fall back.

Good. I didn't want it to.

I use the pressure to walk my feet over its chest, then push against the wall, wrapping my legs around the statue's neck. With strength that I know is not mine, I pull my body up, wrenching my arms on either side of the statue's enormous mistletoe headdress made of stone, and I *twist.*

I feel the sandstone cracking beneath my grip. I feel the rock splintering, like bones popping, and I *pull*, I twist and pull until I take the damn thing's head off with my bare hands, and then, heaving with exertion, the statue crumbles beneath me, shattering, its stone head nothing but dust in my sweaty palms as I land on the ground.

Fritzi rushes to me. "Are you—" she starts, but I point behind her, unable to catch enough breath to warn her.

The last statue, the one with straw stuck into it, steps forward, facing us. Fritzi whirls around, and I push up from the ground, dragging my dusty sword into a defensive stance.

The fight is not over.

But Fritzi puts her hand out, pushes my sword arm down.

I can feel that she's weaker now than before, but the last statue isn't fighting back. Instead, it holds its arms up, and all the bits of straw that had been stuck in it fly up, swirling in a tornado of glinting flecks until it all coalesces in the statue's outstretched palm, turning into...

"The air stone," Fritzi says, eyes on the rock in its grip.

20

FRITZI

The statue holds out the stone. Otto looks at me and waits for my move, the grating of our breaths echoing in the suddenly silent tomb. I can hear Cornelia and Alois talking softly, fussing over a wound she got, and hearing both of their gentle murmurs sets me at ease from worrying about their fates.

My focus goes to the statue. The now motionless statue, still holding that stone out, an offering.

"It was too easy," I whisper.

Otto huffs. I can feel the depletion of my magic now slowly starting to refill, an empty bucket being brought back to full with a steady *drip-drip-drip* of wild magic funneling in. The magic that Otto drew on to fight the statues. I'm glad he had it to call on; I don't regret the terrifyingly low level I can feel my own internal source at now. Other than that, though, we're all still standing. We're all relatively unharmed.

I grab the stone from the statue's palm.

The moment my skin touches it, I blink, and the tomb changes.

Otto vanishes. The murmuring of Alois and Cornelia deadens. The statue in front of me warps, ripples, and in a burst of foggy white light, it's gone.

In its place is a woman with a hefty braid of brown and gray hair that hangs to the floor, various plants interwoven through her plait—yellow agrimony, spiked blessed thistle, fluffy green nettle, all plants for protection and consecration. Her gown is a long, swooping flow of midnight blue, the collar and sleeves set with ivory patterns of stitched animals. She has the same impeccable posture I remember from before, queenly and controlling, the same withering look in her pale blue eyes.

"Hello, Perchta," I say, my voice a croaked whisper.

She still has the stone in her grip. I have my own hand over the top of it, but she doesn't release it into my care.

I risk a glance around. The tomb is transformed. It's just the two of us, the corpse, and the one intact statue back in its alcove. The tables set with finery and food are unmarred and righted, like the feast has only just been laid out, the gifts only recently displayed. A steady white light fills the room now, not the flicker of torches or even the pulse of the sun, but something consuming and resonant and otherworldly.

Perchta narrows her eyes at me. "You should not have come, Friederike Kirch. This stone is not yours to use."

"I don't want to use it," I say. "I want to keep it safe from—"

"*Liar*." She cuts me off with a shout that echoes off the walls. "I see your heart, *champion*—you would use this stone. You would use them all. You would break the Origin Tree, and you would *doom us*."

My instinct is to lurch back, away from her anger, but the moment I try, I can feel my skin tug—it's stuck to the stone, trapping me in front of her. She gives a cruel glare that tells me she will only release me when *she* is ready.

So I harden my shoulders and will myself to meet her gaze.

"I do not want to break the Origin Tree," I try, but I hear the flimsiness in it. "I don't want whatever cataclysm would come from breaking the Origin Tree," I try again, and that at least is true.

Perchta scoffs. "But you would, if given the chance, utterly decimate our ways. You would make it so no witch was bound to the Tree. You think I cannot smell the wild magic on you? That I cannot hear the deadly wishes you make in the dark? You would undo our entire world."

My chest kicks. In fear, yes; each word from her swells her presence until I forget that there was ever anyone else in this chamber but us. She is a goddess, and Holda cannot reach me in this tomb Perchta created to keep the stone safe, and I am so very, very mortal.

But I'm also breathless in grief.

"I don't want to undo our world," I say, pleading. "It is *our* world, mine too. I don't want to destroy anything!"

"You bastardize our ways at every turn!" Perchta shouts. "You—"

"I am not trying to bastardize anything!" Her voice is resonant, so I shout too, desperation finally snapping in me. "I never wanted any of this! I never wanted to be a goddess's champion, I never wanted to get thrown into the middle of your war, *I never wanted to be here*!"

"And yet you are, and you have—"

"Yes. I am." My jaw is tense, muscles winding so tight they vibrate. "I am here. I am here, and I have seen what Holda wants, what *you* and Abnoba want, and I'm not sure any of it is right. I don't want to break our world. But I cannot let the rest of the world continue to suffer when we have the power to help. *That* is what I want. Not to break the Tree. Not to decimate our ways. But to *grow*. To—"

"How is that not shirking our teachings, our way of life? See the way you came into this tomb, the way you fought off my soldiers. This was a test, a test of worthiness for any who would seek the stone, and you *failed*. You have abandoned all your teachings, your spells, and the methods imparted to you on how to access magic properly. You used the bond made between you and your warrior, but even that you have bastardized with wild magic! You have given yourself over to the vilest force we know, and you use it to corrupt the most sacred union between a witch and a warrior, so even the magic your bonded draws on is tainted."

"We aren't—"

"Had you wanted to *pass* my test," Perchta barrels on, color rising in her pale cheeks, "you would have seen that this room holds everything a witch might need to cast the spells to unlock the stone from the statue. The table has herbs for one such as you, Friederike. It has supplies—supplies the priestess, Cornelia, used, when you did not. The way she fought with that soldier, Alois—they were far more in tune with the intentions of a bonded pair than the way you let your warrior nearly drain your magic dry. Did you even try to work *with* your warrior? Did you even try to make a potion? No. You are a danger to us. You and your warrior."

I yank on my hand again, but it holds fast to the stone in Perchta's grip, and I gape up at her with wide, panicked eyes as she towers over me.

"Otto and I have no one to train us," I fumble, my voice losing its bite. "There's no one to—"

"You and your warrior came here and dared to stand in the tomb of one of my greatest champions." Perchta waves at the corpse beside her, wrapped in fine linen, laid out in this room of decadence and death. "You dare to think you would take this stone. You are entitled and selfish, as dangerous as Dieter, and I have let Holda have her experiments. I have let her, even when she failed us so horribly with your brother. But I will not let you lay waste to our ways."

The room darkens. Wind stirs from somewhere up the tunnel and fills the air with a scent like static, like the swell before a lightning strike. My mind is a whirl of terror and primal drive, and I yank at my hand again, again, trying to get away—

But then I hear her.

I hear what she said echo, echo.

Our ways.

Over and over again.

She is the goddess of tradition.

"But—" I lick my lips, mouth dry, and look up at her, fear pausing, like a held breath. "You broke our ways too."

Perchta's furious eyes burn at me. "What did you say?"

A crack forms. A sliver that lets in light, fresh air, and I heave a breath, *feeling,* suddenly, through the fog, and the fear lifts enough that I can *think.*

"You broke our ways too," I repeat. "This tomb—the layout is all wrong. There should be no upper level, no hall. The old teachings were for it to be one room. That's it."

Perchta's jaw works. "You think you can—"

But I'm not done. Not by a long way. That crack widens until all my fear is bathed in righteous fury, anger that sparks from every moment I've been suppressing my true feelings from Philomena, Rochus, Perchta, even Dieter and the hexenjägers and *everyone* who has pointed at who and what I am and forced me to exert every last scrap of my energy trying to conform to their criticism. I have wasted so much *time,* so much precious, fleeting *time* on trying to be accepted by all these different forces that I haven't spared so much as a thought toward how to embrace *who I actually am.*

It hits me in this moment, this breath before the scream, how much I have lost in focusing on how to fit into the demands of others.

Imagine how great I could be, right now, if I had spent all these years not surviving, but *living*.

Tears prick my eyes, and my look shocks another flinch from Perchta. It isn't as satisfying as it should be.

"You hate me for breaking our traditions," I say, voice as unyielding as the stone in our hands. "Yet you have broken more of our traditions than anyone. In this chamber, yes, but beyond too—you let so many perceived infractions slide."

"I am the goddess of rules and traditions," Perchta snaps. "I do not allow those rules to be broken, not by you, not by any who live under—"

"We no longer bury our dead this way. In these grand tombs—we stopped heralding the mighty fallen in this manner, but this was once a tradition, yes? So why did you let us stop doing this? Shouldn't you be punishing us for burying our dead in simple graves now instead of enshrining their bodies like this?"

Perchta's brows go up, a fraction of a pulse.

"Berate me all you want for the rules I have broken." My voice drops until I'm snarling, practically bearing my teeth at her. "But I have done what I needed to do to survive in a world where everyone in positions of power creates arbitrary rules they implement at their leisure. You think you are different from the other forces at work? You think you are better than the hexenjägers, than the Catholic priests, than the Protestant princes? You are all the same. You take out your pathetic need for control on those less strong than you so you can pretend you are better than us when what you really are is *weak*."

The room had paused with Perchta's shock. Now it reawakens, the stirring wind, the growing darkness.

Perchta's face goes red with rising anger. "You would speak this way to a *goddess*?" She drags the last word out, a hiss.

"Yes. I would. Because you have made that title mean *nothing*." The tears heating my eyes finally fall, and when I let my face droop, anger shifts to grief.

I can feel another jolt of surprise go through Perchta. But that surprise hardens into distrust; she thinks I am playing a game.

I have no moves left to make, though. I am tired and strung thin and this is what I am now. This is what I have been since Birresborn, I think. Hollow and empty, a witch, a girl, who watched her world burn to ashes and stood in the rubble, not as some proud symbol of defiance, but because I didn't even have the strength it would've taken to crumble.

All that lack of strength, all that absence, all that *grief*, I feel it now like tilled earth. But I hate the idea that anything good could grow in all this pain—if anything good comes from this, it is not because of what happened.

It is because I choose to create it.

"You have made that title mean nothing," I repeat. I suck in a breath. "But it could mean something. It could mean something *glorious*, Perchta. All the rules and traditions you oversee—we *need* them. I'm not trying to take them away, I swear to you. I love our traditions. I love the way my mother loved them—"

My voice catches, and I feel her loss like a fresh knife.

She would have loved speaking to Perchta like this. She would have loved seeing this barrow. She would have even loved Perchta's guardian monsters—any creature was her friend.

Tears track down my cheeks. I swallow, keep going, knowing I'm not imagining the sudden sheen in Perchta's eyes.

"—and how they are interwoven into all my memories of her and my childhood. She sang me to sleep with our songs. My whole family would gather to cook our recipes. My coven passed down spells and taught the phases of the moon and the best ways of harvesting ingredients. With wild magic, we don't need spells or ingredients, but that doesn't undercut the importance of them as a uniting force. *You* gave us that, Perchta. You gave me happiness in your traditions. I haven't—" I suck in another breath, a gulp, a sob. "I haven't thanked you."

Her surprise holds. Sharpens.

"So thank you," I press on. "Thank you for guarding the things that made my childhood sweet. Thank you for giving me traditions that link me with Liesel, with everyone in the Well. Thank you for connecting us, Perchta. But I wouldn't be connected to the Alamanni, if they were still around, would I? The ancient tribes' traditions differed from ours. All these traditions, all these beautiful things you safeguard—they were not always traditions. They've evolved. They were once concepts that married to other concepts until they became something we could build a foundation on. They were once ideas of *change*, weren't they, Perchta?" I'm breathing heavier, begging her to hear me. "Tradition has always been change."

Perchta's hand, the one holding the stone beneath mine, trembles. Her shocked face doesn't change, her lips in a thin, clasped line.

"You say traditions are sacred, that they cannot be altered, but tradition *is* alteration." Tears roll down my face so when I try to smile at her, I know it is helpless and brittle. "You are the goddess of tradition, but that means you are also the goddess of change, because change is the mark of the success of tradition. It means we survived long enough to evolve."

I bow my head at her. The first time I have ever done so willingly, not out of threat or fear.

"So thank you, Perchta," I say again. "Thank you, Mother, for keeping your children safe enough to let us grow. But we are grown now. And that is because you succeeded. You, the goddess of change and tradition."

"You seek to manipulate me," is all she says, but her voice is rough.

I don't look up, hand still stuck to that stone in her palm. "No. I am tired of fighting you. I don't *want* to fight you. I may be Holda's champion, but I am a witch first, and a witch belongs to all three goddesses. I don't want you to be my enemy. I want you to help me." Now I do look up at her. "Help me make new traditions for our people so we can keep growing."

Perchta's eyes hold on mine. Her face is a mask, as stony as the statues she commanded, as fierce as the monsters that corralled us into this tomb. Her hand, though, trembles under mine, and it is that shake that betrays the emotion in the depths of her eyes, a glossiness that could be agony.

She's afraid. She's as afraid as Holda. They have watched our people get beaten and tortured and burned, imprisoned and exiled and murdered. They have seen it all, done everything they could, over and over, to try to stop it, however misguided their attempts were. But in Perchta's eyes, I see all of the sorrow that went into creating the Origin Tree, all of the terror that has made her the vicious, fearsome goddess of rules that haunted so many children's nightmares.

She tried to use that fear to keep us safe. But it is no longer time for us to be safe.

"I will do everything I can to stop Dieter from breaking the Origin Tree," I promise her. "But I do not think I can do it without you."

A muscle tics in Perchta's jaw.

The darkness that had been creeping into the edges of the room retracts, chased away by the sudden swell of that ethereal white light. It grows, grows, and I have to snap my eyes shut in the piercing clarity of it all—

When I open my eyes, Perchta is gone.

The statue is back in its alcove.

And the air stone is in my hand.

21

OTTO

It all happens in a blink. One minute, Fritzi reaches for the stone the statue holds out; the next, the statue is back in the alcove, and Fritzi is sagging beside me, as if she had just fought a battle herself. Cornelia and Alois don't even notice, don't even stop their bickering over Cornelia's injury, but I can tell.

Something happened.

"Are you all right?" I ask, throwing my arms around her. She leans against me, trusting me to bear her weight for a moment. It is, perhaps, a good thing I am not a witch with all the power Fritzi has; if I were, I would use every ounce of magic in me to carry the two of us far, far away and protect her from ever having to fight again. I am so tired of my Fritzi being driven to the point of exhaustion.

Something in my stance makes Cornelia and Alois look up. "What happened?" Alois asks, noting Fritzi's hunched shoulders.

Cornelia pushes Alois aside and rushes to her. "Fritzi?"

"I'm fine," she says, straightening. She holds out her hand, revealing the air stone. Cornelia sucks in a breath.

"Dieter *cannot* destroy the Origin Tree without all three stones," Cornelia says, relief pitching her voice high. "Oh, thank the Three! He may have the water stone, but this means magic is safe."

"And the earth stone is still protected in the Well," Alois adds. "Two out of three, not bad."

Fritzi and I exchange a look. We have already seen how powerful her brother is with just one stone. It's not enough that we protect magic and the Well. We have to protect the people Dieter is willing to plow down to get what he wants.

Johann's empty eyes, the slight blue tinge to his lips, his lifeless body on the wet stone floor...

"I know," Cornelia says, noting Fritzi's sour face. "But it's *something*. And we can celebrate this for the win it is."

I glance around the room. The shattered remains of the statues crackle underfoot, while the one that offered Fritzi the stone is now standing straight and tall again, its arm molded against its side. "Let's get out of here first," I say.

Cornelia and Alois agree, turning at once to the corridor that opens up to the large room we fell into.

"Are you truly all right?" I ask Fritzi quietly. My muscles are tense; I'm weary from the battle but not as tired as I should be. Thanks to her. She gives me a confident nod of assurance, but if her step falters even once, I will carry her out of this damned barrow.

She doesn't falter, though. Her fingers are white around the stone, clenching it so tightly that I can hardly see its smooth surface beneath her grip, and she quickly catches up with Cornelia and Alois.

The entire area feels darker and claustrophobic. "Does...does this area seem smaller than before?" I ask, looking around.

"Yes," Alois comments. "And..." He points to the corridor we just exited. Rather than a narrow passage and door, the wall is widening, as if the rooms are merging. The tables fold away, the offerings sinking out of sight into the dirt. The alcoves blend into the walls; the statue stutters forward. Every blink brings the linen-wrapped corpse closer, but there's no obvious movement, just a constant readjustment of my eyes. The torches are gone, and with it, all the light except that from the hole above us. The only standing sandstone statue shifts, embedding itself into the earth of the barrow, the shards of its brethren sinking down, lost in the dirt.

"This barrow wasn't just a tomb," Fritzi says, her voice bouncing off the walls as they close in around us. "This was a place Perchta graced. She gave me the stone, and then she left. Which means..."

"The magic that has sustained this barrow, making it larger on the inside, is disappearing," Cornelia finishes. "We have to get out of here before we're buried alive!"

The circular walls line over and over again with layers of earth, each coil tightening around us. But the ground, too, is rising, bringing us closer to the opening.

"You first," Alois tells Cornelia, and before she can protest, he grabs her by the waist, lifts her up so her feet fall on his knees, and pushes her by her rear toward the opening. Hands reach down, and I almost call out a warning, but then I recognize the voices above—Brigitta and the other members of the Watch.

"Come on," I tell Fritzi, grabbing for her. She's going to fight me, insist that Alois go up first, but Alois is on my side. He shoves her to me, and I scoop her up, lifting her lithe body higher even as the dirt under my feet boosts me closer to the top. Our friends grab her wrists and pull her the rest of the way.

I turn to Alois. The walls are so tight now that I cannot throw my arms out on either side. The once vast series of chambers is now one tiny room. There is barely space for both Alois and me to stand, our knees butting against the low bronze couch with the linen-wrapped corpse, the body outline surely nothing but bones, but still, definitely, human.

"You next," I tell him, prepared for a fight, but Alois just nods eagerly, eyes wide and terrified, stepping into my scooped hands and jumping up. His legs kick, hitting me in the shoulder. The hole above us is starting to constrict as well, the passage narrowing.

"Otto!" Fritzi cries, the sound strangled.

With no one to offer me a leg up, I jump on the bronze couch the corpse rests on. I feel the old bones crunching under my feet, and I say a quick mourning prayer, but I have no intention of joining this person in their grave.

Pushing up from the table, I jump toward the hole, arms raised. I can feel hands grabbing my own, yanking, but the dirt closes around me. I kick, trying to raise my body, but there's no room to move my legs. Soil clogs my eyes, my nose, my mouth. I part my lips to shout, but mud washes past my teeth, choking me. I cannot see, cannot hear. Terror floods my mind, and even as I feel the arms pulling me, my body doesn't budge, encased in earth as if the hill itself had formed around me.

A crackle of magic burns in my chest, near my tattoo. A sob claws at my throat, blocked by mud, unable to escape, as I realize that my fight with the statues has drained Fritzi dry of her own magic. It will return, of course, but she cannot save me now.

And then the hill explodes.

A burst of wind so violent that my entire body and the top half of the barrow rips through the earth, dirt and mud and rocks swirling in a tornado that's cut into the ground with a surgeon's precision. My body, which had been tightly constrained, now flies free, my limbs flailing like a rag doll. I go up, high, my back bending awkwardly—

And then the wind stops.

I drop, dimly aware of the thuds of countless clods of earth and pebbles falling onto the ground, skittering over the grass. I have one instant where I remember the way the bones of the corpse crunched under my feet and wonder if my bones, too, will crunch into the dirt, when a billowing burst of wind buffets my fall, pushing my chest up and my legs down, until I settle back on the ground.

I stagger, dropping to my knees. Alois rushes forward, clapping me hard on the back, and I spew bile and mud, choking on rocks that tumble past my teeth. When I breathe, I can still smell dirt. My fingernails are shredded, black with soil and red with blood. My eyes are blurry and burning. Someone brings a skin filled with water, and Brigitta dumps it over my head, washing away some of the dirt that had been pressed into me. My teeth still crunch with grit, and I grab another waterskin, swishing and spitting.

"Thanks," I choke out, my eyes on Fritzi, streaked with dirt from her own ascent. She holds the air stone in her palm.

She had run out of magic, but the stone had given her more.

Fritzi passes the stone to Cornelia and grabs my hand, rubbing my grimy knuckles.

"Well, that was exciting. Let's never, ever, *ever* do that again," Alois says. He stands and offers me a hand to help pull me up.

"By each and every hell of each and every god on this planet or any other, what is going on?" Brigitta snarls, eyes flashing from me to Fritzi to Alois to Cornelia and back. "You four disappear in some mist and then pop out of the ground like daisies?"

"It wasn't like daisies," Alois muttered.

"It felt like I exploded out of the ground," I add.

"You did," Fritzi allows. "Sort of. I had to drive the air *into* the barrow, and then pull it all out again at once."

"What happened to *you*?" Cornelia asks the guard leader. "Did you see the monsters?"

Brigitta shudders. "We all did." She gestures to the Watch members. "Like horrible masks floating in the mists."

"Not masks," I say, remembering the spindly front legs of the running beast, the odd jaw and drooling tongue flapping about. "Full monsters."

Brigitta shakes her head. "We saw only masks, driving us away from the barrow. And the mist was so thick, we could not see or hear everyone. It wasn't until later that we realized you four were well and truly missing."

"Why us?" Alois asks, looking at Cornelia. "The goddesses have chosen Fritzi—well, one did—and Otto's hers, but why us?"

"Perchta is the goddess of tradition," Fritzi says in a low voice. "She likes those who adhere to it."

"Fine, you're a priestess," Alois allows, gesturing at Cornelia, "but I'm not exactly Perchta material."

"You held your own," Cornelia says. My eyes are raw from the dirt, but I think I see her blush.

"Maid, Mother, and Crone, can't you see it?" Fritzi says, exhausted. "You two obviously work well together. You could be bonded. *That's* why Perchta allowed you to go into the barrow. She approves of the bonding tradition, and she's—"

"Playing matchmaker?" Brigitta asks, gaping.

Fritzi shrugs but then casts a sly glance at Cornelia. My eyes are definitely not deceiving me; Cornelia and Alois are both bright red now.

"Well, that would explain things," Brigitta mutters.

"No, it doesn't!" Alois says too loudly.

"Oh, just admit you've been pining over her like a mooncalf."

"I—but—" Alois sputters.

"Really?" Cornelia asks, turning to him, and Alois's attempts at denial taper off into a mouselike squeak.

"Enough!" Brigitta bellows. "I want a report on what happened *now.*"

"We need to regroup," I say through a raspy voice. "But not here."

"I'll cover the basics," Alois offers, and that, at least, satisfies Brigitta. Alois explains with shocking efficiency the basics of the events as we stumble away from the barrow, toward the horses that, somehow, are calmly grazing in the field below. This area feels too open and defenseless, though, and no one protests when I point to the plateau beyond the barrow, the location of the ancient city.

Nothing remains but a few broken walls and random street pavers, but the road up the cliff is accessible, and the trees provide cover. It's a good location. I can see why the tribes met here, why it never fell to the Romans. I can tell the others like it too. They feel safer in the forest. Perhaps there's still a bit of Perchta's protection on this land.

When we reach a small clearing off the ancient road, with the stony remains of a low wall alongside, I suspect that we've actually entered the ruins of some barrack. Fitting, then, that Brigitta declares we'll camp here tonight, with assurances that Cornelia, Alois, Fritzi, and I are to rest only, not participate in the watch.

Cornelia kneels by the fire as soon as it's made, and even though it's not particularly chilly, she stretches her hands to the flames.

Fritzi comes up behind me. "Sit," she orders me. "People who get ripped out of ancient barrows using goddess-blessed elemental magic get to take a break."

"You need to rest too," I say, but I don't protest when she pushes my shoulders down.

"I have something else to do," Fritzi says, giving me a wink as she loops her arm in Alois's to go for a "walk." I don't think Perchta is the only one matchmaking right now.

Cornelia shoots me a sardonic look. "Please don't ask me about him," she says in a low voice.

"I wasn't going to." I pause. "Actually, can I talk to you about the goddesses?"

The priestess straightens. "Of course."

Behind us, the rest of the watch gives us space, as much privacy as we can afford in a camp. I have no idea where Alois and Fritzi have gone.

I glance at the fire. I feel foolish, but I still lean close to the flames and say, "Liesel, if you can hear us right now, please go away. I would like a private conversation."

Cornelia snickers. I have no idea if Liesel *is* actually in the flames, eavesdropping, but I decide to risk it anyway.

I pull out the golden crucifix I keep with me always. "This was my father's," I tell Cornelia.

"Ah," she says, clearly unsure of what else to say.

"I hate him," I say. Her eyes widen, but she doesn't interrupt. "I hate him, currently, still, even though he's dead, and the only comfort I have when I think of him is that he burns in hell." I look down at the gold, warm from my skin. "I have hated him ever since he accused my stepmother of witchcraft and had her burned alive for it. But even though he did it in the name of our God, I did not hate God."

Silence lingers, broken by popping embers. Eventually, Cornelia says, "Do you hate your god now?"

I frown at the crucifix. *Can you hate someone you're no longer sure is real?* Those are the words I cannot quite voice.

"You see your goddesses," I say instead. "*I* have seen your goddesses. At least Holda. And I know Liesel speaks to Abnoba, and I know Fritzi just walked away from a meeting with Perchta. I cannot deny your goddesses exist."

Cornelia's eyes grow soft. "Do you worry that because our goddesses are real, your god may not be?"

I cannot look away from the crucifix. I cannot stop biting my lip, even when it hurts.

Cornelia puts a hand over mine. "Do you know why the goddesses gave us the three stones, warrior?"

I nod. I was in the library when she, Philomena, and Rochus spoke about how the stones are protective, a means to remove magic from our world if it becomes too dangerous.

"They gave us the stones because they wanted to give us a *choice*," Cornelia says, emphasizing the last word when I raise my eyes to hers. "The way I see it, it's impossible to have a choice without options. What use is the gift of magic if it was forced upon us? We chose magic, and we chose the goddesses, and we choose now to fight to continue protecting both."

My jaw is still too tight to speak. Cornelia's smile is sympathetic and full of understanding. She and Fritzi aren't too far apart in age, but there's a deep wisdom to the priestess that I think may come from her different connection to Holda. The goddess chose Fritzi to fight for her, but she chose Cornelia to speak for her.

"Otto," Cornelia says, "I must confess that I don't know terribly much about your religion. But I have read some of the book you worship with."

"The Bible?" I ask.

She nods. "In the beginning, wasn't the whole story of an apple really about choice?"

I suck in a breath, my fingers clenching around the crucifix. The very first story of the Bible, the story of the Garden of Eden, revolved around Adam and Eve's choice to take the apple from the Tree of Life. God could have removed the tree, surely. He could have made Adam and Eve never fall for the temptation. If God is all-powerful, as the priests say, He could have made it so that Adam and Eve simply never had a choice.

But He didn't.

The *point* of the first story of the Bible is that he gave humanity a *choice*.

"Not every witch can hear the goddesses," Cornelia goes on, turning back to the fire. "I counsel some who are upset about it. I recognize that it's not exactly fair for me to be so certain in my beliefs when I have proof of Holda's voice. But at the same time, I envy you, Otto Ernst."

"Me?" I ask, surprised.

"In a way, all of the gods have given us the gift of choice. Except for those of us who've had godliness thrust upon us. I will never know if my faith could ever be as strong as yours, because I have never had to decide whether or not to have faith."

She reaches over and touches the golden crucifix in my palm. "Do you *want* to believe in your god?"

Emotion wells in my throat. *I do.* My rage sustained me through the loss of my mother, the years infiltrating the hexenjägers, the horrors I witnessed. But my faith gave me purpose. My faith gave me peace.

My faith enabled me to act, rather than to burn.

"For what it's worth," Cornelia adds, smiling when she sees my face, "Holda doesn't care who you believe in, or why. She's judged you worthy based on you as a person, not your faith. And the fact that your god's not brought down lightning upon us makes me inclined to believe he finds your actions worthy as well."

"He's not Zeus," I mutter. "I don't think lightning is used as a deterrent."

She shrugs, laughing. "Either way, I'm just glad you wanted to discuss religion instead of..." She doesn't say his name, but red stains her cheeks again.

"Well, if we're talking about choices, I *do* think you could make a worse one than him," I start, prepared to fully lift my fellow guardsman up in the priestess's esteem. "He jokes, but he has a good heart. And he's always the first to fight—not because he's vicious, but because he cares so much about protecting..." My voice trails off as Fritzi and Alois return from the nearby grove. "What on Earth happened to you two?"

They are both absolutely *filthy* in mud, head-to-toe.

Fritzi shoves Alois. "It was *his* fault."

"Was not!" Alois says. "I was *trying* to forage some mushrooms, and—"

"And they were *poisonous*, and this idiot was about to just pop them in his mouth!" Fritzi interjects.

"Yeah, and instead of *telling* me not to, you rammed me so hard—"

"Well, I didn't expect you to just fall over like a startled goat!"

Cornelia, who'd been trying to suppress her laughter, snorts loudly.

Alois's argument stutters and dies on his tongue, and he starts to wipe away some of the mud. Which only smears it more.

Standing, Cornelia offers her hand to him. "Come on," she says, "I can help get you cleaned up."

Alois seems both terrified and excited as he follows her.

I tell Fritzi to wait for me and grab my pack. "There has to be a stream somewhere nearby," I say. No civilization would build an important city like this plateau once was without a source of water. After telling Brigitta we won't go far, I lead Fritzi back into the trees while Cornelia hands Alois a cloth to clean his face.

We wander but are careful to keep the camp in mind, and we don't go too far when we reach a well, stones encircling a hole in the ground with a rotted wooden roof. Whatever bucket had been attached to the crossbeam is long gone, but I lower a wooden tankard from my pack into the abyss with my own rope, and the water we pull up is fresh and clear.

I'm not sure if it's pure enough to drink, but we could at least wash—we both desperately need to clean up. Fritzi quickly takes out the braids that held back her hair, kicks off her boots, and starts to unlace her kirtle, loosening the ties without removing it. It's too chilly for a full bath, but she intends to wash her hair and clean off the streaks of mud at least. The pendant Cornelia gave her swings out, dangling off the silver chain.

She catches me staring at it.

"Is it working?" I ask.

Fritzi shrugs. "I've not... I don't think he's been..." She taps her head. "But maybe he just learned to be quieter about it."

The worry that lines her face fills me with rage. The fact that even when he's not *here* he can still torture her...

But I know she doesn't want to dwell on that. Not now.

"This bath from a well is not exactly the same as baths in *the* Well," I say, tugging the rope back up. I would give a lot for the warm spring water pools among the trees, scented oils and soaps foaming over her body...

"I don't care," Fritzi says. She grabs the tankard, flips her hair over, and dumps it down the back of her head, cold water streaming over her scalp.

"I wish we had soap," she mutters, tossing the tankard back into the well. The cold is already catching up with her, and she squeezes the water out of her hair.

I hand her the rope. Much as I would like to just bring up more water and aid her in an impromptu forest bath, I am feeling the ache and grime of the day as much as her, and soap would, actually, be nice.

I root around in my pack, pulling out a spare tunic for myself and another for Fritzi so she can wrap it around her hair as a makeshift towel.

Something hard pokes my finger. I grab the thing and pull it out.

"What's that?" Fritzi calls as she pulls up more water from the well. "Soap?"

"No." I hold the wooden carving in my hand. "This is..." My voice trails off in wonder.

This is the horse carving I made for Liesel when Fritzi and I first saved her from Dieter, escaping Trier and hiding in the woods. I'd carved the little toy to comfort her, to distract her from the torture she had endured.

It's been worn away—the evergreen needles I'd used for a tail are long gone, and the wood is smoother now than my knife had made it. I hadn't known Liesel kept the carving all this time, but from the looks of it, she not only kept it, she treasured it. It's a little dirty, but that's from her fingers rubbing the wood.

Fritzi comes over, shivering. "Oh," she says, looking down at the carving in my hand. "The dog you made for Liesel."

"Dog?" I gape at her. "It's not a dog!"

"Pig?" she guesses.

"It's a *horse*!" I say. "A noble steed!"

Fritzi snorts. "Trot it back into your bag to find some soap and let's get some of that mud off you."

I tuck the little carving back into my pack and then finally find the soap. I'm far dirtier than her, even with the mud bath she and Alois apparently had. I pull off my tunic as I kneel before Fritzi, and she washes my dirt-encrusted hair for me, chills going down my spine with every pull of fresh water from the dark well. With soap streaming over me, I almost don't hear her when she speaks.

"It's because she loves you."

I look up, risking the soap bubbles in my eyes.

"Liesel," Fritzi says. She blinks rapidly. "It's because she loves you. She hates admitting it, because everyone she loves has been killed. But she loves you. And she wants—*needs*—you to come back."

Fritzi dumps more water on my head, clearing up the suds and not giving me a chance to answer her. I stand, grabbing her hands before she can busy herself with the task of helping me clean again.

"Liesel knows that what we're doing now…must be done," I say, looking in her eyes even as she tries to avoid my gaze.

"I know."

"And Liesel knows that you'll do anything to protect me, and I'll do anything to protect you."

"I know." Her voice is so small.

"And Liesel knows if anything happened— "

"I won't let anything happen to you!" she says, now almost shouting.

"—*if* anything happened, it wouldn't be your fault."

A tear falls down her cheek, so silent and small that I almost don't notice it.

"I…" She starts. Stops. Swallows. Tries again. "I saw the earth take you. And I tried, I tried, Otto, I tried to call up my magic and—"

"And I'd already bled you dry."

She shakes her head furiously. "You did what you had to!"

"We need practice. We need balance, so that we can both fight, together, not with one taking everything from the other."

"If only I could give you a little pocket of magic, all your own." She snorts bitterly, regretting a desire for the impossible. Her face falls, lips pressed tight. Then she adds, "I panicked. I didn't think, I didn't *try,* Otto, I just...I *felt.*"

I wait, unsure of what she means.

Fritzi looks up at me. "I felt sheer terror at losing you, and all I wanted was to rip the world apart and claim you again. And I happened to have the air stone in my hand when I felt that way. *That's* what tore the earth apart, that's what worked. What saved you. The stone. Not me."

I shake my head. "The stone is just a stone. It lay in that barrow for how many centuries, nothing more than a rock. *You* saved me."

"But—"

I press my lips against hers, silencing the doubt on her tongue, wishing I could silence the doubt in her heart.

When we pull away, I can see that old guilt weighing on Fritzi, tugging her shoulders, her soul, down. She let Dieter back into her village, and even though it was him, not her, who slaughtered nearly everyone in her coven, she blames herself. Even though I came to this mission willingly, if anything happens to me, she will blame herself.

Every choice she's made has been to survive.

But that won't stop her from drowning in guilt if I don't.

I tap her chin, gently asking her to look up at me. When she does, I see her eyes are red-rimmed.

"I'm the Catholic, not you."

"You don't have a monopoly on guilt."

"It's not your fault," I whisper. *None of it.*

"I know." Her voice cracks. "But..."

What I want to do next will be.

It's her voice, but it's in my mind. Fighting with her made me more in tune with her thoughts, and this one is especially present.

"What are you planning?" I ask. Shivering, I grab my shirt and pull it over my head. At least I'm a little cleaner now.

"Nothing!" Her eyes go wide, fearful—not of me, I think, but of herself.

"Nothing...yet?" I guess.

Her gaze slides away. "I don't know. Things...are not right. I don't know what the right thing to do is anymore."

"What are the options?" I ask. This is magic, and I don't understand the varied paths it may take. I only know that no matter what, I will be by her side.

"The Origin Tree acts like a dam, ensuring that only so much magic is released into the world, accessed exclusively by the witches who prove their intent with the spells and rituals..." Her voice trails off, and I can tell these thoughts have been swirling inside her for a while. "And what Dieter wants to do is *wrong*, I know that, I *believe* that."

Destroying all the safeguards in place and flooding the world with power in a vain attempt to seize it all for himself.

"But...we can't keep living under the traditional way of doing magic. It isn't enough anymore," Fritzi says, her voice so small I barely catch her words.

"The others speak of wild magic as if it's evil," I tell her. "But you use wild magic, and it's not evil."

"I know."

"Magic is power," I continue. I *felt* that power, filling my muscles, giving me the strength to fight the statues. To *protect* the person I love. "How you use that power is what makes a thing good or evil. Not the power itself."

"Are you sure of that?" Fritzi asks. Her eyes are beseeching, and I can see the war happening in her mind, the questions she barely has the courage to ask while we're alone.

"No," I tell her truthfully. I am not a witch. I do not understand her world, even when I live in it. "But," I add, and hope fills her face, "I believe in you."

She leans her body against mine, her head over my tattoo, listening, I think, for my heartbeat. I want to wrap my arms around her, I want to show her my love, but I also know that the reason why she's letting me support her weight right now is because she is still exhausted from being so drained of magic, and it is my fault. So, instead of pulling her into an embrace, instead of tilting her chin up so I can claim her kisses and calm her mind, I hold her shoulders and push her gently back.

"Can you teach me?" I ask her.

"Teach you what?"

"How to use your magic without draining you. I am your warrior, but I'd rather fight beside you instead of in front of you."

What we don't say is that facing goddess-sent monsters will be nothing against facing Fritzi's brother, and we are not ready for that battle.

"I don't really know how to teach you about magic," Fritzi says in a low, worried voice. "But I can at least show you how I do it."

Fritzi pulls me to a tree near the well, and we sit under its branches, tightly closed buds and new leaves unfurling above us, speckling the light with shadow. The oval leaves are slightly pointed, still small, but I'm pretty sure this is a fruit tree. Perhaps some wanderer tossed an apple core after finishing a snack, and, since this area isn't populated, a tree grew from the seeds, far too close to the well.

We sit so that we face each other, legs crossed, hands open in our laps. I have seen monks pray like this—not the kneeled prayers before the altar, but the quiet personal prayers during a pause in gardening or at the beginning of the day before duty calls, or when alone.

"Magic is like the trees," Fritzi tells me, and I smile, because of course she would use a plant to explain a part of herself. "It takes time to grow new leaves."

"You don't have to show me now," I say quickly. We haven't even slept since escaping the barrow; I shouldn't have brought it up. I asked too much of her then, and I'm asking too much now, and—

She slips her cool fingers through mine and waits for me to meet her eyes before she smiles. "I have enough for this. They call the coven in the Black Forest the Well, but there is a well inside of me, one that is tapped into magic. It refills slower than I'd like, but it does refill."

A well. I feel as if I have one, too, one that I never realized was empty until it was filled with her magic.

Before, during the battle with the soldiers, I reached out for Fritzi's magic subconsciously, and she offered it to me. Now, I close my eyes, and I can feel, somehow, the gentle tapping of *something* inside of me.

It has the same rhythm as my heartbeat.

Rather than grabbing for it, I just...open the door.

Warmth blooms in my chest. I focus on the feeling of it. On cold mornings in Trier, when I worked undercover, I would sometimes gulp strong whiskey for warmth, the burn forcing my body awake. This is like that, but without the sour acid in my throat, without the fire in my lungs. It's all power, all warmth, and no burn.

"You feel it?" she asks softly.

I nod, my eyes still closed.

I breathe in, and when I breathe out, the magic seeps into all of my body, just for a moment, every nerve tingling.

When I open my eyes, the tree above me is heavy with shining red apples.

INTERLUDE

DIETER

I have been waiting so patiently.

Watching only.

See, sister, I can play it *safe* too.

The charm she has now obscures what I could once see so easily. Rude. My sister and I are bonded. She should never hide from me. But no matter what I have done lately, I cannot pinpoint her exact location. I cannot grasp her magic fully. It flutters from my hands like a little bird before I have a chance to pop its head off.

Glimmers. I have seen only flashes of her magic, like lightning in a storm.

That light has been fading.

Her well of magic is so very low right now.

She emptied herself for him.

She emptied herself for *me.*

22

FRITZI

Otto and I both stare up at the fruit he grew. And there is no explaining it away as any other cause, not in early spring like this, not when the tree was bare only moments ago.

"I, um—" I blink, swallow, and manage to drag my eyes to Otto's.

His face is split in a wide smile. "Do I have easier access to plants because of you? Your affinity transfers over into me?"

My lips part. He waits, patient, expecting answers.

"Otto," I say, voice cracking. "I have no idea how any of this works. I don't know how you did—" I jut my chin at the tree. "I barely know how *I* use wild magic, let alone the rules of what is easier for me or you, and how affinity affects it, and—"

"All right." Otto squeezes my hand, his wonder leveling to that steady, resilient surety. Even when I'm floundering and panicked, he believes I'll find the way. How does he trust me so inherently? How can he follow me so unflinchingly when I'm sitting here, admitting to having no answers, to just making this up as I go?

The same way I trust him. An unexplainable thing. A tether that goes beyond the bonding magic, to something innate and foolish and founded in love.

"We don't have to know," Otto continues, his lips lifting on one side, a smile. "Just walk me through what you've been doing when you use wild magic. Maybe it'll work the same for me."

"Well, what did you do to make those?" I look up at the apples again.

Otto follows my gaze. "I was thinking about blooming. Warmth. The Well, and a well inside me, filling. I wasn't necessarily thinking about apples."

I shrug. "When I've used wild magic, I don't always have a direct intention. It's more unconscious, or a demand in the moment. Like the wall of water I used to protect us against Dieter's soldiers in the aqueducts—I'd just wanted protection for us. So maybe controlling wild magic has to do with controlling our intentions beyond thought. We have to control our instincts, those initial kicks of will before they become full seeds."

Otto's jaw sets. "In the heat of battle, that could be difficult."

Holda? I try on instinct. I don't know if our connection is reestablished, being outside of Perchta's tomb, or if the Mother goddess's lingering magic will interfere still—

I am here, she says after a pause. She sounds exhausted. Stretched thin.

I am her champion, yes, but just in the dip of her words, I feel how many other responsibilities she has, and how perilous so many of those things must be. Other witches praying to her. Other souls depending on her.

Never mind, I tell her.

There's another pause. *I will always be here for you, Friederike. You have questions about how best to use the bond between you and Otto. I can—*

No. We can figure it out. What has you so overwhelmed? Other than... everything.

She laughs. I don't think I've ever heard her *laugh* before. It's dry, though, humorless.

Too many things happen that I cannot see, she says. *So my sisters and I attempt to prepare for as many likelihoods as possible.*

They are on your side now? Perchta seemed amenable.

They were never not on my side, Holda says. *They merely forgot where true dangers come from.*

I peel away from my connection with her. Otto and I can explore this bond on our own.

I bite my lip, brow furrowed, and when Otto looks at me again, he frowns.

"What's that look?"

I stand, brushing stray bits of grass from my skirt. We're a ways from the main camp, but the flicker of the orange bonfire can be seen through a few trees, far enough that if we needed to call for help, they would hear.

"I want to try something."

He climbs to his feet and nods me along.

My internal well of magic is still nearly empty. A cavernous, echoing space with a small trickle of magic burbling in. It will continue to fill, but slowly, and what happens if I scrape it dry?

I shake out my hands. "I only have enough magic to do this once for now. Maybe twice."

Otto's frown of interest deepens. "I'm not going to drain you even more. We can practice later—"

"Later when?" I don't mean the bite in my voice. But anxiety tightens my stomach, forces fear past my exhaustion and bruises.

After a beat, Otto concedes, sucking his teeth.

We don't have *later*.

"Eyes closed," I tell him. "Arms up. Fighting stance."

He obeys.

"I'm going to come at you a few times," I say. "One of those times, I'm not going to hold back. I won't tell you which one, but I want you to only draw on magic to truly defend against me once. Your choice which attack it is. Keep your eyes shut."

He settles deeper into a fighting stance. This way, he'll have to be more intentional about how he uses my magic, not merely drawing on it in a continuous stream. It's the best training exercise I can come up with at the moment.

"Ready," he tells me. "Go."

I scoff.

Otto cracks open an eye at me.

"When have you ever been in charge, jäger?"

He smiles. Scheisse, it's nice to see. Will never not be nice to see, the way his lips lift and his eyes glisten.

"My apologies," he says. He closes his eyes again and holds, silent now, but his cheeks are pink, and his lips are still crooked.

I come at him, a punch that barrels through the air. He senses it and ducks, but I'm hardly going for true power with that one. I swing to the other side, throw another punch; he rolls away smoothly.

We continue like that, easy punches coming and going, until I can see his humor fade, his focus sharpen.

The grip he has on my magic tugs. Not him drawing on it yet, just him becoming aware of it in the fight, that he *could* draw on it.

I aim a kick at his thigh and barely brush the fabric of his trousers before rearing back and slamming my fist into the center of his chest, the only true blow I've thrown. It connects, and Otto stumbles back a beat before he reacts, too late to stop me, and I hear the wind go out of him as he grabs at my magic and *pulls*.

Three things happen at once.

Otto realizes he drew too hard, and his eyes fly open with a cry of "Fritzi, I'm sorry—"

I stagger toward him, knocked off course by the absence of magic in my body. Not drained completely, but down to barest dregs, specks only, the incoming trickle mocking, almost, in the way it slows down.

And then a voice.

A caress at the edge of my mind, coiling fingers that brush the brink of my thoughts and lean in close and purr, *Hallo again, Fritzichen. Let down your defenses, did you?*

I rear back, back, trying to get away from the voice, white-hot panic lancing sweat across my body as I stumble to the ground and grab my head. I think Otto says something, the rumble of his voice like thunder in the distance, but I'm all internal now, scrambling through my reserves, so low, *so low*; why did I let myself get so low? I knew I had less magic after the tomb, I knew I was weaker, but I had Cornelia's pendant, and Dieter hadn't been able to get in my head in so long—

Holda! Holda—

But even that connection is brittle. Not enough magic. Not enough strength.

Dieter doesn't speak again. But I can *feel* him here, poking and stretching in my mind, in my body, like a drop of ink spooling out in clear water, tainting everything gray and sickly. I scratch at what little magic I have left and throw it into shielding myself from him, but he's everywhere, there and gone again, I can't chase him, can't catch him.

Leave. I pour all of my will into that one word. *Leave, leave, please leave—*

Shh, Fritzichen, he murmurs. *Just relax.*

I want to fight back. I don't *want* to sleep, not with him *here*, but I'm so tired...so very tired...

My teeth clack against each other, hard.

Coppery blood swims in my mouth, and I spit it out, gagging, and it's only then that I realize Otto is shaking me.

I open my eyes blearily, and he stops, just holding my shoulders, his body wound to spring into action, but what action? Why? What—

Behind him, faces bent in the same look of withheld action and concern, are Brigitta, Alois, and Cornelia.

"What...happened?" I ask, wincing. My tongue is sore; I've bitten it, hard, and while I think the bleeding has stopped, it's swollen.

I ease back from Otto to sit on my own. My chest and shoulder are on fire. I'd loosened my kirtle before to wash, but it's all the way unlaced now.

"Is he gone?" Otto asks urgently.

"I...think so," I say. I hate the whimper that comes, but I hear and feel it and that jolt of sensation stretches out, sending tendrils that shake and twitch across my limbs. I take a breath, but the shaking continues, vibrations that don't stop. I'm cold, that's it; I must be cold.

I reach for the pendant Cornelia gave me. It hangs from the leather string around my neck, but it's thrown to the side, resting on my shoulder.

I'd let my magic get too low. Her protection wasn't enough.

The thought comes to me as innocuously as if I'd thought, *There is rain coming, and I do not have a cloak.* Absent. Unbothered.

Holda? I try.

I do not get a response in words, not this time. I see an image of towering trees and protective plants in a barrier around my mind, the way she tried to fend Dieter off when he overtook me in the council's library. She is fighting to protect me from him. Fighting though I can feel her exhaustion still, ripples of trying to defend against too many things at once.

My teeth chatter.

The cloth of my chemise sticks to my skin.

"Why am I w-wet?" I ask, shaking, shaking. "F-from washing?"

"Liebste." It's out of Otto in a punch of horror, and I note the white pallor to his face.

Cornelia crouches next to me, reaches one hand out, and I brace for her touch, only realizing when she withdraws that I didn't brace, I *flinched*.

"I'm sorry," Otto says, talking fast, panicking. "I'm so sorry, I didn't know how to stop him."

I can't seem to focus. "I know." I blink slowly. "You can't. You don't have m-magic."

No, that's not right. He has my magic. *I* didn't have enough magic.

What is wrong with me? Is Dieter still in my mind? No, that's not it. I almost laugh. I stifle it, but it comes anyway, a high, crooning giggle that makes Otto's already sunken face break even more. Brigitta shares a look with Alois. Cornelia puts a hand to her mouth; her eyes are tearing.

The shaking continues. Muscles cramping, releasing. My head is pounding, and everything's so foggy. Not just my eyes, but all my senses. As if I had been away for a long while, and my body is a neglected house. The fires are cold; there is dust in the corners, cobwebs in the ceiling.

"I had some of your magic, still," Otto whispers. "In my—well? In my body, at least. I sent it back to you. It made you stop enough for Alois and Brigitta to pull you off of me. Then you collapsed."

Pull me off of him?

There are bruises blossoming on his skin, green and purple. Claw marks cover his face and arms, the scratches deep.

A hand lifts in front of my face. My own. I'm holding it up, and I study the nail beds, ragged and caked with dried blood under the torn edges.

"Did I do that to you?" My stomach churns, bile rising, tart against the iron tang of blood still in my mouth.

Cornelia shakes her head. "Only when Otto tried to stop you."

So, yes, then.

His eyes drift down.

My chemise is wet. Right. I'd almost forgotten.

That fog of absence lets me look down at myself.

The wetness isn't from the well water. It's blood. Mine.

I try to peel away my clothes, hissing as the cloth sticks to open wounds. Scraggly lines are crusty with drying blood.

Otto already has a tankard of water out. He twists in front of me with a spare cloth and gently dabs at the cuts.

It's not random.

This wound is a mirror of Otto's tattoo, same shape, same spot. Only there was something on my chest in that spot already, one of the scars my brother gave me, the ones that allowed him access to my magic, to *me*.

He used my fingernails to claw the shape of a tree into it, gouging the scar tissue to make branches that spread up my clavicle, roots cut down into the top of my breast, the skin puffy.

My eyes sting. It takes me a moment to realize it's from tears.

I hold a hand up to one of the branches cut into my body. I can see where my own curved fingernail fits into the red line on my skin.

I did this.

He did this.

It was his actions, but my body.

I am so sorry, Friederike, Holda says, her voice thin. *I should have guarded you more thoroughly. I should not have trusted others to hold against his determination.*

But she can't surround me in her magic all the time. Not with Dieter doing who knows what, and all the magical preparations she should be making to counter that—she can't, *shouldn't*, have to protect me all the time. I should be able to defend myself.

I did this. I dropped my power too low. It was foolish.

Cornelia reaches forward again, tears tracking down her cheeks, but she sniffs, hard, and squares her shoulders as she touches the pendant hanging across my shoulder. "I'll redo the spell," she tells me. "I should have redone it earlier, maybe. I...I'll recast a protection spell every morning from now on—"

There's that noise again, that high-pitched crooning of my manic giggle, and I can't stop it. It comes and comes and I'm shaking so hard the world around me starts to sway.

"Liebste," Otto says. "Can I hold you?"

I nod. *Yes*, and I send it across the bond, I think I do, I'm dissolving beneath these vibrations, this laughter, why can't I stop? It's not funny. None of this is funny. *Why can't I stop laughing?*

Arms come around me. Pull me gently into the cage of his arms, and I wince when the wound on my chest gets jostled.

"I w-was careless," I try. Maybe speaking will help. Maybe I just need to talk. "I sh-shouldn't have let my ma-magic get so low."

Otto smooths his hand up and down my back. "I knew you were low on magic. I shouldn't have—" His hand clamps on my elbow.

"When we get back to the W-well," I manage, "I'll ha-have Rochus and Philomena train us. Or s-someone. Anyone. We can't keep—"

"We can help," Brigitta offers. I've never heard her voice so still. So...empty. "We should have been helping all along. We can put you through training exercises. I can devise ways to test your limits. We'll figure this out."

I nod. Nod again. I can't stop, and that weird, grating laughter carries on in my throat.

"Shh." Otto holds me tighter and I let him, burrowing into his arms and his wide chest. His presence pushes down on my shaking and fear and responsibilities until I let loose one more giggle, and it shatters into a sob.

"I'm here, Liebste, I'm here," he says, because I'm falling apart against him, body shaking now with heaving sobs that come from the very pit of my stomach, making me gag.

I think I talk again. I think I beg him for something, but I don't even know what. I just know I'm exhausted. Physically. Mentally. Brigitta offered to help; Cornelia will cast protection spells; I'm not alone, but I'm so tired, tired of being afraid, tired of fighting, tired of bearing all these burdens and knowing Otto bears them too. And I'm tired of my body, so very, disgustingly tired of *feeling* my body, of wounds hurting and reminding me of Dieter, of the way I can't escape the pain he's left behind. I'm in a cage in this body, and *he* made it that way. I have no idea how to cleanse him out of me. I have no idea how to make this my home again, and he keeps invading it.

"You're still you, Fritzi," Otto says into my hair. How much of that did I say out loud? My sobs slow, body empty of magic and emotion. "You're still you. And I'm yours, too, and I'll do everything I can to bring you back to yourself. You're here now. You're here, Fritzi, and I love you."

He keeps saying that. *You're here, and I love you.*

I suck in a breath. My first full one in who knows how long.

"I love you, too," I say back to him, and it's weak and trembling, and my throat is cracked from sobbing, but he sighs like it's the most beautiful thing he's ever heard.

We're only about a day and a half from Baden-Baden and the Well, but night is falling fast, and we—or at least, Otto, Cornelia, Alois, and I—are exhausted. Brigitta seems torn between wanting to let me rest and wanting to get both the air stone and me back to the Well and under protection as soon as possible. As Brigitta argues with Otto over whether we should risk travel right now, I sit next to the fire.

Cornelia helped me wrap the wound as best we could, but my chemise is stained with blood, and I look like a horror creature, red-drenched and disheveled.

We should leave, exhaustion be damned. Dieter could attack any moment. He could be close; maybe that was why he was able to slip in so easily. He's nearby, stalking, waiting.

He *should be* here already; if he left Trier before we did, even traveling with a large group of hexenjägers, he should have gotten here. Did he not figure out where this stone was? Did he go someplace else? Was Perchta able to keep him away?

Or is he waiting to intercept us near the Well, knowing we'd find the stone, hoping we'll bring it to him, just as he'd hoped to control me into bringing him the earth stone from the Well? Was that his attempt at manipulating me into doing his bidding again?

Cornelia sits next to me, close enough to share body heat.

We shouldn't go back to the Well, I want to say. It's what Dieter wants, for the stones to be with the Tree so he can destroy it. We should run, as far as possible. Brigitta should take the air stone and disappear.

Wait—that's what she's saying to Otto. "...leave and hide so no one knows where it is."

"What if Dieter can track you?" Otto asks. "What then? We wanted to bring the stones to the Well to protect them from him. The Well is still the best place to defend against him, isn't it?"

"We risk him laying an ambush in Baden-Baden or somewhere else nearby upon our return," Brigitta says. "I don't like it. I don't—"

"The earth stone is in the Well. Between that and the air stone, and the defenses already in place, the Well is the safest spot for Fritz—for the stones," Otto corrects.

I wince.

Of course he's thinking about me. How to protect me.

Cornelia is listening too. Everyone is, except maybe Alois, who is lying back with his head pillowed on his arms, eyes shut. He can't be asleep, despite the lines of exhaustion on his face.

As Brigitta and Otto continue to argue, Cornelia leans closer to me. I feel the weight of unspoken words before she says anything, and when she does, it takes my brain a moment to catch up to what she's chosen to say.

"Why did you not tell me you've been using wild magic?"

She saw me use wild magic in the barrow.

I'm grateful, in a way, that she asked me about this now, when I am too wrung out to feel anything like guilt or shame or fear.

"It should not be hard to guess," I say. "Priestess."

Cornelia flinches, mildly hurt, but she nods.

After a beat of silence, she sighs. "You haven't made a single comment about what else happened in the tomb."

The oddity makes me look at her.

"About Alois and I being...*chosen*. Fated." She pulls a face, but blushes. "You said it was the reason we were chosen, but am I truly to believe you have no opinion on that matter?"

I stare at her for another long moment, then feel myself slowly, gradually smile. It's small and trembling, but it's a gulp of fresh air between surges of briny waves.

Cornelia's answering grin of relief tells me she'd hoped I'd respond like this. Distracted. Uplifted.

Even for a moment.

"Oh," I say, and rub at my eyes. "I assumed you were too busy planning your elaborate bonding ceremony. I was going to tease you later."

"Arschloch," she says, but her voice is all fondness.

We listen to Brigitta and Otto talk, their voices softer now, and I don't know what they've decided.

Cornelia looks away. I want her to keep talking. For us to pick at each other, for something to be simple.

"Do you want it? To be bonded with him."

She gives me a flat look. "Oh yes, do allow me to unload my troubles on you." Her eyes go intently to my blood-soaked clothes.

I catch her wrist in my hand as her face falls. "Yes. Please." I'm begging. I don't care.

She bites her lip. Studies me for a beat.

Then she rolls her eyes. "Your bonded spoke with me about his god a bit ago. About choices." She sighs. "I didn't choose to be a priestess, you know."

My brows pull inward and I flick a look at Otto before refocusing on Cornelia. In the orange firelight, I see her eyes go glassy.

"My mother was the priestess before me. She died, and I had been trained to take up her mantle, and so I became it. And I'm *good* at it, aren't I?"

"I think so. Though I am biased, given that you are the only priestess I can truly stand."

Her lips crack in a smile, but her eyes are still sheened with emotion. "I don't truly know what I would have chosen if I wouldn't have done this, and it isn't as though I don't *enjoy* what I do. But what could I have been if I hadn't been pushed into this destiny?"

Her words are such an echo of the thoughts I'd had with Perchta that a shiver rushes over me, keeps me silent.

Do we all fear the same things? Do we all hope for the same release? To make our own choices. To be *free*.

Cornelia shrugs again and wipes the back of her hand on her cheek. "So then, to learn I could be destined to bond with Alois—"

"It isn't destiny," I say. "It's a choice."

"You know as well as I that Philomena and Rochus would not see it that way. The whole of the Well will hear of what happened and think that this means Perchta has *destined* Alois and me to be together. Which... sours it, if I'm being honest. Don't we have a choice in the matter? What if we don't want this?"

"You do want him." I stop. Frown. "Don't you?"

She bites her lip. "But is that only because we were fated to this? Is that only because we were set on this course by the goddesses?"

"You are a priestess—shouldn't this be comforting to you?"

Cornelia huffs a little, rolls her eyes at herself. "It should be. Shouldn't it? And yet, I can't help but wish that we were all on more equal footing. That the goddesses had less control over our paths than we have given them."

"Careful, Nelly," I say, half light, half quaking. "You're awfully close to blasphemy."

"If I were a Catholic, maybe." She nods at Otto, who has convinced

Brigitta to stay, and is now kneeling across the fire from us, talking into it, trying to contact Liesel. "Despite what Rochus and Philomena think, I believe in asking questions. And I'm wondering now what our world would look like if—ugh, I'm not sure what I'm asking. I just hate the idea that anything that might come from Alois and me could be because of an outside force, not because we both *want* it."

"Witch and warrior," I whisper absently. "It's one of the best ways to protect our people. One of our greatest defenses."

Cornelia grunts softly in her throat. "I should be honored then, to be so used." She flinches, looks at me. "I didn't mean—"

I wave it off. "I know what you mean. But it is yet another rule the goddesses imposed on us. You're right to question it. What if we didn't need bonded pairs? What if we could do so, but only if we *chose* to, not because we needed it? What if magic was that for everyone—not something accessed through rituals or only because of our bloodline, but because you simply *chose* to use it?"

"Wild magic," Cornelia whispers.

My instinct is still to deny it. But I force myself to nod.

There are limitations, of course. Wild magic is far from perfect. Only so much can be stored in one body, and when it's low, refilling it is a long process.

I trace the edge of the bandage around my chest. But I'm breathless, suddenly. All the thoughts that have been clogging up my head are too close to fitting together, to spilling out, and Cornelia looks at me strangely.

"I had not thought that big," she says softly. "But...we have gotten this stone to keep it safe from Dieter. Haven't we? Not for any other purpose?"

I pull my knees tighter to my chest, my wound burning. My body remembers the feel of shaking uncontrollably and I shudder in the echo of those vibrations. "Of course."

"Of course." She hums again. Jostles me again. "It is a miracle of miracles that the Mother let you out of the tomb alive, Friederike Kirch."

She has no idea how right she is.

But Perchta did let me out. Even knowing all these thoughts thundering around in my brain.

So maybe it *is* time for a change.

Maybe, against all odds, even the ones I put against myself, I'm meant to bring it about.

Brigitta claps. "There you are!"

The fire heaves just as Brigitta rocks back onto her heels, and it isn't Liesel's face that appears, but Hilde, facing away from us, toward Brigitta.

"Brigitta!" Hilde says. "We've had no news since—"

A tussle, then Liesel's face takes over, and Hilde lets out a sharp chirp.

"You could *ask*, little one!" Hilde says, her voice farther away.

"It's *my* spell—you said hello to her, swoon swoon, now updates, please. Everything's fine here. Where's Fritzi? Otto?"

The fire shifts, then Liesel's face turns to me.

She beams.

Until her eyes drop to my chest, and I can't cover the bandage quickly enough.

But I realize—I *shouldn't* cover it. Even if I could. Liesel is young, yes; we want to keep her safe, of course; but we are long past the time when being kept safe meant lying or withholding information. From her or each other.

"What happened?" Liesel demands.

I look at Brigitta. Otto, standing off to the side. Alois, awake now, and Cornelia, leaning close to me.

My arms start shaking, and I feel that manic force want to bubble up again, but is it a sob, is it a laugh? Whatever it is, it is an unraveling, and it chokes me.

I don't want to talk about it. I don't want to *remember* what I did to myself, to Otto, that Dieter was inside of my head *again.*

But I think of the way Liesel told the council what had happened to us, how she reframed our trauma into an epic tale of bravery and poetic words.

If she can speak, so can I.

"Let Hilde listen in, Liesel," I tell her, eyes tearing. "Something's happened. A few things, actually."

23

OTTO

We travel fast, pushing the horses hard. Glauberg put us east of the Roman Limes, and we have to travel south to get back to the Black Forest and the Well. We cross the Main River outside of Frankfurt and the Neckar River at Heidelberg, keeping the Rhine to our right as we race our horses through the narrow stretches of land between the mountains and the rivers, avoiding settlements when we can.

I keep my horse a pace behind Fritzi's, my eyes on her body, tracking the way she sways on her mount, watching for any sign of her slipping. I call for a halt before anyone else notices the grip on Fritzi's reins loosening; I demand rest before she needs to ask for it, and when Brigitta urges us to drive through, I glare her into silence. It is urgent we get to the Well's protection, vital even, but I will not have Fritzi die of exhaustion to get there.

She knows, or at least can guess, my motivations when we pause a third time. The spires of the Spayer cathedral are just visible across the river, and we're not far from Baden-Baden.

"We can keep going," Fritzi insists.

"No, our horses need—"

"I can keep going," she adds quietly. My brow furrows, but I know better than to argue with her. I raise my arm, signaling to the others that we can continue. It's a mark of how worried we all are that no one, not even Alois, makes a comment as we get back up on our horses.

We don't stop until Baden-Baden. Brigitta, in front, slows us as we skirt the main town. A rider bursts out from one of the hills. I recognize her—a member of the Watch, one Brigitta must have instructed to patrol between the town and the Forest's borders, extending the duties of the guards outside the magical barriers that protect the Well.

"Any activity?" Brigitta demands.

The woman—her name is Lina, I recall—shakes her head. "There was the market in town, of course," she says. "Some merchants came from the north, but they moved on after market day."

Brigitta frowns. "What aren't you telling me?"

"Nothing," Lina says immediately. "Just..."

"Yes?" Brigitta's voice seethes with impatience.

"Folk have been...on edge. I suspect the townspeople in Baden-Baden have noticed our increased patrols. They seem..."

"Suspicious?" Cornelia asks.

Lina nods, but I can tell that's not the word she's looking for. "Philomena and Rochus have taken to the council room, seeking to enhance our warding spells beyond the borders of the forest. We've found an ally in Baden-Baden, and we want to protect them."

"What about the river?" Fritzi asks.

Lina blinks at her. "The river?"

"Has it been...odd? Flooding at all?"

The Rhine is far enough from Baden-Baden that it wouldn't

flood as easily as the Moselle flooded Trier, but there are smaller offshoots that snake through the landscape that could cause just as much damage.

Lina shrugs. "It was a little high a few days ago—"

Fritzi's body tenses, every muscle hard, her jaw clenched.

"—but it rained earlier. Nothing unusual."

Fritzi nods tightly, and, as we leave Lina on patrol and head toward the Forest, her body slowly starts to unwind again.

I know what she's thinking. Dieter has the water stone. He used it to flood the aqueducts in Trier. The air stone, which Fritzi gave to Cornelia for safekeeping, enabled her to rip me from the very earth and toss my body up even when she was otherwise drained of magic. These elemental stones grant *far* more power to a witch than even wild magic. If Dieter was going to lead an attack, he may try to use the powerful river against us. He *could* flood Baden-Baden. And there are smaller rivulets and streams and lakes throughout the Forest. He doesn't care who stands in his way, who he hurts.

I cast my mind back to the rivers we crossed to get here. I'm unfamiliar with those cities and whether the shoreline was higher than normal, but I can't recall any of the locals noting it. I shake my head, dispelling my thoughts. There's no reason to believe Dieter's been using the water stone along our journey or even here. *But if he is, he's smart enough to cover his tracks and keep his use hidden...*

Brigitta stops us again when we reach the magical barrier around the Well, the looming trees of the Black Forest swaying in the wind. She gestures to Cornelia. "If you wouldn't mind," she says as the priestess draws her horse closer.

Cornelia pulls a spell pouch from her belt, raising her arms and whispering words I can't hear. When she finally lowers her arms, she looks at

Brigitta, and then past her, straight to Fritzi. "It's safe," she says. "No one has broken the magic that protects the Well. No enemy has crossed our borders, just like Hilde and Liesel said."

Fritzi eyes the stream nearby. There are dozens of brooks and rivulets winding through the trees, pools of glacial water hidden by mossy banks, countless freshwater springs. Neither Dieter nor any jägers burst from them as we silently continue deeper into the Black Forest.

I didn't realize that there was even more tension wound up tight in Fritzi's body, but I see now how her shoulders drop away from her ears, how her spine relaxes just a fraction more.

As we pass through the final layers of protection and reenter the Well, I feel it too.

Relief.

A part of me wanted to plead with Fritzi to run away—anywhere. Flee to the frozen Siberia or board a ship to the New World or go south, to the Holy City and beyond—anywhere. But I know Dieter will always haunt her, always hunt her, and that there will never be anywhere in the world safer than the heart of the Black Forest, among the coven of witches who protect all magic.

When we reach the main village, members of the guard come for our horses, leading them away with a promise of buckets of cool water and fresh oats, and Hilde rushes out, giving me a quick hug before throwing herself at Brigitta for a longer reunion.

"Liesel's at the schoolhouse," Hilde tells Fritzi, noting her worried glance. "Would you like me to go fetch her?"

I know Fritzi wants to meet with her cousin right away, but she shakes her head. "We should deal with the stone first."

Cornelia comes closer. "Come with me. The council can—"

Fritzi's body tenses again, every muscle tight. "I've told you. I don't want to know where the stones are kept. I trust you, the council, the Watch. I can't ensure that my mind is safe from—"

"I know." Cornelia's voice is gentle but firm. "I will bring the stone to the council, and we will hide it. But I'm certain Rochus and Philomena would want to thank you first. After, we will take the stone and keep it from you..."

And Dieter, spying with Fritzi's eyes.

We head up to the trees, with Alois trailing behind us—not under Brigitta's orders, I presume, but to be closer to Cornelia. We bound over the wooden bridges connecting the village in the trees, and I drop back.

"So, when are you bonding with the priestess?" I ask, nudging Alois in the ribs.

"Shut it," he growls, frantically looking ahead, but Cornelia and Fritzi are deep in conversation and haven't noticed us.

"I had no idea you were so besotted," I say, letting my voice get a little louder. "I wonder what tattoo she'll give you..."

"Shut. Your. Mouth." Despite his words, a lovesick grin smears across his face.

"Maybe a jar of honey, since you're so sweet." I punch his bicep lightly. "Right here. Or perhaps the rune for pie? She could be your Schnucki, your little sweetie pie."

Alois shoves me, and I stumble, barely catching the railing and preventing myself from tumbling through the branches. "Sorry, Schnucki," he says sheepishly, and I can't help but laugh, noting the way his red hair blends with his red neck.

Alois darts ahead once he makes sure I'm all right, side-stepping around Fritzi and Cornelia to reach the council room doors first. I make a big show of sweeping my arms out, bowing like the most pretentious lord of a castle behind the women, and Alois rolls his eyes at me as he pushes the door open. Despite my teasing, he does make sure Cornelia and Fritzi step inside first, then pretends to shut the door in my face.

Inside, the hearth is cold, the only light barely filtering through the closed curtains over the windows.

"What's that smell?" Cornelia asks.

Something sharp and metallic.

Alois lights a tinder, sparking a torch to flame. I grab Fritzi's hand and jerk her close. She slides a little on the floor, wet with—

Blood.

The flickering torchlight bounces off pools of blood drying into a darkening, sticky puddle, leaking from the necks of Rochus and Philomena, lying across the floor. Their robes, caked with dried blood, are the only things that identify them as the priest and priestess of the council.

"Where are their heads?" Alois gasps as Cornelia lets out a choking sob.

Manic hysteria floods me, and I whirl around.

A thud and a wet, rolling sound, followed by another thud. Two heavy objects, skidding through the blood. Philomena's hair wraps around her face from the momentum of being tossed at our feet, but Rochus's beard catches on something, an uneven board or a nail, and the mouth cracks open, teeth sliding through the sticky blood, eyes rolling up at us before the head slides to a slow stop.

I raise my eyes as Dieter strides forward, wiping his hands with a handkerchief as if he had a little dirt on them, not the remains of gore from Rochus and Philomena's decapitated heads.

24

FRITZI

I cannot spare more than a glance for Rochus and Philomena. My body springs into action before I can make rational sense of anything; I flare my hands and fling my intention into the wild magic simmering within me, around me, until one word channels into my focus: *restrain*.

Vines come slithering across the floorboards, punching up through the wood planks. They twine around Dieter's ankles before he lifts the stone nestled in a pouch against his chest and every speck of water within the plants sucks out, beads of moisture hovering in the air, withering the vines to dried husks.

"My turn," Dieter coos, and punches the air between us.

Alois, closest, dives at him. Cornelia cries out while scrambling for spell components in her bag. Otto draws a sword, his face pale as his boots trek through the puddles of blood.

The water Dieter ripped from my vines gathers into an orb as wide as his chest. It slams first into Alois, and he flies back, smashing into a wall of shelves. They all come down around him as he crumbles, vials and jars and plants shattering in the impact when he drops in an unconscious heap on the floor. Cornelia shouts, twisting toward him, and that beat of pause is enough for the water orb to pivot and collide with her, tossing her across the council chamber as effortlessly as if she were an empty flour sack. She spins through the air and crashes somewhere far off, hidden behind tables and furniture.

Otto remains, and I scream, voice tearing against my throat, wordless, senseless, as Dieter bends, controlling the water orb to double back. Otto slashes at it, cuts it in half, but that only serves to make it so two floating, writhing water masses descend on him, one surrounding his sword arm—and one surrounding his head.

He bucks, eyes peeling wide in instant horror within the unsteady ripples of the water orb, mouth moving in the soundless gaping of drowning. Bubbles of air break from his mouth, and the water turns his cry into a muted garble of noise.

"Stop!" I scream and lurch toward him, hands up, already calling wild magic—

Something yanks on my chest. I stumble, make it close enough to grab his arm.

Otto is drawing on my magic.

He collapses to his knees, gagging fruitlessly in the bubble of water, and when I claw at it, droplets come away only to suck right back in. I can feel all of his terror, and even more, I can feel the snap of his control break and the desperate, frenzied way he draws at my magic. I'm not sure he's doing it intentionally; this has plunged him into instinctual panic. My magic is the only thing keeping him alive, but he's draining me, and I'm frozen, letting him do it as he drowns in front of me—

Dieter steps up to us. His face is a snarl of hatred.

"I will kill him, Fritzichen. I will kill him, and you will watch. But he will drain you for me first."

No, *no*—

Tears sting my eyes, heat my cheeks, and I reach for more vines, plants, something to fight with; or the water, I could seize control of the water—

Dieter lifts the water stone, and Otto contorts his body and makes a garbled cry. The magic in me heaves out, and I don't even try to stop it—just let it keep him *alive*.

I'm running out of power. I'm running out, and Dieter has the stone, and what happens when I'm drained dry?

"Stop!" I shout at my brother. "Stop—just *stop this*!"

Dieter towers over me. Alois is unmoving behind me; wherever Cornelia fell, she is quiet. No one else in the Well even knows he's here, do they? How did he get in?

"No," he says. "I don't think I will. See, everything I want will be so much easier to get if I have your help, sister. And I have already tried asking *nicely*."

Otto collapses to the floor, clawing helplessly at his open mouth, droplets of blood now sullying the water of the orb. His eyes roll back in his head, and I crawl toward him, but I'm fading, too, magic funneling out of me in a stream, both him pulling at it in fear and me giving it to him because I don't know what else to do.

Holda, I try, *HOLDA*—

"Oh no," says Dieter. Pain flares, and I rock to the side, his kick to my stomach knocking the breath from my lungs. "She can't hear you anymore, Fritzichen. Not with your magic so low. The only one who can hear you now is *me*."

Otto is dying next to us. My magic strains to help him; he clumsily pulls at it.

Then it's gone.

The last dregs shudder and writhe as Otto clings to the tether, pulls for more, but I have none. *None.*

That emptiness expands, becomes a pit I fall into, panic and horror, *no*—

"Hm." Dieter nudges Otto with his boot. "I would rather kill him, you know. Meine Schwester, I'd rather he die now. But do you think our magic tether would survive that? You're bonded to him, I'm bonded to you, I'm bonded to him, around and around we go. He *does* make you stronger, I think, Fritzichen. As goddess touched as he is. You realize how weak that makes you? That you *need* him."

Dieter drops the water orb.

Otto falls limp. But he's alive. I know he's alive. He's unconscious only; Dieter doesn't want him dead yet; I *need* him alive—

There's a ringing noise, like a bell, like—a scream. I'm screaming, and when I try to scramble over to Otto, Dieter kneels in front of me, grabs a handful of my hair and wrenches my face to look up into his.

The pendant Cornelia gave me dangles from my neck; he yanks it off, tosses it away.

"It's time, meine Schwester," he croons. "*Let me in.*"

No, no, *no, no, NO*—

He frames my face with his hands.

I reach out, trying with whatever is left in me, Holda, *Holda*, help me—or vines, maybe, plants, nutmeg and nettle and mistletoe and *something*—

Something.

Something—

I brought him something.

Dieter smiles. It unfurls across his face, and I see Mama in that smile.

Her affinity was never in plants, but she taught me their uses all the same. Nutmeg and mistletoe and nettle and more. Nutmeg and mistletoe and nettle. Nutmeg and—

What do I need them for?

I've missed him. I miss her. I miss them both, but Dieter is *here* and right now, I can't remember why anything else ever mattered.

He holds out a hand to me, palm flat.

I point off into the council room. Toward a body that fell.

Dieter grins. He leaves me briefly to cross the room. There's shuffling, a thump, no words spoken or cry of alarm.

There's an emotion I should be feeling. The person he's searching—I know her. I know her. He's touching her, and I should feel *something*—

He comes back with another stone in his hand. The air stone, and his smile is the sun. It is a cataclysm of everything I've ever wanted, Mama and my brother, *happy*, and I feel myself smile too.

"Three stones and one spark," he recites, turning the spell into a song. "Water, air, earth. And fire in the heart."

Dieter pulls me to my feet. There are so many bodies on the floor around us.

But my brother is happy, so I am as well.

We walk out of the council room and stand shoulder to shoulder at the balcony railing, looking over the whole of the Well.

People go about their day. Witches living their sad little lives, unaware that Dieter stands in their presence.

They'll learn soon enough.

He slips the air stone into the satchel around his neck. It clunks against the water stone, and there is another I see tucked away with them now too: the earth stone. The one Rochus and Philomena guarded.

Again, an absence of emotion that I should feel. A reaction sparks. My breath quickens, or tries to, wings beating frantically only to—

I stop.

And watch my brother.

He pulls the water stone out and holds it to his lips, rolling it back and forth across his mouth, until he's swaying with the motion of it, like wind bending branches.

"It's time," he sings into the stone, and from far below, at the base of the trees, screams erupt.

I look over the balcony edge. The bloated streams that crisscross the Well begin to burble and roil, bubbles and foam rippling across the surfaces. People nearby, far, far below us, begin to exclaim and point, shouting concern—

It is too late.

The waterways explode in showers of glittering droplets as hexenjägers surge up the banks, the water birthing them straight into the Well.

"I hid them in the water," Dieter tells me, eyes alight in mischief, still swaying, still rolling the stone across his lips. He used to look at me this way in Birresborn, when he'd been naughty, and I would giggle over his antics. "The Well's defenses couldn't stand in water. Not against *this*. Let's leave them to their business, Fritzichen." Dieter turns for the stairs.

Shouts and cries clog the air now, warriors diving into battle, hexenjägers slaughtering them, swords and arrows and cries of pain.

I don't move.

Something, again, something, I should…I should *do something…* about this. Or back in the council room, there's someone I need—

"*Fritzichen*," Dieter snaps.

He's angry.

I jump, shame coursing through me, and when my attention meets his where he stands a few steps down the landing, his smile doesn't reach his eyes.

His teeth show, and he tucks the water stone back into his pouch.

"We're going to be late," he says to me. "And we can't be late, can we?"

I shake my head. No, and he can't be upset, he can't be. I won't let him be.

He nods. Smiles. It hits his eyes now, and I relax.

"Good." He looks down at the battle on the forest floor. "Now go get little Liesel. You can bring her to me, can't you?"

I nod again.

His head bobs as he starts to hum. "Three stones and one spark," he sings. "Water, air, earth, and fire in the heart. Go get my fire, Fritzichen."

Yes. Liesel and Dieter and me. She'll come with me. She'll understand—we have to help him. We have to help him.

I have to help him.

I have to...

I have to.

I have—

25

OTTO

Living near a river, I learned to swim early. My stepmother would laugh at me all summer, shouting that the least I could do was bring some soap with me and bathe once in a while. There were boys from the town I'd swim with sometimes, fishing in the morning, diving into the water when it got hot at midday during those hungry months when the seeds were sown but the harvest wasn't yet in.

One of them almost drowned, the year before my stepmother died, the year before everything changed. It happened quietly, the younger brother of one of the boys pulled under the tow of the current, tiring quickly, slipping beneath the surface. No one noticed at first, and then realization hit, and with it, horror. We frantically screamed his name, searching over the glittering waters of the Moselle, until we heard a shout. Everyone dove for him but I reached him first. He scrambled over me, desperate panic pushing me under the water as he grabbed me, choking and gasping, and I couldn't think, couldn't breathe, but the other boys were there, pulling the younger one off me. I clawed my way to the surface, gulping at air and spewing dirty river water.

I was drowning, just now.

And I flailed with sheer panic, grabbing and jerking at the—

The tether.

The tether between Fritzi and me. The magic. I was terrified, I was panicking, I was *dying*, and I…I drained her of magic.

With *him* in the room.

Oh scheisse, oh no, oh *scheisse.*

I sit up, my hands slipping through something thicker than water, something—

Blood. Pools of it.

Bile rises, but I push it down, swallowing hard. I force my body up, standing, one hand around my sword hilt in a white-knuckled grip.

I scan the room, still struggling to sort my thoughts. Cornelia's up already, bruised and disheveled, checking Alois for injuries. "I'm fine," he says, but he takes her hand to help steady himself.

They turn to look at me, the obvious fear and question in their eyes.

Fritzi's gone. So is Dieter.

He has her.

That's the only thought in my head. It's the only thought I can allow into my mind, because if I don't focus on that, I'll focus on the decapitated corpses of the priest and priestess. I'll fixate on the blood that slicks my boots and I will never process another thought again, not if I don't keep my razor-sharp focus on one fact: *He. Has. Her.*

"He's going to take her to the Origin Tree," Cornelia says, answering my unspoken thoughts. "We have to cut him off—"

"He'll get Liesel first," I say. I remember what they'd all said before, weeks ago, when we first started this quest. There were three stones, one for each goddess—earth, air, water. But the fourth element came from the witches.

Fire.

"He would just need any witch's fire," Cornelia starts to say, shaking her head. "It doesn't have to be—"

"He'll take Liesel." I am bone-certain of this, and while I hate that I know the enemy so well, I do not doubt that he wouldn't love the synchronicity of it, the poetry of his terror.

I turn to the door, a crack of light escaping from the other side. He must have gone that way—the bloody footprints lead in that direction. I motion for Alois and Cornelia to follow me.

I have to be careful. Fritzi has no magic now and nothing to protect her. Nothing but my sword.

Outside, I duck behind a heavy tree branch, my eyes on the fading bloody footprints. Out of the corner of my vision, I see Cornelia and Alois following my lead, taking cover. I can hear—screaming? I dare a look down.

Scheisse. Hexenjägers are *everywhere.* We assumed he would use the water stone as a weapon, but it didn't occur to use that he'd be able to turn the rivers and creeks into a Trojan horse. These hexenjägers are black-cloaked and well-armed as they move like shadows through the witches fighting back, a battle that feels like an even deeper betrayal because it rages through the place I have come to see as home.

As safe.

How is he doing this? He had magic to control people like puppets before, but he lost that power. Is this the water stone? Can Dieter use the liquid within a human body to force it to fight? Or has he found enough vitriolic blood-thirsty monsters of men willing to ignore his own magic in the water to kill the witches he revealed here?

I cannot focus on how he's done this; I must only do what I can now to stop it from getting worse.

Chaos rattles the trees. Shouting, gunfire, magical blasts, horses, crackling fire—

And a voice.

Fritzi.

"Liesel!" she calls across the treetops in a singsong tone. "Come out, come out!"

Fritzi would *never* call to her cousin like that.

But *he* would.

My eyes scan the trees. Most of the buildings among the branches are empty, hollow shells as the residents have all gone to arms on the forest floor below. My heart twinges—*Hilde*. She's a brewer, not a warrior. But Brigitta will protect her...

Fritzi isn't too far away from me—I could reach her with a hard sprint across the bridge nearest me, down a ladder, and over another bridge. But I would give away my cover, and I am absolutely certain that *he* is here, nearby. Hidden as well.

"Fritzi?" Liesel's voice cuts across the cacophony. I only hear it because I'm waiting for it, dreading it.

Fritzi kneels on a bridge, arms spread wide. "Come here, cousin."

"Is that blood on you?"

They're on a landing. My stomach heaves—she's near the school, where the other children of the Well learn magic and math and letters. I see Manegold, the young man who teaches charms to the students, crouching near the window as Liesel takes a tentative step through the door. Wisps of hair and flashes of colored clothing—the children are hiding.

They know something is wrong.

But Liesel trusts Fritzi.

She walks slowly onto the bridge.

"Come to me," Fritzi says, her words muffled by the sounds of the battle below.

I look around frantically. This position on the balcony by the council room has afforded us cover, but now feels too far away. Alois shows me his empty palms—he has only a sword at his hip—and Cornelia's magic isn't ready for this. I have no distance weapons, but if I can locate Dieter—

Liesel steps into Fritzi's arms.

Fritzi picks the girl up, even though her weight is awkward, and she turns. Liesel's eyes are wide, and somehow, while she cannot see Dieter yet, she must know the *wrongness* of Fritzi right now, of this whole situation.

Her worried gaze lands on me.

I see her mouth drop open, fear flooding her as she takes in my appearance—battle-weary, soaked in blood, not beside Fritzi. Her worst fears are confirmed.

Slowly, I raise a finger to my lips. Sticky blood—Rochus or Philomena's—smears on my face. My throat is so tight I can barely breathe; my eyes sting with unshed tears.

Liesel gives me one tiny nod, her curls bobbing on Fritzi's shoulder. Fritzi takes her to a ladder and starts descending.

Dieter is nowhere to be seen.

I step carefully around the branches to another ladder, keeping Liesel's bright yellow curls and Fritzi's braids in sight. Cornelia and Alois stalk behind me, alert, covering me as I narrow my focus.

The minute my feet touch the earth, the battle sweeps by me. I do *not* break eye contact as Fritzi carries Liesel through the heart of the storm.

My sword arm swings down, crashing into an oncoming hexenjäger. I shove, hard, to the right, knocking another back. Behind me, Cornelia screams spells at men who approach, and Alois cuts down the remaining ones with his blade. I stride forward, one long step after another, never once looking away.

Silent tears streak Liesel's face. She knows that Fritzi is not in control of herself. She knows who *is* in control.

But she watches me.

And I will burn this forest to the ground before I let Dieter take either of them.

26

FRITZI

The Well is a battlefield. Swords clash, enemies scream; it is a bloodbath, but I walk through it, limbs stiff with Liesel wrapped in my arms. I walk, and walk, and I think I'm humming, some lilting lullaby Mama always sang to Dieter.

Or, no, it isn't a lullaby—

"Three stones and one spark." Singing, singing. "Water, air, earth. And fire in the heart."

"Fritzi," Liesel whimpers into my neck. "Fritzi, you're scaring me. Stop, please."

"Three stones and one spark. Water, air, earth—"

"Fritzi." She sobs and clings to me. "Fritzi—this is *Dieter*, he has you—let me go, please."

But she doesn't struggle. She holds on to me, an eleven-year-old's tense grip, as I walk us through the battlefield. No one dives at us, no one attacks.

Up ahead, I see my brother, standing beneath an archway of trees. He beams at me, that smile that is the sun, and I walk, keep walking, even as Liesel shivers in my arms. The weight of her presses against a wound on my chest, but the pain is far away. There, but on the horizon. It doesn't matter.

Something tugs at the base of my spine. Revulsion? No, it is smothered in the wash of pride that my brother's smile gives me.

"Good work, sister," Dieter says and looks at Liesel. He reaches a hand out, strokes her hair. "Hello again, cousin."

She glares at him, her jaw set, eyes flashing orange. "Don't touch me."

He clicks his tongue and drops his hand. "Oh, but I don't need to, do I? This way."

I follow.

The sounds of battle fade behind us as we step into a glen. Hexenjägers encircle the space, and as soon as Dieter enters, he nods behind him, and they file out, leaving us alone in a copse of trees that sway in a gentle wind, a small pond undisturbed and peaceful—and the Origin Tree looming over us all.

Its massive roots and reaching branches dominate the glen, leaves clinking against one another, its sheer presence loud even as this space is quiet in reverence.

Memories fight through. This is the place where Otto and I—

Pain lances in my head, and I stumble, almost dropping Liesel. She cries out and tries to scurry out of my arms, but I clamp tighter, regaining my footing.

Dieter frowns at me.

"Three stones and one spark," I hear myself sing. "Water, air, earth. And fire in the heart."

Stop, something says, deep in me; something *screams* it.

He nods. "Good."

He pours the stones out of the satchel, dumping them into his hand.

Behind us, there is a shout. Metal scraping metal.

Dieter glares at the opening to this glen, glares enough that I start to turn, but I can't. I don't.

He says nothing, but when he starts to climb the Tree's massive arching roots, I follow with Liesel in my arms.

She bucks against me. "Let me *go*! This isn't you, Fritzi! *Let me go!*"

Mama, Dieter, and I were so happy. We laughed all the time. We crowded in our small cottage and gorged ourselves on Mama's cooking—something with plums, with cherries, because I remember looking up and Dieter's face was streaked with sticky red, his mouth and teeth—

I hold Liesel. I hold her, and my face is wet, wetness that drips down on her, on my arms around her. She puts her hands on my cheeks, but I am looking up at Dieter, who reaches the Tree's trunk.

There are grooves in the trunk. Three of them. Perfect little circles for perfect little stones.

"Three stones and one spark," I whisper, throat swelling, tears coming stronger.

Dieter places one stone in each hole. The last one clicks into place, and I can *feel* the Tree vibrating beneath and all around us, a sensation that rocks me where I stand on its roots, but I keep my balance, clinging to Liesel.

Part of me expects the Tree to reach its mighty branches down, for it to feel the presence of the stones and react, to fight us off. But it just vibrates still, that hum of life and magic and power, and being this close, the hum is *consuming*. It is enticing, a hum that promises strength and life.

Dieter's eyes are brilliant with need. He hears the hum too. He's always heard it. Maybe that's why he's been the way he is, because there has always been this vibration in his head, begging. And he's here now, one palm flat against the trunk, his face stretching in a giddy grin.

"Now, Liesel," Dieter coos, stroking the bark.

"No," she says into my neck, half whimper, half fury.

Dieter sighs. He glances behind us again.

Swords clash, closer now. Someone shouts.

"Fritzi!"

I want to look over my shoulder. I want to look—

I want to—

I want—

"Little Liesel," Dieter says, but the exasperation in his tone is marred with the slightest swell of anxiety. He faces us, one hand still on the Tree. "You will burn this Tree for me."

"No!" she snaps.

"Yes, you will."

He *pulls* on me, and I shove Liesel at Dieter. He grabs her arm, and she cries out, shock more than anything, but he holds her strong, and I'm standing free on the Tree's roots, balancing on one arch.

"Fritzi!" the voice shouts again, a frenzy of panic.

There's a knife in my hand. Where did it come from?

"Light the Tree on fire, little Liesel," Dieter tells her. "Darling Fritzichen needs you to light the Tree on fire."

The tip of the knife appears in front of my eye. My vision switches from Dieter and Liesel, at the base of the Tree, to the edge of the blade, back and forth, far then close.

"Burn the Tree!" Dieter demands.

Why won't she listen? He needs us. He needs us.

The edge of the blade comes closer to my eye. I can feel my eyelashes flutter against it with each blink.

Tears start to gather as the blade in my hand moves closer, closer.

Dieter needs me to do this. Dieter needs me. My brother needs me.

He needs me.

He needs—

I want—

I have—

The sting of pain. The tip of the blade catches my eyelid, and I flinch so it slides up, cutting through my brow.

Instinct overwhelms *need* and *want* in a sudden surge of *No, no, don't do this—*

Liesel screams. "Fritzi, *stop*!"

"You can stop it," Dieter tells her, cooing into her hair, his arms wrapped around her. "Light the fire. Burn it all down, little Liesel. Witch fire in the heart."

I draw the knife back, and it resets in front of my eye, and I'm shaking now, shaking with holding it back, with needing to gouge out my own eye—Dieter needs me, he needs Liesel, he needs—

He had me in a room in Baden-Baden, chained up. There was no blood then. Only burning, the smell of rendered flesh, his eyes glittering then like they are now.

He left marks on me. He left brands on me there and there and there.

He had me in the library. He pulled me apart in front of Otto.

And again, after Perchta's tomb.

Over and over. His marks everywhere, proof that he is stronger than me, that he will always be more than me, that I will always be his.

My brother needs me to do this.

I want—I *want*—

I see the blood dripping off the tip of the knife that hovers just beyond my eye.

I follow it, looking down. And there is the brand he made, the edge just visible beneath the ruined collar of my chemise and kirtle, and the jagged carving of the Tree still unhealed and roughly bandaged.

I remember the other brands. The other scars.

My body is not mine. My magic is not mine. I belong to him; I am his, and these marks are proof that he dominates me.

No.

Stop.

NO.

That is all I think. Have been thinking for months. *No. Stop. He did this. He has me. He marked me.*

Him, him—

But I am still here.

I am still *here*. Standing.

And these scars.

These scars are *mine*.

These marks are proof that I *escaped* him. That each time he overtook me, I came through.

These scars are badges of survival, and as I look down at them, I scream.

The noise wells from the pit of my stomach, bursting up and through me in a tidal wave of magic and burning, cacophonous rage.

Rage in its purest form, rage stripped to nothing more than single-minded drive and terror.

Rage and reclaiming and banishing, all of it coalescing until that scream shatters every flicker of my brother in my body.

This is *my* body. This is *my* magic.

I belong to *me.*

I drop backward, rocked off balance on a precarious root, and fall, knife toppling from my fingers, body sinking, weightless—

Arms catch me.

I look up, and Otto's blood-streaked face stares down at me.

"Fritzi?" He cradles my cheek in one warm hand.

I nod, and manage a smile, and something in my eyes must silence his worry, because he smiles back.

Dieter's bellow of anger echoes across the glen.

From Otto's arms, I see Cornelia and Alois fighting off hexenjägers in front of the Tree, the battle beginning to trickle over into this peaceful sanctuary. Brigitta is here too, and at her side—Hilde? Brigitta must have been training her, because she wields dual knives with determination.

"Light the Tree!" Dieter shouts, and I spin in Otto's arms, scrambling to my feet on the mossy forest floor as my brother shakes Liesel in a panic. "Light it *now*!"

Liesel's sobs turn to a stone-faced look of fury when she sees me standing, sees the clarity in my eyes.

She twists to glare up at Dieter.

"I won't burn this Tree," she tells him. "But I will burn *you*."

And she puts her hands on his chest and sends him up in flames.

His whole body immediately wreaths in fire, orange and red and deepest blue that snap and pop off his clothes, lick at his hair. Liesel dives away, clambering over the Tree roots until she hurls herself into Otto's arms. He scoops her up, one hand still steadying me, and the three of us watch Dieter burn.

His skin begins to darken and crackle. The smell of burning flesh triggers me back into that room in Baden-Baden—

Then he laughs.

Dieter throws his head back and laughs to the Tree's high branches. It is a tearing, jarring sound, half-mad with pain.

He's still near the Tree. Standing on the roots, close enough to reach out and touch the trunk.

I see it happening slowly, time stretching thin. His hand, shrouded in witch fire, reaching for the bark.

I'm in motion before I can think of a way to stop this. Next to me, Otto shoves Liesel to relative safety and follows me, the two of us climbing, fighting our way up to reach Dieter and stop him before he ignites the Tree. We are close—

Not close enough.

Dieter's hand slams against the trunk of the Tree, right next to the three stones, just as I trip and fall against a root and my bloodied hand slaps to the base of the trunk. Otto's grip on my other arm doesn't budge.

The vibrations in the Tree go silent.

There's a pause.

Like a breath.

Like stillness before a thunderclap.

Then the fire launches across the Tree's bark in a wave of scalding blue and white that ripples down the roots, across the branches, and consumes the entire glen in a flash of incandescent light.

27

OTTO

One moment of pure white heat.

And then—

Nothing.

I blink, whirling around. *Where's Dieter?* I have to stop him, I have to *kill* him, I have to—

That was the wrong question. I don't need to know where Dieter is. I need to know where *I* am.

A hand reaches through the foggy white surrounding me, and before I have a chance to panic, I recognize the feel of the fingers weaving through mine. Fritzi clutches at me, pulls me closer, and she is clearer in focus now, all the red lines of her wounds made starker in the brightness of the light. The brightness fades to misty white, just like—

"Remember when we were tested?" Fritzi murmurs. "Before the goddesses let us into the Well?"

I start to agree with her, and then we see a figure approaching us through the mist, swirling clouds parting in her wake, a stick tapping on the ground with each step. The sound echoes hollowly.

I've met Holda, the Maid; she tested me and forged my tattoo.

I saw Perchta's monsters in Glauberg, another test, that one from the Mother.

"Abnoba," I say. The Crone.

"And you're the warrior," Abnoba replies. Her voice is scratchy, as if she's not used to speaking. She's bent over a cane, her long silver hair sweeping almost to the ground as she hunches. But when she lifts an eye to me, I can tell her vision is clear, even if her face is lined with deep wrinkles.

Without moving, her gaze flicks to Fritzi. "And the champion." Fritzi's fingers tighten around mine. She's on edge and, I know, tired. Drained. Emotionally, physically, magically.

"If I'm a warrior, why did you take us from the battle?" I ask.

"So eager to kill?" Abnoba says. There's no judgment in her voice, only curiosity.

I glance at Fritzi. Dieter is a monster.

Dieter is her brother.

"No," I say, surprised at the truth of it.

Abnoba focuses on Fritzi. I can feel Fritzi trembling—fear of what must be done, I think—and I step forward, shouldering in front of her. I cannot protect her from everything, but scheisse, I wish I could.

Abnoba's wrinkled lips twitch. "I have been most curious about you, warrior," she says, seemingly content to let her attention fall on me instead of Fritzi.

"Oh?" I hate the combative tone in my voice.

"Am I an enemy to you?" the Crone asks.

"Should I treat you as one?"

She laughs, the sound as hollow as the thuds her staff made against the ground...whatever the ground is. It's too shrouded in mist. "I don't think so. But some of your people do." At my blank look, she adds, "You worship a different god."

"Differences do not make enemies, except among fools," I say.

"And you are no fool?" Again with that tone—no accusation, just curiosity.

"I try not to be."

"Many fools do the same." Before I can respond to that, Abnoba smiles again and thumps her staff. "But the real fools are the ones who think they know everything. That *is* one thing I appreciate about your beliefs, human. The idea of the mystic unknowable. It's when people start to believe they know everything that they show their foolish hands the most."

"This philosophy is..." Fritzi heaves a sigh, unwilling to label her thoughts on the conversation. "But I believe we're in the middle of an apocalyptic event that perhaps has a little urgency attached."

"And you are eager to return to what must be done?" Abnoba asks.

Fritzi ducks her head, blond hair falling in her eyes. "No," she says, so quietly I almost miss it.

"Well, that's good, dear," Abnoba says, reaching past me to pat Fritzi on the cheek. "You young ones, always *doing*. It's good to take a moment to pause and think." She turns to me with a twinkle in her eye. "To tell a story. My sisters and I, we are not of your world. But we came here seeking..."

She pauses for so long that Fritzi and I exchange glances, wondering at the way the Crone's voice trails off. "Seeking what?" I ask.

"Oh, different things." Abnoba waves her hand dismissively. "But when we came here, we brought some of our magic. And magic is a wild thing, hm?" She makes a noise at Fritzi, something guttural, and it takes me a moment to realize it's a knowing laugh. "Magic can't be stopped, only delayed. So my sisters and I planted the Tree to slow it down. At the time, this world was very new. We wanted to help humanity grow, but we wanted to protect our children."

"I thought it was Perchta who was the Mother, the protector," I say.

"And I thought you were comfortable with the idea of three gods being one," Abnoba snaps back.

I jut out my chin, giving her the point.

"We did not foresee so many walls," she says after a moment. "A wall to dam magic and mete it out incrementally. A wall to protect the Well. A wall to keep out the Romans. And they made walls, too, the Romans. The limes to push the people back. Walls around your cities, around your amphitheaters, around your homes."

"Walls can protect," I say.

She nods slowly. "They can. But every wall that has ever been made must one day fall."

Fritzi sucks in a breath at that, her hand going clammy. I know what she's thinking. It's my fear too. The wall around the Well *has* fallen. Dieter used the flames engulfing his body to burn the Tree.

I remember the light. It's hard to think in this fuzzy in-between place the goddess has taken us to, but I remember the light.

I remember the fire.

I'm not sure of time anymore. Did the goddess bring us to this liminal space before or after it was too late to do anything about the fire that engulfed the Tree?

"Is...?" I swallow. "Is today the day the Origin Tree falls?"

"What does that matter to you, human with no magic?"

I'm not sure. I'm a soldier, not a general in this war. Fritzi knows—not just what the council wants and what the goddesses want, but what *she* wants. Freedom of magic, magic available to everyone, without the restraints of the rigid rules of the Well. I glance at her, and I'm certain she would know what to say. But she's waiting for me to speak. So is Abnoba.

"What does it matter to you, Otto?" Abnoba asks again, her voice gentler.

"I like having access to magic," I say finally. "I did not realize it before—how can one want something one has never had? Had never believed possible? But I know it's possible now, and it *is* something I want."

Before Fritzi, I never felt that hollow space inside my body that could be filled with magic.

Her magic.

Abnoba's lips twitch, but I don't let her speak. Instead, I continue, "But I don't want it at the cost of Fritzi's magic."

Fritzi's eyes round in question. "My magic—"

I cut her off. "If there were no restraints, if magic was truly accessible to all like Holda wanted, I never would have drained Fritzi, she would never have been open to Dieter's influences, none of this would have happened."

Emotion flickers over Fritzi's face, her expression unreadable.

"I am only meant to use her magic to protect her, and I failed at that." I say the words as if they are a confession, but my eyes are on Fritzi, the only one who can absolve me.

"You lived. I lived. That's enough," she mutters. She means the words to be just for me, but the silence in this place makes her voice echo.

I shake my head. "It's not enough." I turn to Abnoba. "Survival is not enough. Why can't all humans have access to magic? Not just in spells, but the wild magic Fritzi has?" I ask. I hate the whine in my voice, but there's something about Abnoba—her deep wrinkles, her grandmotherly eyes—that makes me feel safe to question her like a child.

The goddess turns to Fritzi. "That is what Holda asked of you, to show witches that wild magic is not evil, and that they have access to more power than we led them to believe."

"Not just witches." Fritzi's eyes flash. "*All* humans should have the choice to access magic." Her voice is firm.

"We originally tried to keep our magic small," Abnoba says. She looks as if she is carefully considering what Fritzi said. "Only a few chosen had access. Gifts can become burdens. And then when those without access started to persecute those with..."

The ancient tribes, the Romans, the battles.

"You tried to create a safe haven," Fritzi says. "The Well."

She nods. "But we also believe in *choice*," Abnoba says, using the word Fritzi had. "We told witches of magic, taught them what the Tree could offer. And then we..." Abnoba takes several steps back, her cane thunking hollowly.

"The people in the Well developed their own governance," she says.

The council.

"Their own rules."

The spells.

"Their own traditions."

The secrets.

She watches me, and I sense that I'm supposed to take more from her speech than just her words. She is old; she is used to waiting, and all of time has stopped anyway, so I consider what she's said.

There is tradition in the Church too. I think of the parishioners who recite prayers in Latin, a language they do not know, the words nothing more than rote memory. The Protestants have translated the Bible from Latin to German, but that text was translated from Greek and Hebrew into Latin already, perhaps other languages beyond that—what meaning was lost in each word's increasingly distant substitution? We kneel when we are told to kneel, we eat when we are told to eat, we move about a calendar with holy days that were originally Roman, originally Greek, originally Pagan.

All in the name of tradition.

But there is comfort in tradition too. I wove advent wreaths with my sister and stepmother. In my village before I left for Trier, I gathered in the town square for dances and feasts—some of my most joyous memories. The Christkindlmarkt was when I started to fall in love with Fritzi. Fresh Lebkuchen sparks warmth and peace at just a whiff of the spices. My sister brews beer with my stepmother's recipe, and in a way, that keeps her alive even when she is gone.

"Some traditions lose their original meaning," I say, "but they're not all wrong."

"And Perchta thought I should let you die," Abnoba says, grinning at me.

My blood runs cold. I cannot forget that, despite her grandmotherly appearance, Abnoba is a goddess. She has stopped time for us in this moment, but I cannot trust her mercy to continue.

"Traditions can be helpful," Abnoba says, nodding as if speaking to herself. "But when they lose all their original meaning..." She looks up, her roving eyes settling on Fritzi. "You, champion, convinced Perchta of that."

Fritzi squeaks in surprise, and that makes Abnoba's face nearly disappear in wrinkles, her grin is so big.

"At best, traditions with no meaning are wasted time," I say. "And at worst, they kill."

"If a tradition would kill my children, then they should kill it first." Abnoba stares into my eyes. "It was not just Fritzi who chose you as a warrior, Otto Ernst."

The weight of the goddess's expectation settles on my shoulders.

"What are you saying we should do?" Fritzi asks.

I feel heat. I don't see the flames of the Origin Tree—all I see is this misty nowhere place—but I think I'm starting to feel the fire.

"Are you saying that we should let the Origin Tree burn?" I ask.

Abnoba laughs. "I'm saying it's going to burn now whether you want it to or not."

"So the world will flood with magic," Fritzi says slowly.

"Yes," Abnoba says, tilting her face to the flames that are gradually becoming visible. "And isn't that wonderful?"

"Are we all going to die?" I ask.

"Oh, definitely," Abnoba says. "Eventually, anyway."

Fear is a tightly coiled snake biting at my guts. "Will the flood of magic kill off all of humanity?" I snap. "There is an apocalypse happening currently, remember?"

Abnoba takes another step closer to me and lifts her walking stick, thunking the knotted top on my chest. Where my tattoo is. "You think this was an accident? You're a human, boy. And you're bonded with a witch. You've felt her magic now. What do you think?" She eyes me, squinting. "We designed traditions to protect, not limit. We taught the witches spells and how to access the Well because they were children then, centuries ago. Children with enemies who wanted to hurt them."

"There are still enemies that want to hurt them," I whisper.

"Yes, but they're not children anymore, are they?" Abnoba's smile turns sad. "Not even little Liesel."

I shake my head mutely.

"Holda would free everything. Perchta would free nothing," Abnoba says, tapping her stick against the wood. "But when you're as old as me, you realize: the only thing left to do is let the children decide for themselves who they want to be."

28

FRITZI

Who they want to be.

I look up at Otto, head ringing with everything he said, everything Abnoba said, all these words and possibilities swirling around me in a storm of building potential.

Who they want to be.

Who do *I* want to be?

The answer has been many things. I wanted to be a good witch. I wanted to be someone my mother was proud of. I wanted to be someone worthy of my brother's attention and love. Then I wanted to survive, to rescue my cousin from the hexenjägers, to be *safe*.

I wanted, and wanted, and sometimes I got what I wanted and sometimes that wanting almost killed me.

But throughout every iteration, I had access to magic in all its varying forms. I had this tool that elevated me even in the darkest, most horrific situations. It gave me a light when all was blue-black, a light that I came to take for granted. A light that I was able to share with Otto, and we may not be the best at using this bond between us, but when I look up at him now, I see the same questions in his eyes.

"Could we…?" I pause, lick my dry lips. "Dieter broke open the Tree. The magic isn't going into him?"

"He will try to direct it," Abnoba says. "But what will you try to do?"

"Magic will flood out into the world," I continue, pieces coming together, "unless we give that magic somewhere else to go."

"Somewhere else?" Otto asks, doubt marring his face. "You? Would you survive it going into you?"

I shake my head. "Not me. Everyone."

His brows go up.

"We could…we could tie it to everyone who belongs to this land," I say to Otto. "Everyone can hold a small well of it in themselves, like you said you could."

"There will still be magic left over." Abnoba twists her walking stick in her long frail fingers. "But the backlash of magic exploding out of the Tree would be lessened significantly."

"So it's possible?" My eyes widen, pleading. "We can give everyone access to magic? Not just witches?"

Abnoba grins. She points between the two of us. "Your mortal is able to access your magic. Bonded pairs could be two witches, sometimes a mortal and a witch, the pairing did not matter. What mattered was the *hearts*. The souls. That is what determines ability with magic. So these mortals you want to give our magic to—some will be receptive. Some won't know anything has changed."

"But they'll have the chance." I suck in a shaky breath. "Everyone will have the chance to use magic if they want it. We can do this."

I turn to Otto, grab both his hands, something tight and feverish welling up in me. My mouth opens, and I start to explain what I'm thinking, a fumbled, delirious plan, but he squeezes my hands and smiles.

That smile silences me. That smile is a caress on my cheek, a warm beam of sunlight. The connection between us vibrates with that warmth, and I feel his understanding, his acceptance, his surety.

"How?" he asks me, but then he turns the question to Abnoba. "How do we funnel the magic out to everyone?"

Abnoba lifts her hand, and suddenly, she's holding an apple. She takes a bite with a crack and crunch, juices flowing down her chin. "How, indeed?"

Otto made the apple tree bloom when we were trying to practice him accessing my magic. We talked about intent, and will, and instinct.

"We've barely figured out how to use our bond," I say.

"Will it hurt her?" Otto asks over me. "Will it—"

Abnoba smiles at us. "I do think you'll be just fine."

The whiteness around surges brighter, brighter, so bright I have to slam my eyes shut to avoid the piercing intensity—

The smell of smoke has me yanking my eyes open, and I'm sprawled back on the Origin Tree's roots, my hand on the trunk, Otto next to me, his arm around my waist. The Tree burns, the air sullied with gray smoke and the stench of ash, flames of orange licking up the bark.

And there, not an arm's length away, is my brother, slumped at the base of the Tree, his skin charred and bleeding.

I can feel his tether to the Tree's magic. It's a weak, brittle thing, a clumsy final grasp at magic he can no longer host or access, not since I cut off his bond with me. A final, divisive rendering that can never be undone.

He's dying. I can feel that too. The slow drain of his life. The smell of his burning flesh.

His eyes meet mine, startling blue against the burnt black and cracked red of his face, and he sneers at me, reaching one trembling hand until he rests it on the Tree over his head, palm flat against the bark.

"Can you feel it, Fritzichen?" he croaks. Then laughs, a sharp, aching guffaw. "No. You can't, can you? It's *mine.*"

He's taking the magic. He's pulling the Tree's magic into him, it's the only thing keeping him alive, and I scramble to my feet, Otto with me.

I put my back to my brother. He doesn't matter now. Maybe he never did, and I only thought he did because I wanted to love him.

But I want other things now.

I *need* other things. And I'm choosing this, to grab Otto's hands and stop him from moving higher up the Tree, toward Dieter.

"Wait." I look up into his eyes. The Tree burns next to us. Dieter lies at the base just across the roots from us, draining the magic into him. It's a pull on the air, a physical jerk in my chest; it's such a potent *feeling* that the air should be awash in sparks and glitter and flashes, but there is nothing to see, magic effervescent and ethereal. Somewhere beyond the flames, voices shout, weapons clash—hexenjägers and witches, fighting.

But I cup Otto's jaw in my hands and pull his forehead to mine and breathe.

"This is our magic," I tell him. "Not his. *Ours.* All of ours."

"That's our intention," he says. "That's our will."

Otto settles his hands on my waist and gasps, his fingers clamping tighter, and heat radiates off his chest—off his tattoo.

I reach out along our bond, and then beyond it, entwining to point into the distance together.

First, Dieter. Our tether winds around him, snuffs out his final grasp at magic like it's nothing more than a candle flame. For all the destruction he caused, that's as strong as he ever truly was—a single flicker, a weak, unsustainable spark. Cut off, he lets out one pained cry, and that desperate hold he had on his dying body begins to slip away.

For a moment, I'm drawn out of my focus. I'm pulled to stare at him again, watching the light leave his heavy blue eyes, eyes that I swear once sparkled with joy, eyes that used to entice and promise.

I don't think that version of my brother ever really existed; I think I cobbled together that memory of him, wanting so badly to not fear him, to not hate him.

Hate is all that remains now. Not even fear. And maybe I *should* be fearful, on some level, that I can look at him and feel only burning hatred—but that is reclaiming in a way too. This is all he deserves from me. Just enough hatred to stop him. Just enough energy to end this.

His eyelids flicker, then softly close.

The flood of power that had been feeding into him shifts now, widening—without his will against it, it bucks like a furious horse, kicking and wild.

Otto and I stagger, feet slipping on the Tree's roots, flames still burning, brushing up against the edges of our boots, long fingers of it reaching for our arms and faces. But we stay focused, locked together, all of our concentration on that tether, our tether, and now, this magic. Our magic.

Out, I think. We think. *Go*.

Out into the world. Out into people like those we passed in our travels, people just trying to endure. Out into people like those hiding in Trier, cowering under the persecution of the hexenjägers. Out even into the hexenjägers themselves, people who have never considered that there is another way; they have that way now, they have a path that is not lined with hate. Out, out, into hearts and souls.

Faces flash in my mind. All the people who were in the prison with me before Otto blew up the aqueducts. And the children near his house-fort, little Mia and her brother.

Then another face comes, one I know is from Otto, the kick of grief that accompanies it: Johann. What could have happened if he'd had magic during the fight with Dieter under the city?

Out, out; our combined will tethers like our bond.

I see witches too. Witches in the Well, and others, still scattered, few and in hiding. I see the rules they have been forced to adhere to that limited their power in ways they aren't even aware of. I see that potential inside each of them, the sudden filling where they had previously only been able to draw in such magic through rigid customs and ceremony. They are full now, full to bursting with power, and tears trickle down my face as I feel their awe and wonder.

The kicking, bucking wildness of the Origin Tree's magic breaks into an all-out sprint, surging, unburdened, unrestricted. It rips my breath away, sucks against the air in a whirlwind that douses the fire, spinning bits of ash and debris around us in a windstorm. It spins, spins, gusts stronger, and in that wind, I spot the three stones whirling around us, caught in the dance of the magic evolving.

Just as quickly as the storm came, it stops.

The magic has left the Tree. It has somewhere else to go now.

The wind settles. The stones drop with heavy thuds to the roots around us, where they come to rest, unchanged.

Otto and I stay there, locked with our foreheads together, panting and hearts racing. I only give us a moment's pause before I rear back and look him all over, patting his chest.

"Are you all right?" I demand. "Did that hurt you?"

He pushes air out his nose. "Did it hurt *me*? What about *you*? You're the one usually—"

He stops. Pushes on his chest. Panic leeches into my body until he smiles, wide and beaming.

"I can feel it," he whispers. "Fritzi—I can feel the magic in me. It's—not yours, not like when I draw on you. It's—" His smile flickers. Tears glisten in his eyes. "It's *mine*."

Behind us, a cry goes up.

We both whirl on the Tree's roots to see a few remaining hexenjägers on their knees at swordpoint by Brigitta's guards. The witches are cheering their victory, a victory I can hear echoed throughout the Well, beyond this little glen.

Liesel scrambles up the roots and throws herself around my waist, arms locked tight. "I'm sorry, I'm so sorry—I shouldn't have burned him; I shouldn't have used fire—"

I wrap my arms around her shoulders. "Liesel, it wasn't your fault. It's all right." I exhale, shaking, and feel those words. "Everything's all right now."

In the tangle of guards before us, I spot Hilde, bloodstained but smiling. Cornelia leans on Alois; the two of them give a tentative smile.

Then their eyes lift beyond me, to the Tree, and their faces pulse wide with shock.

I turn. Otto follows my gaze and what wonder he'd had sharpens.

The Tree is split in three pieces. What was once a massive, ageless pillar of magic is now an unraveled heap of charred wood, branches split off, leaves gone.

And at the base, locked beneath a fallen branch, is my brother's body.

I look away, and hug Liesel to me tighter.

"Everything's all right now," I whisper again.

Otto tucks his arms around us both as guards begin to move towards us. I think I hear Brigitta shout a question from farther off, demanding explanation. And it will come. So much will come now—explanation, momentum, forward motion.

But for now, for this moment, I lean into Otto's arms and feel Liesel bury her face into my stomach, and—

Movement catches my eyes in the trees surrounding this glen.

Three shapes, nearly translucent, like ghosts in mist. One bent over a walking stick. One proud and rigid. And one smiling, eyes glistening, cheeks damp.

Holda bows her head at me.

Thank you, I hear in my head, her voice familiar, comforting.

I nod at her.

A twist of concern seizes in my chest. *Are you leaving now? Did the Tree hold you here? Will I still be able to speak with you?*

Her smile is half relief, half pure joy. *You can always speak to me, Friederike. Now, I have other people who can speak to me too. Thanks to you and your warrior.*

She bows deeper. A long, slow curtsy.

Abnoba mimics her, gray hair rippling.

After a beat, Perchta lowers as well, her face stoic, severe.

I blink, and they vanish.

"Are you all right?" Otto cocks his head into my field of vision.

I smile, cheeks aching, and I nod, because I am. We are.

Under the shadow of the destroyed Origin Tree, in this hidden sanctuary of magic, at the beginning of this promise for a better world, I do the only thing there is left to do.

I thrust up onto my toes and kiss the man I love.

EPILOGUE

OTTO

THREE MONTHS LATER

I first came to Trier to infiltrate the hexenjägers and take them down from within. The second time I came to this city, it was to find and kill Dieter Kirch. I have never visited Trier without a mission.

This time is no different.

"Do you think it will be difficult to find them?" Fritzi asks me in a low voice as we pass through the gates of the city. There are guards here, but they are not hexenjägers.

There are no more hexenjägers.

"I'm not sure," I confess. I veer left, past the remains of the basilica that Fritzi and I blew apart in an attempt to save the accused witches due to be burned under Dieter's reign of terror. That ancient structure may be rebuilt, although some of the rubble has already been scavenged by resourceful workers looking for cheap materials.

Fritzi sees my glance and slips her hand in mine. How long ago that feels now. How desperate I was.

How alone.

"There you are!" Alois calls, darting over, Cornelia at his heels. Alois skids to a stop in front of me, his face grave. "Have you or have you not had apfelkraut before?"

"Of course I have," I say. The fruit spread is delicious on fresh bread; my stepmother used to make some at the end of every summer.

Alois's eyes narrow, and I notice for the first time that he has a jar of the sweet stuff in his hand, purchased from some merchant, no doubt. "How *dare* you keep this a secret from me? I need bushels of the stuff delivered to the Well immediately!" He eats some straight out of the jar, sticky, dark red syrup staining his lips.

I laugh at him. "You know, my sister could make you some. She has my stepmother's recipe."

"Yes, but then Brigitta would get all of it." Alois pouts.

"There's nothing stopping you from getting the recipe and making it yourself," Cornelia says. "It *is* quite good."

Alois whirls around to her. "I can!" he exclaims, eyes full of wonder. His gaze turns inward, as if the secrets of the universe have been revealed to him. "I can make some myself, and then eat it all myself."

"You have to share with me," Cornelia tells him sternly.

He stares up at her with adoration. "Of course!"

"This is a very good development," Cornelia tells Fritzi.

"Having fresh apfelkraut and brotchen at the assembly meetings will be wonderful," Fritzi says. The two women bend their heads together, discussing possibilities. After the deaths of Rochus and Philomena, as well as the destruction of the Origin Tree, Cornelia and the coven at the Well voted to dissolve the council. Now Fritzi and Cornelia moderate a monthly assembly of anyone who wants to discuss matters, a more open forum that relies on honesty and group efforts rather than secrets and control.

Alois is long gone by the time Cornelia looks up. "Where did he go?"

I point toward a shop. Cornelia heaves a sigh. "We're *supposed* to be fostering new alliances," she mutters, chasing after him.

"He'll be fine." Fritzi slips her hand through mine. A new archbishop was selected a month ago and will be arriving from the Vatican soon. We are staying in Trier long enough for Fritzi and Cornelia to have a meeting with the recently appointed religious leader of the diocese, and there is hope that a new sort of peace can be reached between those who use magic and those who choose not to. It is early days yet, and while the new archbishop has seemed receptive, we shall have to wait and see. Our steps toward introducing people to magic have been hesitant and careful. It's not yet widely known or understood. Cornelia and Fritzi have practiced various different scenarios for how to soothe the prejudices that once scarred this city.

Trier will not be forgotten.

Not again.

"Come on," Fritzi says, tugging on my arm. We have our own mission to complete today.

Together, down the hill, away from the cathedral. The last time I was here, I was racing toward the church where Johann had hidden his message in plain sight. I push the memory of how he died away. I will have to face the guilt, the sorrow, I know.

But not today.

Today, I have a different task in mind.

As we reach the city square, Fritzi shifts a little closer to me. It's hot now, and I realize this is the first time we've been in the city together without cloaks obscuring our identities. Just a scrap of material, but pulling the hood up had felt like armor. Striding over the ancient Roman cobblestones now makes me feel both free and exposed. I throw my arm over Fritzi's shoulder.

"So much has changed," she says, looking around in wonder. The market square is now being used as it was intended—as a communal meeting place, a shared space for citizens to barter for goods, chat among neighbors, discuss ideas.

I stumble and look down. The cobblestone at my feet is slightly taller than the others, a paler stone. A replacement for the cobblestone that had been removed so that stakes could be set into the earth. The rocks nearby are black; the weather has not yet removed all the char on the surface, making the new stone even starker and more noticeable than the others.

I hope it stays like this, I think, moving more carefully so I don't trip on the other stones that mark the places where stakes stood. There are no names, nothing more than a rock to trip on, but it's a grave marker nonetheless.

Fritzi slips out of my hold, heading past the apothecary, toward the opposite side of the square. The Judengasse is still mostly empty; our world may have magic now, but it is still cruel. The people here are no longer burning witches, but they have not allowed Jews back inside the city walls. The knowledge of this is not enough; I must at least try to foster change.

As if guessing at some of my dark thoughts, Fritzi shoots me an encouraging smile, leading the way as we wind around the curving alley. We pause, both looking around.

I feel a tug on my sleeve, and I jump. Little Mia, the orphan girl who's worked as a spy and a watch for me, grins up, clearly pleased that she escaped my notice until she forced my attention.

"You came back," she says, and this time her expression is one of joy, a feeling I know is mirrored on my own face. I was worried it would be difficult to find her—she could have left the city or fallen victim to the hexenjägers after I left or been hurt in the floods... But she's here, alive, safe.

"Of course I came back," I say, kneeling in the street in front of her. "I promised I would."

"To stay?" she asks.

I shake my head, and her smile falters. "Not forever," I clarify. "But I wanted to help you."

Her eyes flick to my waist, where my coin bag is tied to my belt. "Good. The farmer my brother was working for decided he doesn't need him anymore."

"Well, I can help with that." However, we both know gold will only help for so long.

"But there's more," Fritzi says.

Mia looks wary. The street, even in the shadowed alley of the Judengasse, is not the place to discuss this. She makes a whistling sound, and I see her little brother creep out from behind a shed. She motions for him to join us.

Mia is fiercely protective of her brother. He's younger than her, and his arm is an obvious mark of difference. I've seen him a few times, but have never been properly introduced.

"Hello," I say, holding my hand out to him. "My name is Otto."

"I'm Johann," he says.

I suck my breath in through my teeth.

I feel Fritzi through our tether, her sympathy and hope all mixed into one unnameable emotion.

The housefort I once used is still unoccupied, and my ramshackle collection of shabby crates still works as a ladder. I lead our small group there, hoping for privacy. Once we're safely inside the housefort, we sit in a circle on the dusty floor. I brush aside some splinters of wood as the children sit down across from us.

I glance at Fritzi. We've practiced what we want to say, how best to approach this topic. But it feels tenuous, this hope for magic.

"You know the hexenjägers burned witches," Fritzi starts.

Mia's jaw is tight, her eyes shiny. "Witches aren't real," she grinds out. This is the argument she's had to make for years, because her own father tried to have her brother burned at the stake. She reaches for him now, gripping his good hand. "It's wrong to try to kill people just because they're different!"

"I know," Fritzi says gently. "It *is* wrong. But..."

"No," Mia says, her little voice rising. She whirls toward me. "What are you trying to say? I thought you wanted to help my brother and me, I thought—"

"That's not what she means," I say, reaching for her. "Burning *anyone* is wrong. There is *no* question of that. She meant that witches are real."

That stops her. The girl gapes at me, then slowly turns to Fritzi, eyes wide. "I heard stories, but I thought they were all just that. Stories."

Fritzi shakes her head.

"Really?" Johann asks in a small voice.

"Really," I say.

Fritzi's already pulled out a pouch from her belt, cupping her palm and pouring the contents out. Dirt, sprinkled with seeds, rests in her hand. Mia stares at her, doubtful. I know the only reason the girl hasn't said anything or fled is because of the strangeness of Fritzi's actions—what harm can come from a fistful of dirt?

And then a green tendril pushes up. It grows rapidly, taller and taller, a tight pink bud forming on the tip as new leaves spiral off the stem. Mia stares, unnerved. I reach across her and pluck the flower into my own hand. The bud bursts open as the rush of magic pours from me, no longer a limited well but a river I can tap into.

After three months of working together, the magic comes easily, flowing between Fritzi and me. It's not just simple things like this either. Together, we made sure the fruit trees in the Well created a double harvest—which will be perfect for Alois's new venture into apfelkraut.

"How...?" Mia starts, agape. "What devilry is this?"

"Not devilry," I say, unconsciously touching the crucifix I wear around my neck. "But magic."

Johann leans forward eagerly, eyes wide. Mia stutters as I hand her the flower. She looks as if she wants to throw it down, but she cannot compel herself to do so, especially not when her brother touches the petals with such reverence.

"Magic is good," Fritzi says. "Or, it can be. And it's something you can do now too."

"Me?" she gasps.

Everyone. Everyone can do magic now. Everyone has access to the ability to change and grow and *become*.

"You only have to reach for it," I say.

Acknowledgments

The Fate of Magic concludes our first duology together, and with it, a massive chapter in both our lives. A chapter filled with global strife and struggle, personal victories and lows, and all manner of mind-blowingly unexpected revelations that left us with the lesson we hope this book has imparted to you:

You don't have to look far for magic.

You don't even have to look outward at all.

It's here, with you, in so many small moments of success, failure, discovery, and, most importantly, survival.

You only have to reach for it.

We owe this book to a truly epic group of people fondly known as the DREAM TEAM:

To Amy Stapp, Sara's agent, for being an endlessly optimistic cheerleader, strategist, supporter, and just all around anthropomorphized butterfly of a human being.

To Merrilee Heifetz, Beth's agent, for being a champion of books and keeper of knowledge, and to Rebecca Eskildsen, for keeping us all organized and together.

To Annie Berger and Jenny Lopez, whose calm, steady guidance helped transform both books in ways we never could have achieved on our own. We are endlessly honored to have gotten to work with you on our books. It is truly rare to have a vision so clearly shared and to see that vision come to fruition in the most brilliant way possible.

To Taryn Fagerness, for showing our witch and witch hunter the world, and to Jill Gillett, our film agent, for working to bring this story to life.

To the extended Sourcebooks crew, our village, the pillars of our DREAM TEAM: Karen, Rebecca, Michelle, Delaney, Caitlin, Emily, Deanna, Margaret, Valerie, Emily, Thea, Susan, and Aimee; and all the bookstore owners, reps, and salespeople who championed our book from the start (looking at you, Nissa, and the wonderful people at Beth's favorite bookstore, Malaprops).

Special shout-out to Kiki Rockwell: your folksy, Germanic, witchy music is in and of itself a gift, and Sara remains a giggly fangirl mess because of your support.

From Sara, to Beth: We wrote a mother-flipping duology, my dude. We wrote it during these years, and not only that, we hit so many professional goals, I'm running out of ways to celebrate. Thank you for teaming up with me. Thank you for putting up with my inability to keep historical facts straight. Most of all, thank you for being you, and for coming on this magical journey with me.

From Beth, to Sara: Everything I love about writing and making up stories is doubled when you're involved, and all the hardest parts are made twice as easy! I never knew that the best thing about co-writing is the sheer joy of getting to live in a new world with someone else, and to have this story be such a light during dark times and then to get to magnify that glow with you is something I'm not skilled enough to put into words (at least not by myself). Thank you for reining in my pages of historical notes and reminding me to add in more kissing. I may have brought the history, but you brought the magic.

About the Authors

Sara Raasch has known she was destined for bookish things since the age of five, when her friends had a lemonade stand and she tagged along to sell her hand-drawn picture books too. Not much has changed since then. Her friends still cock concerned eyebrows when she attempts to draw things, and her enthusiasm for the written word still drives her to extreme measures. She is the *New York Times* bestselling author of the YA fantasy trilogy Snow Like Ashes as well as four other books for teens (none feature her hand-drawn pictures). Her favorite German food is Pfeffernüsse—so many of her childhood memories are connected to the anise scent of those cookies that her grandmother used to bake.

Beth Revis is the *New York Times* and *USA Today* bestselling author of numerous science fiction and fantasy novels for teens and adults. Her debut, *Across the Universe*, has been translated into more than twenty languages, and her works have been honored by the Junior Library Guild, and received stars from *Kirkus*, *Publishers Weekly*, *Booklist*, and more. Co-owner of Wordsmith Workshops, which aids aspiring novelists, Beth currently lives in North Carolina with her son, husband, and dog. Her favorite German food is spaetzle and zimtsterne, and in researching this novel, she was able to trace her own family roots to a village outside of Bernkastel.

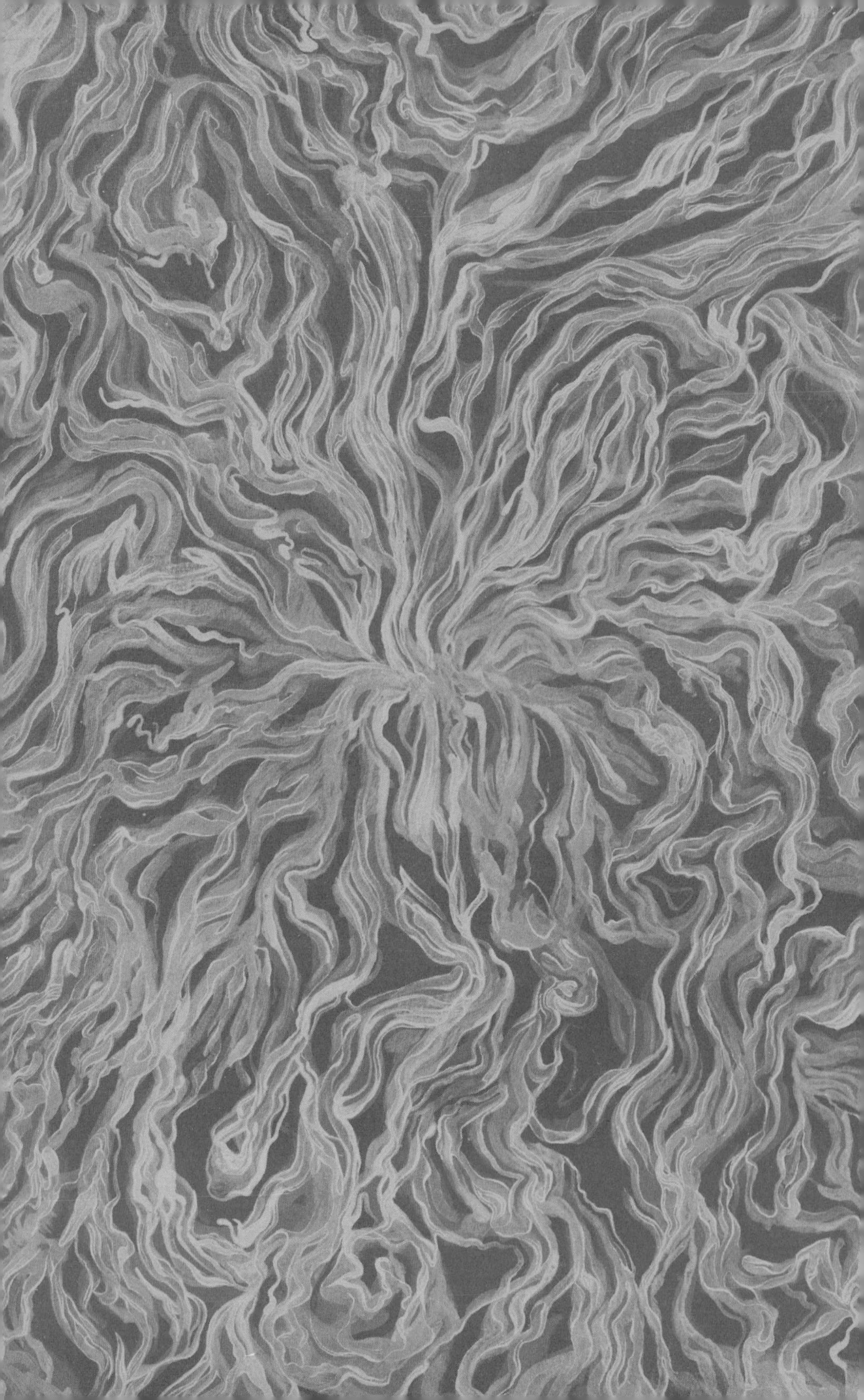